Sweet jayne

K WEBSTER

Books by Author K Webster

The Breaking the Rules Series:
Broken (Book 1)
Wrong (Book 2)
Scarred (Book 3)
Mistake (Book 4)
Crushed (Book 5 – a novella)

The Vegas Aces Series:
Rock Country (Book 1)
Rock Heart (Book 2)
Rock Bottom (Book 3)

The Becoming Her Series:
Becoming Lady Thomas (Book 1)
Becoming Countess Dumont (Book 2)
Becoming Mrs. Benedict (Book 3)

Alpha & Omega Duet:
Alpha & Omega (part one)
Omega & Love (part two)

War & Peace:
This is War, Baby (part one)
This is Love, Baby (part two)

"Harmony would only come with destruction."
—Shannon A. Thompson, *Death Before Daylight*

Dedication

To my husband. My rock.
Thank you for always hearing me. Always.
Even when you don't know what I'm saying
and even when I don't actually say anything at all.
You. Always. Hear. Me.

Prologue

Nadia

I FUCKING HATE DONOVAN JAYNE.

A furious scream is lodged in my throat, but one desperate, pleading look from my mother, and I'm trotting away from the asshole in our expensive kitchen toward the front door with my lips firmly pressed together.

Words like, *Fuck you*, or *Eat shit and die*, or *Stop checking out your seventeen-year-old stepdaughter, you prick*, all remain unsaid and poised on the tip of my tongue that craves to lash out at him. If it weren't for my mother actually loving the asshole, I'd have already given him a piece of my mind.

But she does love him—or so she says. And Mamá deserves any morsel of happiness she can get. She's been unhappy for so long. Ever since Papá died in an accident at the mill he worked at, just outside of Buenos Aires six years ago, she's been lost. The pretty smile that used to light up her face had darkened. It was by chance that she ran into the cocky hotel and resort magnate, Donovan Jayne. She'd been working as a housekeeper at one of the biggest hotels in Argentina. During her rounds, she pushed through his door, ready to collect the dirty towels thinking no one was in at the time. He was just coming out of the bathroom after a shower as she was entering. She apologized profusely and went to leave, but he wouldn't let her go. Love at first sight, they both claim.

Gag.

How anyone could love that self-centered asshole is beyond me. He not only uprooted us and moved us to Colorado to marry her, but I also had to leave all of my friends behind during my last year of high school. We'd gone from our simple two-bedroom apartment which Mamá was able to afford in the city on her meager housekeeping salary to a breathtaking mansion on a fucking mountain. But, her smile is back again. Mamá smiles like she did when Papá was still alive and that's the only reason I put up with Donovan's shit.

And by shit, I mean his possessiveness over his "family." The way he struts around this town showing us off like we're a couple of prized horses. But when someone so much as looks at us remotely wrong, he turns into a narcissistic idiot who reminds them who owns this town. *We do,* he says. Quite frankly, I'm embarrassed to be a part of the "we."

Ten more months. I can suck it up, bite my tongue, and let him pull my strings for ten more months. And then I'm off to college. I'm not sure where I'll go yet but it will most definitely be far, far away from Donovan and his superiority complex.

"Nadia Jayne!"

I cringe on the bottom step of the front porch and consider running the rest of the way to the bus stop to avoid having to talk to him. But Donovan doesn't give up so easily. He's shrewd and determined. It's best to let him spout his bullshit and then move on. So, instead, I lift my chin and turn to regard him with a raised eyebrow, no doubt revealing my disdain for him.

"What?" I hiss out my question, hoping the venom in my voice stings.

A small flinch at my tone is the only indication I've hurt him before he quickly masks it away with a look of indifference. He must've gotten ready for work early this morning, as he's already donning a pristine dark grey suit. I've never, not once, seen him *not* in a suit. For thirty-six, he's well-built and handsome. His dark hair is styled in a way that's meant to look messy and his grey-blue eyes are piercing. Always calculating and determining his next move. I'm not blind to the fact that his physical traits are attractive. But it's what's on the inside that makes him a creep. And he's the biggest damn creep around. I've seen the way he looks at me as if he wants to fuck me.

His eyes linger on my bare legs, unhidden by my ridiculously short school uniform because I've purposefully rolled it up as not to appear to look like an old maid on my first day, before he drags them up to meet my simmering gaze. "You forgot your lunch money," he says, waving a crisp hundred-dollar bill at me, "and you forgot to give your old man a hug goodbye."

Anger causes my chest to heat up. I can feel it clawing up my neck, revealing itself to him. His smirk tells me he knows he's struck a chord with me. I fist my hands at my sides to keep from doing something stupid like flipping him off. I'm already grounded from the car he bought me after we officially moved here this summer. I hadn't even gotten to drive it once. *"You talk back around here and your privileges get taken away. My house, my rules."* Fuck him and his house rules.

"You're not my dad," I snap. Visions of my own loving father flit through my head and I feel the familiar ache in my chest at losing him.

He takes a few steps toward me and flashes me a wide grin, revealing perfect, white teeth. "Technically I *am* your daddy. If you forgot, maybe you should check your ID again."

Tears well in my eyes but I clench my jaw. I won't let them spill over and give him the satisfaction of knowing that he can so easily rile me up. But he's right. Donovan's good at what he does. He swoops in, buys property—in this case, my mother and me—and stamps his name all over it. The asshole made sure he legally adopted me so I would bear the Jayne name too.

I'm no longer Nadia Blanco.

As of two months ago, I'm officially Nadia Jayne.

With a huff, I stomp up the steps and make my way up to where he's standing. His eyes glimmer with excitement as I approach. Five bucks says he's sporting a hard-on, too. More heat floods through me, this time making its way to my cheeks, and I shiver at that idea. God, my poor mother.

He holds out the money but when I reach for it, he clutches onto my wrist. His gaze darkens and he affixes me with a firm glare. "Don't embarrass me. The principal at your school sits on the board of my company. I won't have you tarnishing the Jayne name," he says coolly. "I wouldn't want to have to spank you over my knee for being a bad girl."

My jaw drops and I gape at him. I knew the bastard was a pervert but he's crossed over onto a whole new plane of twistedness.

"Oh, don't act so shocked, Nadia. You know I'm not opposed to disciplining you. If I remember correctly, you're still grounded from your car because of your attitude. I'd be more than happy to try other methods of punishment. Clearly, your attitude still fucking sucks. Maybe a little ass whipping will be good for you."

When I try to wriggle my hand out of his grasp, he grips it tighter and pulls me closer. His cologne invades my lungs and I nearly choke from the potent smell.

"¡Te odio!" I hiss. *I hate you.* Jerking my hand away, I take several steps back.

The corner of his mouth lifts up in a devilishly handsome grin. "Tell me you'll be a good girl."

I glare at him and nod my head, not giving him the satisfaction of my words. His eyes lazily skim over my face and stop at my lips.

"Good," he says, his smile faltering and his eyes finding mine again. "Have a great first day of school, sunshine." His gaze softens for a brief moment. For one tiny second I think Donovan Jayne may even be human. Not some asshole I've been forced to obey until the day I turn eighteen and can bolt. "Come here." His voice is hoarse this time.

With his arrogance taking a surprising backseat for once, I find myself going to him willingly. Almost seeking his comfort for some odd reason. When I'm close enough, he eats up the rest of the distance with his long legs and then his powerful arms are around me, pulling me against his solid chest. The stiffness I always carry when I'm around him melts away as he hugs me. Our hug is different this time. It's not forced for once. His scent, like always, cloaks me and I know from experience I'll smell him all day long. A constant reminder of his iron grip on my life. Today, though, I'm hoping it will give me even an ounce of his confidence as I attempt to make new friends in my new school.

"The boys are all beneath you here," he says with a playful growl. "I know this because I grew up here. Stay away from them. They don't deserve you."

A small smile tugs at my lips. That's probably the sweetest thing he's ever said to me. I lift my head up and look into his eyes that sparkle with an emotion I can never quite put my finger on. "Maybe I'm not into boys." I quirk up an eyebrow in a challenging way.

His soft features pinch into a hard scowl, momentarily stunning me. "You shouldn't be into anyone. School should be your primary focus. I'll forbid you from dating—boys or girls—if your grades start to suffer."

God, I hate him. How could I have so easily forgotten?

Before releasing me, he pats my ass with one hand and kisses the top of my head. As soon as he pulls away, I snatch the money from his hold and storm away from him. It isn't until I'm halfway down the long gravel driveway that I realize tears are streaking down my cheeks.

"Nadia," he calls out to me, a hint of remorse in his voice.

Swiping away a tear, I turn to regard him. His face has an apology written all over it but his stubborn mouth refuses to let it out.

"What?" I prod.

He scrubs at his cheeks with his palms, an almost angry scowl forming after. His steps are rushed as he strides back over to the front door and swings it open, calling out to me over his shoulder. "Have a good day at school."

I don't respond as the door slams behind him but instead wave him off. If it weren't for him and his "undying" bullshit love for my mother, I'd be texting with my friend Julienne as we speak, trying to figure out a way to skip out on our last class of the day. Instead, I'm in another country, going to a brand new school, and completely friendless with nobody to talk to aside from my mother and annoyingly good-looking stepfather. *Thanks, Daddy.*

Once I reach the road beside the mailbox, I sit down in the grass and ignore the cold morning dew soaking my bottom through my skirt. I swipe the tears away with the back of my hand and try to overlook the fact that my stepfather is a prick. It was stupid to think there was an actual likable person behind the suit and hard eyes. Doubt I'll ever make the mistake of letting my guard down again.

"Please don't tell me you live *there*," a voice calls out from the road.

I look up to the sound of the young voice and see a girl who looks to be around my age walking toward me. Her hair is dyed black on top and pale blonde underneath. She's got it pulled up in a messy bun that reveals multiple piercings in her ears. The school uniform she's wearing looks just like mine, but wrinkly and slightly baggy.

"Please tell me you're here to help me run away," I joke back.

Her eyebrows furrow together as she approaches and

inspects me. "Why are you crying?"

I drop my gaze to my lap and tug at a loose thread on my skirt. "I hate my stepdad."

She plops down beside me and mimics my cross-legged position. I watch with fascination as she pulls out a pack of cigarettes and lights one. "Funny. I hate my stepdad, too."

A puff of smoke surrounds us as she exhales. We sit in silence for a moment while she smokes and I plan ways to kill Donovan.

Finally, she says, "I'm Kasey."

She hands me her cigarette and I gingerly take it from her. I'm not a smoker but I don't want to scare away my first potential friend with being snooty.

"Nadia."

I take a puff and then cough before handing her back the cigarette.

"You new to Aspen High?" she questions.

Glancing up at her, I take in her features. Despite the dark eyeliner and heavy purple lipstick, a pretty face hides beneath. Her hazel eyes look sad, as if she has a whole life-time of stories to tell.

"Yep. I moved here from Argentina this summer."

Her eyebrows furrow together in confusion. "You don't sound foreign."

I laugh and roll my eyes. "What exactly does foreign sound like?"

Her cheeks turn slightly pink but she tries to hide her embarrassment with another puff of her cigarette. "I don't know. Like, you don't speak another language or have an accent or whatever."

"Los Americanos pueden ser tan ignorantes," I tell her

with a smile. *Americans can be so ignorant.* "Is that better?"

She scrunches her nose up at me. "What did you say?"

"I insulted you," I say shrugging my shoulders. "It takes out all the fun if I tell you."

"Bitch," she says with a grin and flips me off.

I run my fingers through my long, dark locks that are still smooth from straightening them this morning. "In my old school, we had to learn both English and Spanish. Everyone there could speak both languages fluently. My mother always drilled into me that knowing multiple languages would help me be successful one day, especially if I went to college in another country like the U.S. Her dream, not mine. I guess her dream came true."

She laughs. "College. Must be nice to have that option."

"Everyone has that option," I say with a frown, furrowing my brows together.

She stands quickly and flicks the half-smoked cigarette into the street. "Not when you're trailer trash," she says and points at a mobile home through the tree line across the road. "When you're poor, your only option is to find a job in this shitty-ass town and pop out a couple of babies. Your destiny, when you're like me, is being some asshole's punching bag. A wife to a drunk who beats you. You have no future. No love. Happily fucking ever after. Just ask my mom."

I lift my chin to see her visibly shaking. Not really knowing anything about this girl and also not wanting to upset her, I rush to blurt out the first thing that comes to mind. "Cheers," I say with a sneer, "to moms everywhere who married fucking assholes."

She snaps her gaze to mine and a small smile plays at her lips. With a few rapid blinks, she chases away the despondency in her eyes and is once again composed. "Cheers."

"You know," I tell her as I pick a blade of wet grass and try to tie it in a knot, "you could go to college. You don't have to be like your mom."

A sardonic chuckle is tossed back at me. "God, you sound like Taylor," she says wistfully but then her bottom lip trembles.

"Who's Taylor?" I question, wondering about her sudden mood change.

She gapes at me as if I've lost my mind but then waves off the question. "He's just someone I used to know." I sense the lie in her words. He was more than that. Much more than that. "Besides," she says, changing the subject, "what money would I go to college with, anyway?"

This time it's me who looks at her like she just crawled out from under a rock. "Um, grants? Scholarships? Duh."

She shrugs her shoulders. "Maybe. But college isn't what I want to do."

I wait for her to elaborate but she doesn't. Finally, after a few minutes, I ask. "Well, what do you want to do then?"

She turns to regard me with a look of embarrassment, her teeth tugging at her bottom lip. The expression makes her seem younger, a stark contrast to her harsh makeup. Kasey hides behind the emo look for some reason. I wonder what she'd look like with her natural hair color, whatever that may be.

"You'll just laugh at me."

I roll my eyes. "Fine, I'll go first. Mine is laughable too. We can laugh together."

The corners of her lips draw up into a small smile. "Okay then."

"I always wanted to be a cook. Maybe a sous chef or a pastry chef. I'm not one hundred percent sure, but I love food. Clearly," I mutter and motion at my curvy body.

She places her hands on her hips and arches a brow at me. "Are you kidding me right now? I'd kill to have your body. I'm still waiting for the boob fairy to show up and sprinkle me with some titty dust. But obviously she accidentally spilled the whole jar on you."

We both burst out into a fit of giggles and I swipe at tears—this time from laughter.

"Be careful what you wish for," I tease. "Now tell me already."

She lights up another cigarette as if she's working up the courage to start talking. After a couple of drags, she meets my gaze. "I want to work at a day care."

"That seems completely doable. Is this like a gothic day care?" I question with a grin. "Would all the babies wear Metallica T-shirts and cuss? Would they take smoke breaks instead of recess?"

"Bite me." She laughs and kicks some rocks from my driveway toward me.

I'm still smiling when a squeal of tires draws my attention down the road. Kasey flicks her still burning cigarette into the street and we both watch as a black SUV comes barreling down the street, headed our way.

"Slow down, asshole!" she yells and flips off the vehicle as it nears.

A screeching of the tires deafens me as it comes to a complete stop right in front of where I'm sitting beside the mailbox. The door is wrenched open, and I see black combat boots first before seeing who they belong to.

Flickering my gaze over to Kasey, I notice the nervousness on her face as she starts to take a step back. When I jerk my head back over to the car, I see why.

A big man, dressed entirely in black with a ski mask covering his face, is charging for her. It happens so quickly that I'm frozen with my ass planted on the earth and I can only watch what's unfolding right in front of me. She lets out an ear-piercing screech as he runs for her. Kasey doesn't make it far before he's got his massive arms wrapped around her middle. Her long legs kick wildly around her as he drags her back toward the car. The moment her terrified gaze meets mine, I jolt into action.

"No! Stop!" I scream as I scramble to my knees when he passes by me. "Let her go."

He grunts in exertion at her struggling but has the ability to meet my stare. The eyes behind the mask are wild and crazed. I'm trying to get a better look at the man when he raises his knee in the air. The bottom of his gigantic boot slams into my cheek with the force of a hurricane. Blackness explodes in front of me, blinding me from the man who is forcefully kidnapping my friend, and I fall back into the grass, slamming my head against the ground.

As I try to regain my wits, I hear a car door slam once as he shoves her into the vehicle. Another slam sounds after he climbs back in. The SUV screeches into drive and hauls ass down the road. A wave of dizziness washes over me but I quickly roll to my side to try and read the license plate.

Too blurry.

Too far away.

Another blanket of darkness clouds my vision and I black out.

I'm not sure if it's minutes or hours later when I hear Donovan's concerned voice and I slowly regain consciousness.

"Nadia, baby," he murmurs as he cradles my head in his hand. "What happened?"

My eyes are fixated on the road where Kasey's half-smoked cigarette rolls around in the wind, the cherry still red on the end. When I don't respond, he slides his arms beneath me and pulls me into them against his chest. Normally, I hate Donovan but right now, I need him.

I need him to hold me like Papá would have.

To tell me everything's going to be okay.

For him to assure me that Kasey and the man who took her were all just a silly figment of my teenage imagination.

"Selene!" Donovan hollers to Mamá. "Call 911! I think Nadia was assaulted. Her nose is bleeding and she's disoriented."

His dark eyebrows are pinched together in genuine concern and it comforts me.

"Kasey," I murmur and blink slowly. A massive migraine is wrapping its evil claws around my skull and crushing in on me. "He took Kasey."

His eyes widen and he darts his gaze back down the street as if to see the vehicle that's now long gone. When he turns to look back down at me, he presses a chaste kiss to my forehead and then pins me with a searing stare. "Shhh. We'll tell the police. But you're safe now, Nadia. I'll make sure nothing happens to you." He then curses, "Jesus Christ, it could have been you instead."

I want to feel comforted that it wasn't me but I don't. All

I can think about is her terrified expression. The fact that someone took her. How, if the police aren't able to find her and soon, she'll never get to hold the babies at the day care like she dreamed about.

Someone could abuse her. Rape her even.

And what's worse, they may kill her.

Kasey was right.

She has no future.

Donovan carries me up the steps of our house where moments earlier he was acting like a pervert and fondling my ass. It seems so miniscule in comparison to what Kasey is now facing—being taken by some twisted predator. While I was annoyed and creeped out over my stepdad, she's probably scared out of her fucking mind in the clutches of a lunatic. I really am just a spoiled brat. A girl who doesn't know how good she really has it.

"Please help me find her," I beg him with tears in my eyes.

He stares at me for a long minute, a frown tarnishing his otherwise handsome face. When he eventually snaps out of whatever thought held him, he nods. "I'll do what I can, baby. I swear to fucking God, I will do everything in my power to find her." The intensity in his vow to find a random girl who is a stranger to him shocks me. A newfound respect for him begins taking root deep inside me.

In this moment, I realize Donovan might not be so bad. The glimmer of the man he'd shown me earlier is making a reappearance. I see the promise in his penetrating gaze—a promise to make me happy. To indulge his little girl.

And if sucking up to Donovan is what it takes to find Kasey, then that's what I'll do.

I have to save her.

I swear to God, I'll find and save her somehow.

She'll have her future.

Her happy ending.

I'll make sure of it.

One

Kasper

Nearly ten years later...

H ATE.
A four letter word that has consumed nine years of my life.

Nine fucking years.

It's dictated my every thought, my every action, and my every move. I've faded into a ghost of the person I was before and gladly taken on a new image. A new persona.

I've become a nightmare.

Sure, you could call me one of the good guys. But I know better. Despite my career choices and the way I carry myself for all to see, I'm something dark and bitter beneath the surface. Beneath the lopsided grins and cocky exterior, I'm a hell storm of fury and rage.

My fire burns for one person.

So bright and brilliant—exceedingly hot.

I crave to decimate everything in her path, including

her.

I've made it my life's mission to destroy hers. I don't want to kill her. Nah, that'd be too fucking easy for the bitch. Instead, I want to take every single thing she cares about and ruin it. I want her to watch as I rip and tear her entire life to shreds, only to then stomp what's left into the dirt.

She needs to pay for being a stupid, useless cunt.

"You still coming by on Saturday for the game?" Rhodes questions from the doorway of my office. "Ashley was pissed she made pigs in a blanket just for you, only for you to not show up last weekend. You know how emotional her pregnant ass gets, Ghost."

I smirk at him and shrug my shoulders. Jason Rhodes and I go way back. All the way to our high school years. He's one of the few guys at the station I actually like and don't mind hanging out with. "I don't know, man. You know how it gets this time of year. Everyone wants shit built so they can enjoy it for spring. I've already done two decks and a gazebo and we're only two weeks into November. If I'm free, I'll stop by."

He shakes his head. "You work too much. What, being lieutenant and Chief's bitch isn't enough? You just have to spend all your free time building shit too?" His radio beeps and he responds that he's en route. Before he turns to leave, he flashes me a mischievous grin. "Ash said Cassidy will be there. She's been wanting to get back on your cold dick since you porked her at my thirtieth birthday party last month."

"Blow me, Detective," I grunt, grabbing my dick. "Don't you have better shit to do than worry about my sex life?"

He chuckles and saunters down the hallway leading away from my office and calls over his shoulder, "Just think

about it. Blow-jobs, lil' smokies, and a lot of beer. What better way to spend a Saturday night?"

When he's gone, the smile falls from my lips and I flip
the file closed I'd been working on. I pinch the bridge of
my nose and close my eyes. Just like always, my mind flits
to her.

The bitch.

The one responsible for my sister.

Gut-churning hatred filled my insides.

With a huff, I open my eyes and start slamming files
into my drawers. My shift ended a half hour ago and I'm
tired as hell. I just want to go home, do a little research, and
pass the fuck out.

Once my desk is cleared, I pull my drawer key from my
pocket and open it. Inside is one single file. A file that I've
obsessed over ever since I joined the Aspen Police Department five years ago. At the time, I thought it held answers
to the questions that plagued me. I assumed I'd unravel the
mysteries nobody else had been able to.

Instead, I found *her* statement.

I found *her* pictures.

I found *her* high-dollar lawyer's business card and *her*
stepfather's information. Fucking Donovan Jayne of all people.

But nowhere did I find any clues about the prick who
took Kasey. The stupid bitch simply watched while some
sick fuck stole my sister and did nothing. Absolutely nothing. She watched as he—*the man who was dressed all in
black wearing a mask*—shoved Kasey into his black SUV—
no make or model—and drove away.

"I don't remember."

"*I don't know.*"

Those two phrases were used more times than I could count in her report. But that's a lie because I did count. In fact, I highlighted every single time she *didn't remember*. All twenty-six times. And all eighteen times she *didn't know*.

The rich bitch went on to have a fucking fabulous life.

Meanwhile, my little sister was probably dismembered and at the bottom of some fucking lake right now.

With a roar, I slam my fist on my desk, causing my cold cup of coffee to slosh and splatter onto the file. I flip to the back and run my fingers over the last date recorded. The last time I had eyes on the dumb bitch. She'd gone to college for a few years in LA. Then, she'd come back to Colorado to work at the Aspen Pines Lodge at the top of the mountain with Donovan. I thought it would be my chance. That I could finally seize the opportunity to make her life a living hell. I'd even put plans in motion to make that happen.

But then she fucking vanished.

For three goddamned years.

And I've been trying to locate her ever since.

My phone buzzes and I see a text from my mother which causes the stale coffee in my stomach to sour.

Mom: I miss you. Come see us at The Joint.

Rolling my eyes, I ignore her text and shove the file back into my desk. Once it's locked up, I shoot her a reply.

Me: Maybe. Is asshole there?

I stand from my desk and stretch before swiping my keys from the corner. I'm not in the mood to see Dale today but I know Mom will just harass the fuck out of me until I come visit, so I decide to drop by for a few minutes to get it out of the way, on my way home from work. Before I leave my office, I do a cursory sweep to make sure nothing is out of place. Rhodes makes fun of me, says I'm a sociopath or some shit, but I pay him no attention. It's that observant nature that makes me a good detective and what got me promoted to lieutenant at the early age of twenty-nine last year. My attention to detail is a trait of mine that has served me well in this life. I'd like to teach that bitch a lesson or two about paying fucking attention to important details.

I'm about to leave the room when I notice that the nameplate on my desk has been moved. With an annoyed grunt, I adjust the metal so Lieutenant Kasper Grant is perfectly straight. Whichever fucking asshole did this, I'm going to hurt. A smile plays at my lips knowing it was probably Rhodes. I'll get the prick back later.

I shut my office door and lock it before striding down the hallway. As I pass Chief's doorway, he calls out to me.

"Ghost, can you come here a second?"

With a sigh, I turn and stride into his office. His face is contorted into a frown as he stares at his phone. I wait patiently until his features relax, and then he regards me, a brilliant bullshit smile on his face. He thinks he can fool me along with everyone else. But he forgets that I've known him forever. I know his shiny smiles and easygoing personality are anything but genuine. They're forced. All a part of what comes with his prestigious job as police chief. Who the hell am I to judge, though? People change. Apparently Logan wants to be someone nicer now. He's got the whole town fooled, so I guess he's doing a pretty damn good job.

"You headed home?" he asks as he tucks his phone into the breast pocket of his white button-up dress shirt. The pin on his shirt that displays his name, Chief Logan Baldwin, sits neat and straight. It's one of the reasons I get along with Logan. He too sees the value in the details. Together, we've brainstormed on some tricky-ass cases and have found answers many of our detectives had overlooked. I may not believe his plastic smiles, but he's a damn good cop. That I can respect.

"I'm going to head up to The Joint and visit Mom for a bit," I tell him as I run my fingers through my overgrown, almost black hair. I need to get it cut but ever since I fucked Regina over the product bar of the salon after hours a couple of weeks ago, she's been clingy and downright stalking my ass. If I go in to get my hair cut, she'll want to suck my dick or who knows what else. And quite frankly, she wasn't very good at it the first time. I'm not eager for a second go. I'll just have to take my ass to Quick Cuts or have Ashley do it next time I visit.

"Ah, The Joint. Dale going to be there?" he questions, his brows furrowing. We both fucking hate Dale. Due to a conflict of interest, I'm not allowed to personally haul Dale in, being that he's my stepfather and all. But, on the several occasions, when he's whipped up on Mom, and she's called me crying, I've had Logan handle the hauling for me. It's one thing for your boss to know you're the product of a white trash family. It's a whole other thing for all of your subordinates to know, too. Most of these assholes don't like taking orders from "the kid," as some of them call me. If they knew about my fucked-up family, they'd be more than glad to hold that over my head and I'd lose any and all respect that I've worked my ass off to gain. So Logan steps in when I need him to and I owe him big for that.

"Probably. I'll try not to kill him," I joke. "What do you

need?"

"Can you ride by Jimmy Salem's building? He's out of town on business. Called and said one of his neighbors told him she'd seen some kids trying to break in. Probably just that, kids, but take a look for me, will you? Jimmy and I go way back, so I told him we'd check it out. I'd do it myself but I have to deal with something rather urgent." He stands and slides on his jacket.

"Sure," I tell him as I turn to leave. "See you tomorrow."

His desk phone rings and soon, he's barking out orders to one of the uniforms. Leaving him to deal with the issue on his own, I stride out of the building toward my department-issued Camaro. Logan and I drive the only two unmarked police cars in the department, whereas the rest of the guys drive typical squad cars. When he'd handed me the keys to the black muscle machine, I nearly fucking died. I'd always heard police departments were lacking on funds.

Not ours.

Somehow, Logan manages to garner substantial support from the community. With his inherent charm and good looks, he smiles his way into some big-ass donations.

Hell, I'm not complaining.

I hit the button to unlock the vehicle and it beeps in response. As I climb into the car, my thoughts go back to *her*. The one who was too stupid to remember a license plate. Or to recall one tiny fucking detail that could have led the police to my sister. Anyfuckingthing.

Picking up my iPod, I flip through my music until I find "(Don't Fear) The Reaper" by Blue Oyster Cult and then set off on my ride.

I wonder where the hell she's been these last three years.

I've stalked her social media accounts and even watched Donovan's office at the lodge, hoping she might show up there one day. Nothing. She's completely gone off the grid. I even briefly considered interrogating Donovan on her whereabouts, but I know he would only lawyer up and refuse to answer like he does with everything else. Then, I'd have Logan on my ass which I don't need. If Logan knew I was still obsessing over this case from nearly a decade ago, he'd probably order a psych evaluation.

I don't need a psych evaluation.

I just need my sister back.

I'm lost in thoughts of her while I make a pass through Jimmy Salem's parking lot. A few beer cans litter the place, evidence of some kids having a recent party, but nothing looks disturbed. After a quick sweep, flashing my light to the dark corners of the building, I pull back on the road to head toward The Joint. My mind is numb once again as I contemplate where she's gone.

As I slow at a four-way stop sign, something big and white comes barreling through off to my right, headlights bouncing as it nears. My eyes zero in on the big-ass Ford 250 which is speeding toward the intersection with no signs of stopping. It plows past me and as it flies past, I recognize the vinyl king's crown decal on the back window that's revealed under the red brake light.

No fucking way.

I pop my flasher on the dash and peel out after the vehicle. Sure enough, as I follow behind it, I recognize the truck to be Logan's. Problem is, I know he's driving the department issue Tahoe today, not his truck.

Did someone actually steal the police chief's vehicle?

What a fucking moron.

Adrenaline surges through my veins as I speed after the truck. It doesn't show any signs of slowing even though I'm tailing its ass with my red and blue lights flashing. I end up following it for a half mile before I realize that whoever's behind the wheel is just driving faster and has no plans to pull over. Knowing there's a curve coming up soon, I yank my wheel to the right and gas it past the truck. As we reach the curve, driving side by side, I start inching into the right lane. I don't want to damage mine or Logan's vehicle but I'm not about to let this person get away. When I barely bump the side of the truck, it jerks off to the right and sails into a ditch. Slamming on my brakes, I pull off to the side a little ways ahead of the truck and jump out of the car. Headlights blind me, so I draw out my 9 mm Glock and aim it at the vehicle.

"Hands on the steering wheel!" I shout as I slowly make my way to the truck.

Since it's getting dark, I can't see through the windshield. The hairs stand up on the back of my neck as I approach. Whoever it is, the fucker is going to pay for making me scratch up my car.

When I reach the driver's side window, I peer in. A woman with dark hair is slumped over the steering wheel. My heart thunders in my chest as I tap the glass with my weapon.

"Ma'am," I bark out, "put your hands where I can see them."

Her body quakes and I wonder if she's having a goddamned seizure. With eyes on her, I yank on the door handle. The door swings open and all hell breaks loose. She launches herself at me, knocking my gun from my hand but not before a shot fires off into the trees. As soon as my ass hits the grass, she scrambles to her feet and takes off in a sprint. With a grunt, I jump to my feet, scoop up my gun, and begin running after her.

"Stop or I'll shoot!" I snarl after her as I charge in her direction.

She's short, probably a good six inches shorter than my six-foot frame but she runs like the devil. The headlights shining on her reveal toned legs beneath a floral print dress and cowboy boots. How the fuck she's running in boots is beyond me.

I close in on her, my legs eating up the distance easily, and I tackle her to the dirt.

"Ah!" she cries out the moment her face impacts the ground.

I shove a knee against the small of her back and wrangle her squirming arms into cuffs. As soon as she's secured, I roll her over onto her back so I can Mirandize her. "You have the right to remain—"

She spits in my face, silencing me. "Let me go! I have to go! Now!"

Her panicked tone sends my heart thudding in my chest. But when I push her hair out of her face and lock eyes with her dark, chocolate-colored orbs, my heart ceases to beat. Familiar rage chases away my moment of shock and I fist my hands at my sides.

I fucking found her.

Sweet Nadia Jayne all grown up.

Anger consumes me and I grab her jaw with my fingers, biting into her flesh hard enough to make her yelp.

"You're going to jail you stupid, stupid woman. You stole the police chief's truck," I sneer and bare my teeth at her.

My fingers twitch to grip her neck and choke the fucking life out of her. Fuck serve and protect. More like punish and abuse when it comes to Nadia Jayne.

"Please," she begs, hot tears running from her eyes. "You don't understand. I need to get out of here."

I release her jaw and smirk. "You're not going anywhere except to the station where I'll fingerprint your ass and your rich little daddy can have fun trying to bail you out."

Her eyes widen in horror. "You know Donovan? Please don't call him. I'm begging you, from one decent human being to another. He can't know I'm here in Aspen. You don't understand..."

A niggling inside of me causes me to take pause. I don't like the way she pleads with me—the way it works its way inside of me. This dumb bitch has the tongue of a goddamned serpent. She let my sister disappear and I cannot forget that.

Ignoring her, I pull my phone out and call Logan. "You'll never believe this," I say with a laugh. "I'm straddling a woman who stole your truck. Donovan Jayne's kid. Can you believe it? I'd like to see him buy his way out of—"

"You have Nadia?" His tone is cool, not at all what I expected.

"I have her detained on Plantation Road, by The Joint. She tried to fucking flee, Logan," I snap, my anger returning like a storm thundering in.

He curses into the phone. "Get her off the ground, goddammit. I'll be there in ten minutes."

When I hang up and shove my phone back into my pocket, I look down to find her face contorted into one of those ugly-cry expressions chicks sometimes make. It irritates me and I want to really give her something to fucking cry about. If I kicked her in the face like that prick who stole my sister did nine years ago, I wonder if she'd forget this whole scene too.

Her supposed forgetful nature seems like such a cop-out.

I would make sure she never forgot the way my boot felt as I crushed her skull.

"Get up," I snap as I rise to my feet dragging her up with me.

She's a fucking mess—her hair a wild entanglement of leaves and snot running from her nose all over her face.

"What did you do?" she questions through her hiccupping sobs.

I frown at her. "I did my job."

She hangs her head in defeat and stays that way until Logan's Tahoe comes barreling down the road toward us. He screeches to a halt and climbs out. Nadia stiffens in my grip but doesn't lift her gaze to meet his. His glare is hateful when his eyes shift to me, and I stare at him, dumbfounded for a moment. I don't get a chance to ask him what the hell is going on because after another second, he shoulders past me and pulls her into his arms.

"Oh, baby," he coos and strokes her hair. "Are you okay?"

She breaks down, as in knees collapsing, gut wrenching wails kind of breaking down, and it makes me sick. I don't know what's going on but I do know she's playing him. What she did was illegal and I stand behind chasing her ass.

The part about wanting to choke her to death was for my own personal vendetta.

"Look, Chief," I mutter to Logan, "she ran a stop sign and was going well over the posted thirty-five miles per hour speed limit. When I finally ran her off the road, she attacked me, ran, and then resisted arrest."

He turns and glares at me as if he wasn't listening to a word I just said. "Un-cuff her."

Clenching my jaw, I yank my key out and unlock the cuffs. Her hands are trembling. This bitch is good. *Too good.* "Now what?"

"She's my Dale," he says, and nods his head over in the direction of The Joint, just down the road. "This is between us, Ghost. Just like it's between us when I have to deal with your stepfather beating the shit out of your mother. *Nadia* stays between us. Do you understand?"

I give him a clipped nod but my gaze falls on her. "You doing a favor for Donovan?"

His Cheshire cat grin doesn't escape me, even though it's quick. He slips his hands into her messy hair and tilts her head back. I watch in shock as he kisses her softly on the lips. Her lip wobbles but she kisses him back, her breathy sigh echoing in the dark. When they finish their weird-ass kiss, he turns to me, a confident smile spread across his face.

"Lieutenant," he says with a chuckle, "meet my fiancée. Cat's officially out of the bag."

And things just got a million times more complicated.

Two

Nadia

LOGAN BALDWIN IS A GODDAMNED LIAR.

And an oh-so-good one, too.

I listened with a mix of awe and horror as he revealed to the man named Ghost that I was his fiancée. On one hand, I should be fist pumping the air. Joyous for such a leap of progress toward my ultimate goal. But I'm not. Instead, I'm terrified of the wrath that will inevitably follow.

We've gone public.

Going public means all eyes on us.

Donovan and Mamá back in my life. A vision of Donovan's pained, steely grey-blue eyes is at the forefront of my mind. Those eyes haunt me but they also remind me—they remind me of my purpose.

He'll come for me eventually.

The thought it is both terrifying and pleasing in one confusing mix of emotions.

It is absolutely crucial, though, that he stays away. I *need* for him to stay away.

"The axel's broken," Logan grunts from his position, crouched on his hands and knees as he peers under his truck.

My heart rate picks up when he stands back up and saunters over to Ghost. The other officer's eyes haven't strayed from mine. I hate the way he stares at me—like he can see into my head, the same head that holds the secrets I'm desperate to protect. Having people find out about Logan and I could be a good thing. But something tells me I'll need to keep my distance from the man with the jade-colored, knowing eyes and unsmiling face.

I shiver, the night air chilling my bones as the adrenaline wears off. Ghost frowns at me. And Logan snaps his head over to me, his eyes flickering with that rage he masks so well.

The sound of Logan clearing his throat breaks the silence that had fallen over us. "Call a tow truck, will you? I need to get Nadia home. She's freezing to death out here. Just have Bill invoice me."

Ghost nods and pulls his cell from his pocket, his gaze never leaving mine. When Logan touches the small of my back to guide me back to the Tahoe, I flinch. His gentle fingers barely brushing against my lower back are more terrifying than his heavy hand.

I remain quiet as he helps me into the vehicle. He climbs in a few seconds later, and soon we're weaving down the dark road. Chewing on my lip, I try to formulate the right words. Words I hope will keep him calm.

The eagle-eyed cop fades in the side mirror as silence fills the Tahoe. The ominous mood surrounding us darkens the night further. "You do realize what you've done, don't you?" he questions in a measured tone, his eyes on the road and both hands gripping the steering wheel tightly.

My heart rate quickens and I let out a small whimper. "Logan, please... I swear on everything I love that I'll play the part for you. They'll never know."

His eyes dart over to mine for a moment before they're back on the road again. "Oh, believe me, I have no doubt about that. You're going to have to convince everyone in this whole goddamned town about your depth of feeling for me. No backing down now."

My hands tremble in my lap. I quickly clasp them together so he doesn't pick up on the overwhelming fear that nearly consumes me. Logan feeds off of fear and I don't want to strengthen the beast. I need to weaken him. Use the skills I've perfected over time and make him feel reassured.

"I promise I'll be perfect for you, Logan."

He nods and the rest of the drive is silent. I know in that twisted head of his, he's contemplating my punishment. Beatings. Whippings. Orgasm deprivation. Near suffocation over and over again.

Those are preferable.

Always my choice.

Because when it comes to Logan, he knows my weaknesses. With Logan, his psychological punishments are much worse. He knows my Achilles heel and isn't afraid to cut me where it hurts the most.

"Donovan is going to be a problem," he says as he puts on the blinker to turn into his driveway. "I'm going to have to figure out how to deal with that one." The moonlight shines down on the large, stunning estate. If it wasn't the place that housed my worst nightmares, I'd be in love with the architectural beauty of it. It's a delicate mix of rustic country meets modern elegance, which is a common décor choice here in Aspen among the wealthy.

And Logan is among the wealthy. He's practically their leader amid the local Aspen community. Well, he and Donovan are.

He tells everyone he's a trust fund kid—because clearly, he couldn't ever afford a house like this on a police chief's salary. And just like all of his other lies, they believe it. There was a time when I trusted and believed in him too.

Until he turned my world upside down.

He pulls into his three-car garage beside "The Beast," as he calls that vehicle. The space where his truck once sat remains empty. As soon as the overhead door closes, caging us inside of his fortress, I swallow down the panic flopping around in my belly like a fish on the bank. It's time to breathe and face the music. And this isn't the good kind of music. No Led Zeppelin here crooning away in my head. Instead, raging Pantera is what threatens to crush me.

But the time for crying is over.

The armor is going up.

This warrior princess is strapping up for battle.

"How will you punish me?" I question when I climb out of the Tahoe and slam the door.

He's already striding into the house, ignoring my words. I trot after him, hoping to distract him in some way from the inevitable. By the time I make it into his room, he's yanking off his tie and tossing it on the bed. With practiced finesse, he pops each button on his white dress shirt until it's completely undone and he peels it from his muscled frame.

Logan is forty-five years old, the same age as Donovan,

and has the body of a thirty-year-old. He's lean in all the right places but his muscles are more sculpted and defined on his arms, shoulders, and abs. As he stands in his slacks and white sleeveless undershirt, I admire his monstrous beauty. Despite the undershirt covering up most of his body, his sleeve of tattoos on his left arm is visible and my eyes fixate on the words.

Harmony after annihilation.

Those words are my focus. When he does his worst, I focus on those words. My constant reminder.

Just like now.

His tattoos are a colorful piece of artwork surrounding that profound phrase. The phoenix which takes up most of his arm bears his dark eyes, symbolic of the man before me. Within the flames permanently licking his skin encompassing the hellish bird are names. Reminders. My reasons. I fixate on my favorite one and steel my heart, preparing myself for annihilation.

"Logan, what are you going to do? You're too quiet."

He peels off the undershirt and once again, my eyes are drawn to his masculine physique. More tattoos cover his chest and abdomen. His chest is mostly free of hair aside from the dark trail centered in the V of his lower abdomen.

The man is beautiful.

But on the inside, he's a wolf in sheep's clothing.

Wicked darkness cloaked in smiling light.

And yet, I still have a sick, sliver of love for him.

It doesn't make sense, but when his dark, familiar eyes meet mine, it does. I can look past those menacing eyes and see perfection. Beauty. Innocence. It's pure—untainted and uncorrupted—and I'd do anything for that untarnished part of him.

"Who says I want to punish you?" he questions, the thick cord of muscle on his neck tightening.

Dread washes over me and I rush over to him. "Please, Logan. I'm begging you. Hurt me."

His gaze meets mine and he smirks. I hate his smirks. When I hear the jingle of his belt, I nearly sob in relief. But when he yanks it from the loops of his pants and wraps it tightly around his fist, panic once again chokes me. He pushes past me, out of his bedroom and down the hallway. I know where he's going. I can't let things escalate that far.

"No!" I cry out and launch myself against his back before he reaches the door to the basement. "Not down there. For the love of God, just fuck me up. Fuck me up on the kitchen floor or your bed or the back porch. I don't care. Just do it up here."

He shakes me off of him and I slip between him and the door. His eyes are darkened with rage and his breathing is so heavy he's visibly shaking. Desperate to distract him from what I know is coming, I grab his thick cock through his work slacks.

"Choke me with your cock, Logan," I beg with fat tears welling in my eyes.

He laughs, the sound cruel and humorless. "I'm not in a choking mood."

I grab on to his fist holding the belt and stand on my toes to try and meet his vacant glare. "Make me bleed," I implore him firmly, rapidly blinking the tears away. "Make me bleed with this." I squeeze the leather he's holding and then lick my lips.

His anger lessens marginally and his features slightly

relax. I pounce, not wasting any time, and wrap my arms around his neck. He dips his head to meet my lips and I kiss him hard. I throw all of my energy into distracting him from breaking my soul a little more than he already has.

I'm a wolf too, you see.

The games Logan plays are no longer difficult to understand.

In fact, sometimes I think I'm starting to win.

His tongue spears into my mouth and I let out a moan as he kisses me hungrily. And I am pleased for the simple fact he's reciprocating. When I hop to wrap my short legs around his firm waist, he grabs on to my ass with a punishing grip. I yelp, which only spurs him on because he loves to hear me scream and he strides away from the basement toward his bedroom. My heart leaps into my throat because his bedroom is the safest room in the house. It means he's feeling softer than usual which surprises me.

Maybe I'm finally getting to him.

When we finally reach his bed, he pushes me onto it. I bounce on the mattress and then jerk my gaze to his, waiting for his next move. He starts undressing the rest of the way, baring his large cock to me, but I wait patiently for his next order.

"Leave the boots on. Everything else goes," he says, his tone curt, as he takes his cock in his free hand.

I focus on the way he strokes himself as I go up on my knees to peel off my dress. At one time, his dick had been too big. Too scary. Too much. It'd been enough punishment alone. But over time, I grew used to the way he filled and stretched every hole in my body. I'd learned how to turn myself on so I could accept him more easily. It was the only way. With Logan, you just have to accept that he's going to destroy you from the inside out. Once I finally made peace with that, it soon became easier to take all of the crooked, brutal parts of him.

"Now, lie face down across the bottom of the bed."

I scramble to heed his instructions and wait for the pain that will inevitably come. But then it doesn't come. Not right away. Instead, he teases my flesh by dragging the leather of his belt along my spine toward my ass. I focus on the way it tickles my skin and imagine his mouth on my clit, sucking and tasting. Just the idea of him between my legs has me growing wet.

I absolutely need to be wet.

"Did you get the shit you needed from the store?" he asks softly.

I shudder at his tone but nod. "Yeah, it's in my purse. I can add it to the meal and then put it in the oven as soon as you're done with my punishment."

Crack!

Fire rips across my skin as the belt cracks against my ass. I scream but don't dare move. His heavy hand is more preferable than the other implements he has at his disposal.

"One thing, doll. You had to get one thing. What took you so long? Do I need to remind you what happens when you run late?" he demands with a hiss, his finger flicking the sore flesh where he whipped me.

Gritting my teeth against the pain, I shake my head emphatically. "I never need a reminder. You know that. It was the stupid train. I was doing great on time until the train held me up. Please," I beg, "you have to believe me."

"*Hmmmm...* If you aren't guilty, then why are you begging for punishment?" His question throws me off guard and I stutter trying to find the right answer.

"I, uh, I—"

Crack!

This time his hit lands on the middle of my back and it hurts like hell. I clutch onto the bedding to keep from scrambling away from him. Seeking escape is not an option.

"Tell me why the fuck I'm whipping you, Nadia, if you're so fucking innocent," he seethes, his breath coming out in ragged huffs.

A sob gets caught in my throat but I swallow it down. "B-B-Because I like it when you hurt me," I lie and push my ass into the air. "I need the pain."

Clearly, I'm a masochist. But I have my reasons.

"Is that so?" he questions with a chuckle and runs the leather of his belt down along the crack of my ass. "Are you wet?"

"Yes," I tell him, "and I crave for you to fuck me."

He pops my ass playfully with the belt and I squeak in surprise. I was expecting another lashing. But then his fingers, two of his thick digits, are pushing into my pussy, completely distracting me from any thoughts of punishment. He glides them in and out easily because my being wet for him wasn't a lie. My body is under my command and I can control it as needed.

"Lie down on your back in the middle of the bed," he says suddenly as he wrenches his fingers from inside me.

Without hesitation, I scramble over to the middle of the bed and wince when I lay down on my newly inflicted welts. His dark eyes peruse over my large breasts, down over my flat tummy and wide hips, to my pussy.

"So beautiful. How'd you manage to trick me into becoming my fiancée?" he questions as he climbs on to the bed. He gently spreads my knees apart and hooks my legs around his waist. I swallow down my anxiety when he loops the belt around my neck. It isn't tight...*yet*.

"I didn't trick you. I just want to be with you all the time. I'm glad people will know I belong to you," I tell him with a practiced smile.

He yanks on the belt hard enough to pull me into a sitting position by my neck. My fingers naturally claw at the leather to loosen its grip. The air I was so easily breathing seconds before is completely cut off and my tongue hangs out as if in a search of just one tiny breath.

"Damn straight you belong to me," he snarls as he uses his other hand to guide me onto his cock. I slide down easily over him and he grunts in pleasure. "It'll be a nightmare, though, once Donovan gets wind of this. He doesn't share well."

Stars are glittering in my vision as I struggle to breathe. My first reaction is to get rid of the belt, but when I can't loosen it, I grab on to the back of his hair and attempt to pull him from me. He hisses at me but doesn't release me. Instead, he slams us down on the bed and he fucks me into the mattress, his grip never waning on the belt. When I go to push at his face to get him to release my throat, he bares his teeth to my forearm and bites down like a wild beast.

More searing pain jolts through me but I can't scream. My sobs, my screams, my pleas are all lodged in my throat below where the belt is cutting them off. I can feel the blood trickling down my arm and I start to grow dizzy.

My body goes limp beneath him. I don't remember him

coming. I fade off into the darkness of my mind. It's warm and quiet there. Safe. *He's* there.

"That's not a word." His eyebrow is arched up in challenge.

I stare at the Scrabble board and frown. "Where I come from, it is."

He smirks and shakes his head. "The things I allow…"

Smiling triumphantly, I accept all sixty-four points. "Your turn, loser."

His eyes are on the board and I take a moment to risk a glance at him. I like when he's relaxed and playful. "Keep talking, little girl. I'll still win and then what?"

"You're not going to win," I scoff.

His lips quirk up into a smile and he tugs at the knot in his tie, loosening it. The action steals my attention for a moment. "And if I do?"

Heat burns up my neck as a brief, wicked thought flits through my head. One I'd never allow myself to say aloud. I swallow down my embarrassment and meet his stare.

"You won't. But I'll humor you. If you do, what do you want?"

He reaches across the table to pull some tiles from the bag and accidentally brushes his hand against mine. Just an accident. I think. My cheeks must be blazing crimson at this point but a jolt of excitement courses through me at his touch. Our eyes meet, his searching mine with an unexpected heat behind them. Such an intense, foreign heat. I think. "If I win, you have to…" He looks off, somewhere behind me, as if he were considering this seriously. "Wash my car."

I'm already shaking my head and arguing. "It's ninety degrees out there, easily!"

He contemplates my words and his lips twitch with amusement. *"You can wear your swimsuit if you want. I'm easy. You know I'd never let you suffer."* At this, he winks. *Playfully.* I think.

I clench my thighs together and refrain from fanning the heat away from me, which seems to have crept inside on this unusually warm late October evening. "I'm going to win," I assure him. I think.

But then, I spend his entire next move wondering how I can let him catch up. Because, I do, in fact want to lose. Anything to see that hungry look in his eyes when he mentioned me wearing my bathing suit. And he was hungry. For me. I think.

I think *I want him to see me like that, barely dressed. And I'm not sure why.*

I think *he wants to see me like that, barely dressed. And I'm not sure why.*

"Mine," he says in a low, gravelly voice, which makes me shiver.

My eyes fly to his in shock but then I stupidly realize "mine" was his word, not a declaration... of any other sort. Oh. However, there's no mistaking the glint in his eyes. Primal and shameless. Starved. For me. I think.

He most definitely wants me.

I think.

Does it make me a bad person if I think *I want him too?*

"Shhh," his deep voice coos as I drag my eyelids open, stealing me from my warm memories.

He's still inside of me but he's removed the belt from my neck. His eyes shine with something I've never seen before. Adoration maybe? Pride?

My throat is hoarse and scratchy. I'd kill for some water right now but I'm too weak to move. I tense when he starts peppering kisses all over my face and then down along my sore throat. He makes his way to my collarbone and when he reaches the top of my full breast, he sucks the upper part of it hard into his mouth. I want to cry out but I'm too worn out to do much protesting. He sucks and sucks until I know I'll have a big-ass bruise for days.

"I'm ready for dinner, doll. I have some cases to look over but I want to watch you cook in nothing but those cowboy boots you're wearing," he says with a playful growl. "So fucking hot."

He climbs off of me and saunters off toward the bathroom, his sculpted ass tightening with each step. I attempt to sit up and manage to bring my shaky hand toward me to examine it properly. His teeth marks left a red, angry mark, and in some parts of his bite, he punctured the skin. Blood continues to seep from the wounds and I can only stare at it.

I don't realize he's returned until he pulls my hand from my gaze. His brows furrow as he inspects the wound. My belly flops when he brings my wrist to his mouth. I brace myself for him to hurt me again but instead, he runs his tongue along the flesh and licks up the blood. He flashes me a wolfish smile.

"Clean this up so it doesn't get infected," he instructs and climbs off the bed to start dressing. "Wrap it in some gauze and then start dinner. I'm fucking starving."

I let out a relieved sigh the moment he leaves the bedroom and dutifully do as he says. It isn't until I've cleaned my arm and am wrapping it in gauze that I allow myself to smile in celebration of my small victory.

I did it.

I fucking did it.

Logan was enraged beyond logical reason, yet I had the ability to bring him back down to earth. To me. This is progress. We may be going public with our relationship, but I won't let that ruin my carefully laid out plans. It'll be trickier, especially when Donovan assuredly shows up, but I have do this.

I need to do this.

My heart depends on it.

The fragility of my perfectly sculpted plan is hanging precariously in the balance of others who could ruin everything. People are nosy, especially the good-looking cop who ran me off the road. His eyes were calculating. Perceptive. Aware. Not one who seems to miss a single detail. I just pray to God I can fool him too.

The lives of the ones I love depend on my ability to play a part.

Three

Kasper

I HIT THE LOCK ON THE CAMARO AND STRIDE INTO THE police department with hot coffee in hand. Last night, I'd lain in bed for hours thinking about Nadia. She'd grown up since I'd last had eyes on her but she was still the stupid bitch from before. What pisses me off, though, is that she's been off the grid for three goddamn years only to just pop right back up. It doesn't make sense. I wanted to throttle the answers from her last night but the moment I learned she was with Logan, I knew things would have to play out much differently.

I would need to be careful.

This morning, I woke up with a new attitude. It didn't matter where she'd been. All that matters is where she is now. She's right under my nose and I can finally start implementing my plan to make her pay.

I yearn to collect her debt to me.

I've seen Chief's house. It's big and the man is loaded—how is the question. People seem to forget he wasn't always this way. At one time, he wasn't any better off financially than me and my family are. But he's rich now and nobody seems to question how or when it happened. Of course Nadia would move from one sugar daddy right into the arms of another. A sly little cunt is all she is. Everything is one big show and she's their little star. Acting the stupid, emotional damsel in distress back when she could have been revealing clues about Kasey. Then, hiding behind the domineering presence of her prick stepfather, Donovan Jayne—a fucking thorn in my side—when the media storm about my sister's kidnapping became too much for her fragile fucking self to take. And now, she's the police chief's perfect princess despite her breaking the goddamned law.

"Ghost," Lena, the department receptionist, greets as I walk into the building. "Head on over to the conference room. Chief is making a statement to the press. He came in with Jayne's stepdaughter." Her eyes widen and her dyed red eyebrows fly to her hairline which perfectly matches her brows. "This town is going to have a field day with this one," she mumbles as she shifts through papers on her desk. "He's like twenty years older than her. Why are we even having a press conference over this?"

Who the hell knows anymore in this town? I grunt but storm past her, ignoring her question. "Don't be a gossip, Lena."

Striding past my office, I eat up the distance to the conference room with long and purposeful steps. As I approach, I can see everyone in the department squished inside, including a couple of reporters from the local news stations. But Lena's right. Since when *is* the police chief's engagement newsworthy? The whole thing is fucking weird.

"The Jayne girl grew up to be a hot piece of ass," Bart Stokes, mutters to me as I squeeze into the room. "Have you seen the tits on that one?"

Jerking my head to him, I sear him with a scathing glare. "Maybe Chief would like to hear that comment?"

His cheeks redden—the devious smile falling off his face—and he drops his gaze to the floor. I've followed her life for so long that I almost feel a proprietary sense of ownership over her. She's *mine* to ruin and destroy. It's already bad enough Logan's marrying her. I don't need every other asshole in this precinct falling for the duplicitous bitch.

I want to be the one to make her fall.

And I know just how I'm going to do it, too.

Pushing through the crowd, I make my way to the front. Logan is imposing his commanding presence over the audience in his dress uniform. Neatly styled hair. Clean shaven. The complete embodiment of police perfection. When I finally bring her down, Logan too will no doubt suffer for her sins. It will get ugly and there will be consequences for my actions. But I will ride out of this town in a blaze of glory, my vengeance in hand, knowing that justice has been served against this gold-digging whore.

"Thank you all for coming today," Logan's voice thunders. "I know this is a little out of the ordinary for you all, but I have an important announcement and wanted everyone in on the great news. I'm getting married." He flashes a white smile which earns responding camera flashes. The man is a natural in front of a crowd. "Please meet my fiancée, Nadia Jayne. You may all recognize her as the daughter of my good friend and hotel and resort tycoon, Donovan Jayne. We plan to marry in the spring and I can't wait to start my life with this incredible woman."

Cameras flash and my eyes finally fall to her. No longer does she look to be the little broken bird from last night. No, today she's got her armor up and rewards the crowd with a winning smile she no doubt learned from Logan. Her hair is no longer messy but hangs in long, silky waves over her full tits, framing the soft features on her face. Her face is painted with a bunch of expensive looking makeup, certainly not the kind my sister used to wear, and she almost looks pretty. To everyone else. I can see how they'd think she was hot. Her eyes scan the people in the room and when they find mine, they stop. I watch with fascination as her pupils dilate and her pouty lips, which are stained red, part open.

Those lips will be the first step in her fall.

Her perfect, white teeth bite down on her bottom lip creating a beautiful contrast. Those lips are the color of blood and I feel my cock twitch at the idea of spilling some of hers. How fucking amazing would it be to run my sharp pocketknife along her throat and puncture the skin below her right ear. I could gather up her tainted blood with the pad of my finger and smear it around her mouth to see if it really does match her whorish lipstick. Would she suck herself off of my finger?

A shameful heat creeps up my neck as I realize I've given myself a hard-on fantasizing about her blood. As if realizing I'm turned on by her, she bats her eyelashes in an innocent way and sends me a meek smile. The smile is only meant for me, and it only serves to add fuel to my fire of hate.

How dare she try and play me at my own game?

I scowl at her until she breaks our gaze, a frown marring her enticing features. Logan continues rambling but I don't hear a word of it. I need to get the fuck out of here.

I need to think.

Prioritize.

Set my plan into motion.

Pushing back through the crowd, I escape the suffocating presence of her and unlock my office. Closing the door behind me, I remove my coat and roll up the sleeves of my dress shirt. I slip my iPhone into the dock and turn on some Led Zeppelin. As "Stairway to Heaven" starts playing, I begin to relax. Surprisingly enough, my love for seventies music was something I'd gotten from Donovan. Back when his brother worshipped the ground he walked on, and as a result, so did I. Funny how things change. That all seems like a lifetime ago. I'm staring out the window, contemplating my next move with lingering thoughts of my old friend hanging in the air, when a small knock on the door jerks me from my thoughts.

"Come in," I bark out but remain turned away from the door.

The door clicks open and the muscles in my back tense. It's her. I recognize the way my body flares to life with a hatred that makes me tremble when she is near.

"Um, Ghost?" she calls from the doorway. "Things were getting a little hectic in there. Logan asked me to come sit in your office until he's finished."

I turn to regard her and have to physically force the look of disdain from my features. My plan won't work if I start by scaring the shit out of her. With a sigh, I motion for her to sit down at one of the chairs across from my desk. "Close the door behind you."

She presses it shut and leans against it, folding her arms

over her chest. The white cardigan she wears over a peach colored dress gapes between each button. It's a pathetic attempt at hiding her generous breasts. When she clears her throat, I snap my gaze to hers, realizing I've been blatantly staring at her chest. To disarm her, I flash her a grin that works for every chick. One of those lopsided, smug grins that melts women like butter in my presence.

And thankfully, Nadia is no exception.

"Led Zeppelin," she says with a smile. "I approve."

"So glad I have your approval." My chest tightens and I clench my teeth. I don't need her goddamned approval but I placate her anyway.

Her lips part open again and she tears her gaze from mine, focusing on the nameplate on my desk, but when she reads it, her brows furrow as if something just clicked in her pretty little head.

Did someone finally learn how to pay attention?

Where were these fucking skills a decade ago?

I wonder if she's putting together the fact that I'm Kasey's brother. If she's afraid of me for that very reason, she should be. Because of her lack of description of the man who took my sister, she single-handedly ruined my life. Surely, she senses I'll ruin hers too. The thick curtain of hate hangs between us with no intention of being pulled away. It will always remain in front of me, veiling the beautiful woman before me with the constant reminder of her fortuitous mistake.

My sister was my everything. She and I had lost so much together. We had been bound by a grief that made our hearts bleed together. It was my responsibility to take care of her, just as my best friend had vowed to at one time.

He gave up everything for her and I was hell bent on picking up where he left off. I owed it to him and to her. As soon as college was over, I was going to come back for her and make sure she had the life she deserved—a life Dale and Mom could never give her while they loved the bottle more than they loved her. I'd had it all planned out. Kasey wouldn't have had to feel hopeless anymore. The heartache would have eventually gone away. I was going to fix my sister and keep her safe forever.

The rage ripples through me, heightened while in Nadia's presence, but I have to get my emotions in check. To watch her fall, I'll need her trust and eventual adoration. It will be more climactic. Beautiful. Deserving.

Needing to put my plan into action, I stride over to her, crowding her space. I'm shocked when I inhale the sweet scent of lemon. I half expected her to smell like sour deceit.

"How long have you two been dating?" I question. I'm standing close enough for my breath to blow some of her hair from her face. The urge to push the dark strand out of her eyes is strong.

She lifts her chin and her brown eyes lock onto mine. They widen and dart around almost frantically. You'd think I'd just asked her where she hid a body because the guilt and horror on her face is plain as day.

"A couple of months...like Logan was saying during his um, speech." Her voice is soft, timid even. I like the way her chest heaves in my presence as if she knows deep down what I'm thinking. Of how I want to obliterate her perfect little life and spit the remains in her face once my dirty work is done.

My eyes become fixated on her lie-spouting mouth.

When she swallows, I can't help but stare at her slender throat. But the moment I see a dark shadow ringing her neck, I furrow my brows. I'm wondering why the fuck she's slapped on a shitload of makeup to cover up a bruise.

"What's this?" I ask and drag my finger somewhat forcefully along the bruise, smearing the makeup away.

"¡Mierda!" She winces at the touch, making my cock twitch at her show of pain, and her eyes narrow. "Nothing," she lies.

I seize her throat with my hand but don't squeeze. Gently, I press against the bruise and watch with glee as she clenches her jaw in pain. Her bottom lip wobbles and I have the urge to bite it so it'll stop. Now my cock aches as it stretches the fabric of my slacks, eager to play with the stupid whore.

"What are you hiding?" Dipping forward, I inhale her lemony scent and briefly wonder if she tastes tart or sweet.

"I'm not hiding anything." More lies. She squirms but I don't release my grip on her neck. I'm not squeezing her, just simply restraining her.

"Are you happy?" My question carries an angry hiss, my lips just a breath away from hers. I could bite her lip easily right now. The craving to do so is making my entire body tense with need. I want to hurt and punish her.

Her eyes find mine and she nods. "Yes."

I should hate that she's happy while my sister is dead somewhere probably in a shallow grave with bugs eating at her remains. But what thrills me is that she's lying. Her transparency makes her deceit obvious. She's not happy. And that makes not only my plan easier. It puts a genuine smile of pleasure on my lips.

She deserves to hurt and ache. To cry and scream. Nadia Jayne deserves not one sliver of happiness.

"Liar," I say with a laugh. "Are you a kinky girl, sweet Jayne?"

Her woe-is-me and I'm-so-fucking-innocent façade falls as she pins me with a glare. "Don't call me that."

I throw my head back and laugh at her haughty attitude. "What? Jayne? I thought you loved being Donovan's little girl? What's Daddy think about you fucking his friend?"

"That's enough," she snaps. Her entire body ripples as if she's seconds away from clawing my eyes out. But she remains still, a picture of self-restraint.

I wonder what Logan would think if I fucked his sweet little fiancée right up against this door. Made her scream for the entire precinct to hear. Her flawless reputation would be tarnished in minutes and the game would be over.

As much as I'd love to push my dick into her pussy and mutter how much I fucking hate her in her ear, I know I'll take greater pleasure in her slow demise. She doesn't deserve for it to all be over in one swoop. I want to cut her only to let her heal. Then, I want to pick her scab over and over again until all her blood has run dry. I want to scar her for life.

Her head is mine to fuck with.

She's certainly pickled mine the fuck up.

"Awww," I taunt, my lips near hers. "Sweet Jayne's getting upset. Who will come to her rescue this time?"

"I don't need anyone to rescue me," she seethes. "Especially not some dirty cop who uses his authority to push around women." The sudden bite in her voice shocks me.

I shake my head in disgust. I'm nothing like that asshole

Dale. "I *do not* push around women." *Just you, Nadia.*

"You're *all* the same here."

We glare at each other for a moment. But then she goes to shove me away. I grab her wrist and push it against the door behind her to keep her in place. We're not done with this conversation.

"Ow," she yelps and her hard gaze falls. "Don't push around women, huh?"

"I guess you're right," I huff, annoyed that I'm no better than my stepfather at the moment. I'm battling with that inner thought when I become distracted. Warmth surrounds my thumb and I flick my stare over to where my hand covers her wrist. I stare in sick fascination as blood seeps through the white fabric of her cardigan around my thumb.

"You are nothing like what I've been told about you from…" she huffs and shakes away her frustration before lifting her chin. Her words become cool. "You're nothing like your reputation states."

I grunt at her jab and press into her wound. "I don't know who you've been talking to. Are you hurt?" The smile on my face is instantaneous at the sight of her bleeding. She doesn't fight me when I draw her arm from the door and bring it to me. When I push her sleeve up, she tries and fails to tug it away. I'm stronger and determined to inspect her injury. I don't bother with being gentle as I unwrap the gauze, my inner monster eager to see her blood. She's probably cut herself for attention. One of her many tricks.

But when I fully remove the bandage and it drifts to the floor, I'm shocked at what I'm seeing and the smile is wiped right from my face. Rage bubbles inside, although for once, it isn't aimed at her.

She doesn't hurt herself. Someone else does.

Teeth marks ravage the flesh and it's heavily bruised around the bite marks. This wasn't a simple love bite. Some kinky display of affection.

Someone bit the fuck out of her.

Someone wanted to tear through her like a rabid dog and devour her like a meal.

A growl rumbles in my throat.

"Are you having an affair behind Logan's back?" I demand, my gaze hardening. The Logan I know doesn't hurt people. And what would he think if his precious girl was fucking around on him. Maybe ruining her will be a lot easier than I originally thought it would be.

She gapes at me in shock. "Absolutely not and don't you dare insinuate such a thing."

I search her eyes for deceit and find nothing. But if she's not sleeping around, that means he inflicted these bruises. Chief and I go way back. He may be cocky, but he's not the type to do this shit. *Or so I thought...*

"Did he do this to you?"

Her eyes flit behind me and I follow her gaze to a picture of my sister on my back credenza. I almost wince in shame. If only Kase could see me now. Would she stare in horror like she would when Dale would beat on Mom? The way Nadia is staring at me now? Swallowing down my discomfort, I avoid placing Nadia and Kasey in the same category. Nadia is *not* a victim. I have to keep that fact clear in my head.

"Yes," she murmurs, her voice quivering with embarrassment, "but I asked him to."

Our eyes meet again and I furrow my brows together.

Her eyes seem to be pleading with me to understand.

"I see," I say softly. And I do. I see that she's hiding something. I'm not sure what exactly, but my instinct tells me it has everything to do with Logan. I've seen the same look in my own mother's eyes. Desperation and terror. Despite him being a model leader, hell, even someone I've learned to look up to over the past decade, I know everyone has their skeletons. As a matter of fact, I have some pretty fucking scary ones hanging in my own closet. Skeletons I attempt to hide from everyone. It appears that the king here in Aspen has a dirty little secret. Problem is, he knows mine too.

He has to know about my obsession with her.

Of course he fucking knows.

He was one of the responding officers at Kasey's crime scene. Logan Baldwin has always known she was my sister—and not just because we go way back to when I was a teenager. Logan knows this because my gasoline of vengeance is soaking this cold case, just begging for me to light a fire under it. When I checked out the file from the precinct basement, my name was signed on the log.

His attention to detail is as proficient as mine.

Surely, he knows I've been tailing her all these years.

So why in the hell did he hide the fact he was even with her until now? Is this some fucking mind game? I'd thought he'd grown up since becoming a leader in the community. I had long since pushed away how I remembered him as a teen and embraced the man he'd become. Yet now, I can't help but wonder what's truly lurking behind Logan's Cheshire cat grins and good 'ol boy persona.

One thing's for sure. I *will* find out.

Her eyes meet mine and her lip quivers as she glances at

the door. When she looks back at me, a chill ripples through her and her eyes flicker with fear. Not fear of me, though. For once in the last goddamned decade, I'm not trying to hurt her. This time, I feel an overwhelming urge to protect her. From him.

Why?

Because she's *mine* to destroy.

Not his.

It would be pointless for him to damage her before I get my chance. I can't wait to see the look on Logan's face when he realizes he's been had. When I'm balls deep in his pretty little fiancée and he has to witness the fucking act himself. Two birds, one stone. Mr. Perfect will be revealed for who he truly is—a goddamned woman beater like Dale.

This is going to be fun.

And therapeutic as fuck.

Stepping away from her, I grab a tissue from my desk and wipe her blood from my thumb. She watches me warily.

"I have some work to do," I tell her as I toss the bloody tissue, which does in fact match her plump crimson stained lips like I thought, into the trashcan. "Stay in here as long as you need." I swipe my iPhone from the dock and stalk out of the room without another word.

Time to start finally finding some answers.

Four

Nadia

ONCE HE'S GONE, I GLANCE OVER AT KASEY'S PICTURE again. I'd known her brother's name was Kasper but when he was introduced to me as Ghost, I hadn't connected those two pieces until I saw his nameplate. This could have been a moment to reach out to him. To befriend him after everything. But it's clear he has some hate/lust thing going on. I mean, I can understand why he wouldn't like me, but I don't understand his intensity or the heated interest in his stare. I could feel it practically rolling from him in waves. He clearly hates me though. I won't be making friends with him anytime soon.

What is it about me anyway that attracts the wrong type of men?

Do I have a flashing aura around me only they can see?

Mamá used to tell me all the time that our spirits had auras. That you could tell a lot about a person from the kind of light they projected. Mine must blink neon yellow and say "Hey! Over here! Come fuck with me! I'm asking for it!"

It has to be true because Kasper, the not-so-friendly ghost, just proved it. The way he called me sweet Jayne, a term of endearment I've only ever heard from one other man, struck an emotional nerve. A harsh and devastating reminder of my past. After a clipped, semi polite goodbye, he stormed out of his office, leaving me to quickly rewrap my wound. The longer he's away from me, the less my judgment is clouded by his intense presence. Had Logan walked in on whatever it is Kasper and I were doing, he would have been enraged.

And I cannot have Logan lose control.

Not now.

Not ever.

My whole existence revolves around making him happy until the time is right. To get him to trust me just long enough. To watch him slip up just once.

And then I'll fly in like an avenging angel and take my bloody heart out of his hands once and for all.

"You ready?"

Logan's deep voice startles me and I nearly drop Kasper's nameplate. It's juvenile how they all call him Ghost. *Ghost* sounds serene and simple and calm. Kasper sounds like the name of a crazy person. More fitting actually.

But despite him acting like a jerk, I can't help but feel hopeful. A tiny part of me realizes connecting with him could be exactly what I need. He seems like a perceptive man.

"Yes," I squeak out and cross my arms, careful to hide the blood stain on my cardigan. "Is everything okay?"

My eyes flicker to where he keeps his phone in his breast pocket. One hour. One short fucking hour is all it takes these days to send me into a panic.

He flashes me a wicked, knowing grin before pulling the phone out and tapping a few buttons. "Good thing you reminded me. I almost forgot." Once he pushes it back into his pocket, I let out a breath of relief.

I smile tightly at him. He never forgets. Ever. Because if just once he did forget, I could make my play. It would be a race against time but if it worked, I could untangle my heart from his and bury him once and for all. But if my play didn't work in time? If I failed, the cost would be unmeasurable. Brutal. Life-altering. Deadly. And that is exactly why I wait.

"Where's Ghost?" he questions.

Frowning at his words, I shrug my shoulders. "I don't know. He seems like an angry man. I don't think he likes me for some reason."

Logan's eyes narrow as he scrutinizes me. "Well, he's a damn good cop and he did think you stole my truck. I chastised him in front of you. Most men don't take well to being embarrassed in front of a woman they desire."

I bristle at his comment and scoff. "He does not...*desire* me. I think he'd prefer to hurt me if he had the chance."

Logan's gaze jerks to mine and he glowers at me. "Only *I* can hurt you."

Blinking rapidly, I realize I just let my guard down. For once, Logan wasn't my nightmare—someone else was—and I easily confided in him like a friend. The mistake is a horrible one I can't ever make again.

"No," I agree and launch myself into his arms. "Only you, mi amor."

His possessive growl calms me. He strides us over to the desk after locking the office door and shoves Kasper's nameplate out of the way before laying me down on the cool surface.

"What are you doing?" I hiss and my eyes flick over to door.

He laughs but it's anything but warm and friendly. "I'm fucking you on my subordinate's desk."

I want to argue but I've already gotten on Logan's bad side enough in the last twenty-four hours. "What if someone comes in?"

He grabs my hips and flips me over onto my belly. I grab onto the edge of the desk as he pushes my dress up over my ass. "Kasper left. Besides, it's locked. Nobody's coming in."

His fingers hook the top of my panties and he shoves them down my thighs letting them fall to my ankles on their own. I try to focus on Kasper's meticulously organized office, anything to take my mind from what I suspect Logan's about to do. There's no mental preparation that can get me ready for this. I can force myself to get turned on all I want but unless he has lube, which I know he doesn't, it's going to hurt like hell.

The key is to focus on anything but the pain.

Turning my head to the side, I stare at a shiny silver pen sitting in a stand. Kasper's name has been engraved on it and it's spotless. Completely free of fingerprints or smudges. I try to fixate on the fancy font of the *K* and ignore the painful way Logan's dick pokes at the tight ring of muscles between my ass cheeks.

"Is that pen more interesting than me, doll?"

I shake my head in denial but he's already snatching it from its stand. Snapping my eyes closed, I pray he's gentle. When I feel the cold metal slide against my clit, I let out a sigh of relief. His free hand grips my ass cheek painfully as he teases my sensitive nub that now begins to throb. Logan either gives me no orgasms at all as a sick form of punishment, or he forces them on me. They're never for my enjoyment. They're always a way to torment me.

"You like Ghost's pen on your pussy?" he taunts. "You like making that mean man pay for upsetting you?" I'm thankful he misinterprets my distaste for his lieutenant as just that, dislike versus the unusual way the man had my heart racing with hope, such a glorious fucking feeling. It was almost like being thrown a life jacket before being tossed to sea. There would be no drowning with someone like Kasper on my side. I just have to figure out a way to get him there.

As much as I'd hated how rude he was with me, I liked the flash of anger in his eyes upon seeing what Logan had done to my wrist. It was as if he wanted to be the one to own me and hated the very fact that another man did instead. Despite his actions, I knew it was something I could work with. I've certainly worked with much worse.

"Oh!" I cry out when he pushes the cold metal into my pussy. "¡Jesucristo!" I don't try to stop Logan's torturous assault on me. This is his show and at least presently, he's not hurting me. I can suffer through being fucked with a pen. When his other hand slips from my ass and curls around me to touch my throbbing clit, I let out a small moan.

"I think you like making him pay, you dirty little girl. Are you going to come all over his pen? Imagine how pissed he'll be when he goes to write with it and finds it sticky with your cum. Do you think he'll be angry? Or do you think he'll suck on it?"

My nerve endings flare to life as Logan taunts me. The need to climax is overwhelming and I squirm against his touch. I close my eyes and let the sensations overtake me. A jolt of pleasure crackles through me and I shudder with a heavenly orgasm. It's been a long time since Logan's let me get off properly.

He continues to slowly fuck me with the pen until I'm a useless heap of muscle sprawled out on the desk. With a pop, he slips out the pen and carefully places it back in the holder. I let out a mewl as he rams his cock into my pussy. The pleasure is intense and I almost think I could get off from him fucking me this way but I know better than to delude myself.

Logan's only warming himself up.

I force myself to relax just as he slides his now lubed up dick from me. Without any warning, he pushes into my asshole with little resistance on my part. I was ready and waiting. We've danced to this same song too many times to count and as long as his dick is wet, I can take it.

Normally when he fucks my ass, I just drift off to my happy place. I dream of irises with shards of sliver and flecks of blue. I get lost in lingering scents of love and my whole reason in this life. Because usually, when he takes my ass, it's all for him. He doesn't need me to participate.

But today?

Today, Logan is a new breed.

He's a man I don't understand, certainly not the man I've learned to observe for the past three years. I need to know why, this time, he's playing with my clit as he fucks me. I need to understand how, this time, he's making sure I enjoy it too.

Is it his way of marking me in Kasper's office? Is he somehow jealous of him? Or is he softening toward me?

The third question has my heart stopping altogether. If he's softening, then it's working. Everything I do has a purpose and I refuse to give up. I need to make him fall in love with me. Because that unlocks my entire world.

All I need are six little numbers.

And fifteen minutes.

I close my eyes only to be launched into a memory that happily steals me from the present.

"You're fifteen minutes late," a deep voice growls from the kitchen.

I let out a squeak of surprise and walk into the dark room. In the shadows, he stares at me with his hip leaned against the countertop.

"I didn't realize I had a curfew," I huff out in defense. "I thought we were friends, Donovan. Not to mention the fact that I'm eighteen."

He lets out a breath of air and scrubs his face with his palms. "Of course we're friends. I was just worried. You texted me and said you'd be here fifteen minutes ago. After what happened with Kasey, I tend to panic."

Warmth floods through me. I toss my purse onto the countertop and make my way over to him. Once I'm near, I wrap my arms around his waist to hug him. A year ago, I would have laughed at the idea of willingly being this comfortable around Donovan. But things change. People change. "I'm sorry."

His palms circle my back and he chuckles. "I overreacted. I'm sorry too."

Smiling, I look up at him. The moonlight shines in from

the window and lights up part of his face. He's a good-looking
man, no doubt about it. My mom is lucky to have him.

"Now that we got that out of the way," I say, but don't
make any moves to break free from our embrace, "I think I
found a clue."

He cocks an eyebrow up in question. "What's that?"

I bite down on my bottom lip before speaking. "I spoke
with Kasey's stepfather Dale."

At the mention of Dale, his brows furl together angrily.
His entire body tenses. When I go to step back, his fingers
grip the back of my shirt to keep me in place, sending a thrill
humming down my spine.

"You spoke to that prick without me?" he hisses. "I don't
trust him around anyone I love."

My heart pounds at the mention of his love for me and I
instinctively place my palms on the front of his chest to calm
him. He tears his gaze from mine to briefly stare up at the
ceiling. I'm not sure why he's acting so strangely.

"You're not hearing me," I huff in exasperation.

He's quiet for a long moment as his gaze lingers on my
lips. "I always hear you, baby. Even when I don't know what
the hell you're saying."

When he smiles, I let out a rush of air and try to still
my thundering heart. "It was fine. Karla was there so I wasn't
alone with him. I just wanted to ask them a few questions
about where they were that morning. The police already ques-
tioned them but I needed to know…for myself. Do you understand? I feel responsible for what happened to Kasey. If only
I…"

His fingers trace along my throat from just below my ear
to my exposed collar bone sending currents of unusual plea-

sure surging through me. I'm momentarily dazed. I have no idea what I was even talking about. All I can think about is the way Donovan's touch is so soft and possessive. When our eyes meet, neither of us speaks. His shimmering icy irises drop to my lips and he licks his own. A heat—so foreign and overwhelming—seems to blaze its way through me. "You're not responsible, baby."

For one brief moment, I'd say he wants to kiss me.

Before I can give much thought to it, I hear footsteps thumping down the stairs. I tear myself from his grip and stumble back a few steps. A second later, light blinds me.

"What are you two up to in the dark? You weren't going to wake me if you turned on some lights," Mamá chides as she enters the kitchen.

She places a quick kiss on my cheek and then takes a bottle of water from the refrigerator. My eyes find Donovan to gauge his reaction. His jaw is clenched and I swear he looks as though he's in pain as he now grips the countertop, avoiding my mother's stare.

"I was just talking to Donovan about a lead I'd followed up on," I explain, a slight quiver of embarrassment in my voice. "But it doesn't matter. It ended up being a waste of my time."

She chuckles. "You two and your detective games. You definitely have that in common."

Donovan snaps his head toward her and glares. The room chills several degrees from the look on his face. She simply shrugs her shoulders and leaves without a word to her husband. As soon as she's gone, he turns his attention toward me. When I shiver under his intense expression, he seems to snap out of his daze. He runs his fingers through his hair and *stalks off muttering an "I'm sorry" on his way out.*

My stomach churns at his abrupt dismissal. I want to chase after him and ask him what's wrong. But something tells me I need to drop it for the night. Not to mention, I have a mountain of homework to catch up on.

Flipping off the light, I make my way through the dark house toward my bedroom. I pass by the guest room on the way. A sliver of light filters into the hallway. It makes my heart ache that they don't sleep in the same bedroom. I don't understand it and am too afraid of what the answer would be if I ask why.

I should keep going toward my bedroom but curiosity has me taking a few steps back. Peeking in, I glance around the small space. Donovan stands with his back to the door as he sheds his shirt. His back muscles flex with each movement, and this time, heat floods through me straight between my legs. When I hear the jingle of his belt as he unfastens his pants, I part my lips open to let out a sigh. Soon his pants are on the floor and his sculpted ass, in nothing but a pair of black boxer briefs, is what I'm staring at. He then steps out of the slacks and strides toward the bathroom.

A part of me wishes he would have just taken off his boxers too while in the room. I wanted to see his bare backside.

What kind of perverted girl does that make me?

I swallow down the embarrassment of where my thoughts were headed and scurry back to my room. Back to where I can touch myself in the darkness. Where I'm safe to fantasize about whatever the hell I want.

My memory fades and it takes a moment to realize where I'm at. Logan pinches my sensitive clit causing me to immediately shudder beneath him. Another orgasm slices through me, this time causing the muscles in my rectum to ripple with pleasure. Blinding white ecstasy sears through me and I moan a little too loudly in the small office. Logan's cock seems to double in size and he grunts as he explodes with his release inside of me.

His cock softens and he pulls it slowly from me. My legs are weak and I feel oddly satiated.

"Come on, tick tock," he says as he pulls his pants back up. "We need to get you home."

The shocking reminder of the time startles me into action and I quickly pull my panties up, ignoring the way his cum from my ass soaks them, so I can make the walk of shame through the precinct.

"I'm going to eat my supper in the basement. Care to join me?" he questions as he fills a tray with the food I cooked. His eyes are almost sad which alarms me.

Bile rises in my throat but I swallow it down and force a smile. "No, I'd prefer to stay up here. Maybe clean up a little."

He chuckles and raises a brow that makes his features seem more handsome. Boyish even. I try not to cringe. "Are you afraid I might accidentally leave you down there?" he asks feigning an innocence we both know he has long since possessed. He abandons his tray and saunters over to me, wrapping his arms around my waist. "Is my baby doll getting comfortable with playing wifey already?"

I stand on my toes and kiss his full lips. "Maybe," I tell him, injecting a hint of playfulness into my voice.

His hands slide into my hair and he groans as he kisses me deeply. If I can get him to fuck me really quick, he'll be too tired to think of much else tonight. The rest of the night will go smoothly as a result.

Earlier, when we'd come home, he'd taken a quick shower before heading back to work. I took my time and scrubbed his scent from my body. The entire time, under the hot rain, I contemplated what my next move would be. Am I brave enough to sneak out of bed and try to get to his phone in the middle of the night? Could I manage to sweet talk the information out of him? Perhaps even get him wasted somehow, and drive the things I need to know right out of his stubborn head?

Of course no answers came to me while in the shower.

When it comes to Logan, he's the ruler of my world. I have to bow at his feet until my time to overthrow the dictator comes along. I've been patient. Have craved that moment for three long years. One day soon, my prison sentence will be over.

"Today, in your lieutenant's office," I say forcing a breathy sigh against his lips, "was so hot. I've been horny for you ever since."

He pulls away and his brows pinch together. "Really?" He rears his head back from mine marginally, studying me. I maintain my façade of poised interest. "Why didn't you call? You didn't look that horny while you swept the entire house and then spent hours cleaning the baseboards after I went back to work. You know I watch your every move."

I suck in a sharp breath of air. *Yes, I knew he was watching.* There are cameras all over his house. In my bedroom and in the adjacent bathroom, his bedroom, and one in the living room that also captures the dining room. He doesn't need to have a camera in the kitchen because he knows I love being in there. I've never once done anything to make him think I'd ever dream of running or of trying to hurt him. Dutifully, I clean and cook for him. Every day. And when he comes home, I let him fuck me however and whenever. The only time I ever step foot out of the house is when it's under his specific instruction. I absolutely hate leaving the house, but at least twice a week, he sends me on an errand to fetch something or other.

"Do you ever work?" I joke and flash him a wide grin. "Maybe next time I'll clean naked. That'll distract you. Voy a ser tu criada coqueta." *I'll be your flirty maid.*

My attempt to be cute and coy works because a moment later, he's shoved me to my knees, right there in the middle of the kitchen, his supper forgotten. He rips open his fly and yanks down his pants, releasing his engorged cock and ramming it down my throat. I dig my nails into his thighs and take him deep, just the way he likes it. If he comes down my throat, then I've done my job.

All part of the plan.

He thrusts into my face, forcing the back of my head against the cabinet behind me and begins brutally fucking my mouth. Hot tears streak from my eyes but I take it. Because I have to. When I hear his desperate groan, I prepare my throat and let his hot seed run down the back of it. His cock finally stops twitching and he slips from my mouth, my slobber still tethering us together.

"You really are trying to be the perfect wife," he says with a half grin and ruffles my hair like I'm a damn dog. "Good girl."

I smile as he pulls his pants back up, grabs the tray, and heads for the basement.

Don't think about it.

Closing my eyes, I remain still for a few minutes to compose myself. He's down there now. Eating. In his fucked up little cave.

Don't fucking think about it!

I grit my teeth to keep from screaming in frustration because I can't *not* think about it. No matter how strong I try to be, there are some things I can't block out. It's an impossible feat. Nobody is that strong. Not even me.

Bang! Bang! Bang! Bang!

I pop my eyes open and quickly stand up. Logan's down in the basement so I know he can't hear the door. If he happens to look at his phone, he'll see me open the door on the camera feed but something tells me he'll be too preoccupied.

Smoothing my hair down and taking a calming breath, I affix a smile and prepare myself to greet whoever is at the door. He'd warned me that we may start having unwanted visitors soon and to always be on my game. I rush over to the front door and open it quickly, prepared to send the visitors on their way.

Logan's napping, I'll tell them. *Come visit another time*, I'll say.

I half expect to see his neighbor Ruby from down the road who likes to deliver casseroles from time to time because she thinks he's a lonely bachelor. But instead, I lock eyes with *him*.

Donovan Jayne.

His grey-blue eyes widen momentarily before his gaze

hardens. "Where in the fuck have you been for the last three years, Nadia? The letter you sent explaining how you needed to 'go find yourself' was bullshit, wasn't it?"

It was complete bullshit. He's right. I take a step back and glance over his shoulder. Thankfully, Mamá isn't with him. I don't think I could take seeing her. Not after so long. It would break me and I absolutely cannot break. Not when I'm so close.

"I'm in love and we're getting married," I blurt out, ignoring his mentioning the letter, the quiver in my voice belying my words.

He scowls and shakes his head. "Not to him you're not. Not with Logan fucking Baldwin. Over my dead body!"

"Please," I beg and hold my hands up defensively. "Just leave, *mi cielo*."

His entire body freezes at my words. After Kasey was taken all those years ago, Donovan had made good on his promise to help me search for her. He'd spent an ungodly amount of money on private investigators and donations to the police department, so they could utilize the very best search methods at their disposal. He protected me when I needed it most as a young woman. I'd never spoken against him again. Our relationship developed into...a very close one.

I love Donovan and owe him a lot.

Everything in fact.

Which is why I need him to get the hell out of here before he ruins it all.

"Donovan, please," I try again, my voice growing shrill with anxiety. "I'm okay. I promise. Confia en mi." *Trust me.*

Ignoring my words, he storms inside the house and

draws me into his arms. His embrace is greedy and starved. But none of that matters now because I have a job to do. Selfish for one brief second of happiness though, I inhale his clean scent and let it take root in my lungs. When he starts pressing kisses into my hair, I clutch onto the back of his suit jacket and take a welcome reprieve of a few more seconds with him.

He's the only comfort in this world I can physically touch.

All of my other comforts are just out of reach.

"You're coming home, baby. Now." His voice is a possessive growl and he pulls away to stare down at me. "Grab your purse or whatever. I'll take you back home."

I'm already shaking my head before he even gets the words out. "N-N-No! I love Logan and am marrying him!"

His face falls, devastation contorting his features, but when I hear heavy footsteps approaching, he snaps his gaze to Logan who I can sense with every part of my being as he enters the room. Donovan's face turns murderous and his entire body tenses with rage.

"You motherfucker!" Donovan roars and pushes past me, charging for Logan.

I shriek and scramble out of the way. Logan, somehow seems to seethe with unleashed fury. Having Donovan on his turf is too close for comfort.

Donovan manages to swing a fist at Logan but he's not quick enough. Logan ducks out of the way and shoves Donovan from him. He grunts, quickly facing Logan again and charges. "You can't marry her because she's mine!"

Logan snarls and his fist connects with Donovan's jaw, a loud crack echoing in the room. I should help Donovan but I'm not about to get in the middle of two furious storms raging against each other. "She's a grown-ass woman now and certainly not yours anymore, so get the fuck over it!"

Donovan charges again and his shoulder impacts Logan's chest. He tackles him hard against the wall, sending Logan's back smashing through the Sheetrock.

"You were one of my best friends!" Donovan snarls. "You knew she was off limits. I had to find out about this on the goddamned news."

Logan manages to swing a fist at Donovan who narrowly ducks out of the way. More Sheetrock explodes, this time at Logan's hand.

"I'm still your friend, asshole," Logan spits and cracks his knuckles. "But you need to get the fuck off my property and calm your ass down before I have my boys bring you in."

Donovan runs his fingers through his always gelled-to-perfection hair, messing it up completely. I've never seen him so furious. Not like this. Sure, he's had moments where his powerful exterior falls away and reveals a vulnerable man. But it doesn't happen often. Unfortunately, it only happens when it concerns me.

I'm Donovan's weakness.

The very sword he'd impale himself on if it came to it.

"I want to talk to Nadia alone," Donovan hisses, his eyes flitting over to me. Assessing me. Washing over me. Checking to make sure I'm okay. It's the way Donovan is. He protects and takes care of what belongs to him. Always and without fail.

"Not going to fucking happen," Logan snaps. "Not when you're so pissed off."

Donovan screams again and launches himself at Logan. They crash down the hallway past the basement door through the entryway to my bedroom. The door is nearly ripped from its hinges and they both fall into the room with a grunt. I hurry after them to make sure they aren't killing each other.

Logan manages to straddle Donovan and back hand him. But Donovan's a big boy and he shoves Logan away. He yanks a gun from the back of his pants and points it at Logan, his chest heaving with intent—intent to kill—and I cry out as I rush him. If he kills Logan, he kills me. My heart will cease to beat.

"No!" I shriek and tackle him onto my bed, knocking the gun from his hand onto the floor. We're a tangled mess of limbs and his arms instinctively wrap around my back.

"Oh, God," he grunts, his breath coming out in labored breaths. "How did this happen? How did you fall for *him*?"

I hear a familiar click of metal and I stiffen in Donovan's arms.

"Let her go and get the *fuck* out of my house." Logan's voice is low and scathing.

Donovan grips me harder but I struggle and squirm until I'm out of his arms. My eyes dart all around as I take in the scene before me. Donovan, the big, strong powerful man on his back, stares up at me from the bed, betrayal marring his features. And Logan stands over him pointing his dropped gun at his face.

"This isn't over," Donovan snaps and scrambles to his feet. He storms over to me and quickly hugs me once more before he stalks out of the house. The front door slams as he leaves and my weak heart goes with him.

Logan strides over to me and uses the barrel of Donovan's gun to lift my chin. My eyes lock with the monstrous ones I'd been so good at containing. His beast is running wild and free. And it's starving. Starving for me.

"You're in so much fucking trouble, bad girl."

Five

Kasper

YESTERDAY, I LOST CONTROL. I'D HAD THE BITCH IN MY grasp and I fucking lost it. I nearly kissed her for fuck's sake. And when I'd seen her bruises and the way Logan tore through her flesh with his teeth, I was infuriated.

I'd like to lie to myself and claim it was because he was ruining her before I could get my hands on her. But that wasn't it. All night, I lay in bed and contemplated my new-found anger that for once wasn't directed at her. I thought about Mom and Dale. The eerily similar relationship between Logan and Nadia. My mind had been a mess thinking about ways to fucking save her like I could never do for my own mother.

Fucking ridiculous in hindsight.

This morning though, I woke up with my head back in the game. My new plan was formulating and beginning to take shape. A plan to impregnate Nadia and spend the rest of my life terrorizing her for child visitation and all the other bullshit that goes along with shared custody. So goddamned tempting. I wouldn't simply mess up her world for now, I could mess it up until the day she dies. Every time she looked at her child, she'd be reminded of me. Just like every time I look at her, I'm reminded of my sister who she couldn't help.

I'll be her worst fucking nightmare.

At least she wouldn't get beat on...

The thought sobers me up, once again my own personal experiences clouding my judgment, and I shake it away. I need to slowly work my way into her heart. Make her love me even. She'll fall for me, head over fucking heels. I will be her security. Her love. Her safety. Once she's finally settled in my arms, my child growing in her stomach, maybe even a ring on her finger, I'll dump her.

Dramatically.

Suddenly.

And watch her whole world crumble around her.

I will remind her she's just a stupid bitch and if she'd ever learn to pay attention, she would have noticed it was all a fucking act. An act that resulted in her destruction, all in the name of revenge.

"Isn't that right, Ghost?" Logan's voice booms, jerking me from my daydreaming about his fiancée.

Fucking woman beater.

I drag my gaze to meet his and nod. "Tourist season is always a bitch. I agree, extra patrol, especially on the weekends. Are we in a position to hire more unis?"

His eyes flicker in surprise, probably at the fact that I *was* listening and heard every word of his speech. But he knows me better than that. I don't miss a single thing. Ever.

"Yeah, HR is already interviewing. Until then, I'll assign

some boys to rotate shifts," he tells me as he stands from his desk. He walks over to the door and closes it before coming to sit back down. "I need your help with something. On the down low. Between us."

I sit up in my seat and affix him with a curious stare. "What's up?"

"Donovan fucking Jayne," he says with a growl. "Bastard showed up last night at the house. I was in the basement and Nadia unknowingly let him in. He went ape shit on her and damn near threw her over his shoulder caveman style. Luckily, I got him out of there."

My eyes sweep over him. His easygoing demeanor he usually wears is gone. I've seen this murderous scowl on his face once before when I was with my best friend. We watched as Logan kicked the shit out of some pimply kid at the rec center. It took Donovan and a couple of other guys to pull him off. I'd never heard what set him off but it was eye-opening to see someone who was normally fairly calm in an all-out rage.

He keeps his beast contained in public, that's for damn sure.

These days, though, it appears Logan is having a hard time keeping his smile affixed and his shoulders relaxed. In fact, he's struggling to keep what I now know is a mask in place.

"What does this have to do with me?" I ask, rubbing at a knot at the base of my neck.

He sighs and pulls his phone from his pocket when a timer goes off. I watch him poke at six numbers before he shoves it back into his pocket. "We sort of had a brawl. The house is torn all to shit. I was wondering if maybe you could come by tonight and take a look. Maybe take some measurements and get some crap to fix it. I'll pay double your normal rate if you push any of your clients out of the way and help me out."

The idea of spending more time with Nadia is tempting. And actually perfectly fits my plan. "Sure, man."

"That's not all," he tells me and steeples his fingers together as he rests his elbows on his desk. "During the day, while you're on duty, I want eyes on Donovan. I want you to watch his every move and report back to me if he does anything stupid. If I have to put his ass away, I will. Nobody is taking Nadia away from me. Not even her perverted stepdaddy."

I clench my teeth to keep from smirking.

I'm taking her away, asshole.

Instead of revealing the seething rage that simmers below the surface, I flash him an easy smile and stand. "On it, Chief."

I leave his office and stalk back to mine. Once I've pushed through the door, my gaze instantly surveys the space. The very first thing I notice is the scent. A lingering smell of sex. Familiar. Enticing.

Kicking the door closed behind me, I stride over to my desk. My nameplate has been shoved away but aside from that, the space appears to be untouched. I sit at my desk and my eyes zero in on blood.

Blood from her wrist.

Smeared across the edge of my desk.

That motherfucker had sex with her on my desk.

Fury explodes within me and I clench my fists. Everything in me screams to storm back into his office and bash his goddamned skull in. To rip away his good cop mask and reveal to the entire precinct what sort of monster lies within.

But I don't.

Instead, I take a deep breath and lean back in my desk chair. My eyes land on my pen and I pluck it from its stand. I've had this pen since before I left for college. Kasey saved up all of her babysitting money and bought it for me as a going away present for college. It's special to me. Very fucking special.

It's streaked and my heart thumps in my chest. Curiously, I draw it up to my face just under my nose and inhale. A growl rumbles in my throat. It reeks of sex. With an annoyed sigh, I grab a tissue and set to cleaning the damn thing off. This display of marking his property in my office is a good indication of his beast tearing through its cage. Eventually people will see him for who he really is. Once the pen is safely back in its holder, still smelling like her, I stand and leave my office as I attempt to harness my anger for her. With Logan doing stupid shit at every turn, he's making me lose my focus.

And I need to focus.

To remember the plan.

I'll make her so crazy in love she'll gladly give up her abusive man for someone like me.

A small grin plays at my lips as I stride out of the building toward my car, a cold chill swooping down from the mountains, freezing my already frigid heart.

Time to play, sweet Jayne.

Today, following Donovan around, was a waste of my god-damn time. He'd just sat up in his big office all day at the Aspen Pines Lodge he owns at the top of the mountain. When he left for lunch, he was on the phone the entire time, pacing and yelling at whoever was on the other line. I'm sure he's trying to find a way to get his precious stepdaughter back. Probably recruiting the best damn lawyers or some shit. Problem is, though, he doesn't realize just how powerful Logan is. Logan gets what he wants. Always. Donovan isn't big enough to take that away from him.

Lucky for me, I am.

And I will.

I will take the pretty little she-devil right from under him.

It's going to be satisfying to watch it all crumble.

I'm pulled from my thoughts once I turn onto Logan's driveway. He'd said to come after work to take some measurements so I could purchase the materials necessary. When I texted him to let him know I was on my way, he'd been short in his response, telling me he got hung up at the office and he'd see me shortly.

The smile on my lips is immediate as I put my car in park and climb out. I'll have a few minutes with Nadia alone. Just enough time to rile her up a bit.

I bang on the door and then a few minutes later, she answers, shock morphing her features. My eyes peruse down her tight, low-cut long-sleeved dress that hits her mid-thigh. The material is bright orange and makes her skin seem even tanner than usual.

"You do realize it's supposed to snow today?" I ask, raising a brow at her wardrobe choice.

She frowns and folds her arms across her chest. "It's warm inside. What do you want?"

Ignoring her rudeness, I shoulder past her into the house and saunter over to a large hole in the wall. Music plays in the background—some Dean Martin crap—and I shake my head. "This is going to be fun," I groan, putting my hands on my hips.

I hear the door slam behind me and her bare feet padding across the wood floor. "You should probably leave."

She comes to stand beside me and I turn to her and smirk. "Your *fiancé* asked me to come over and take some measurements. You wouldn't want to upset him again," I tell her with a low hiss. "He might bite your jugular next time."

"Hijo de puta..." she retorts in Spanish and I make note to look it up later. An annoyed huff then escapes her and she comes to stand in front of me. "Very funny. But just so you know, you're being recorded. Don't try anything like you did in your office yesterday. I can assure you he won't be happy." She lifts her chin and meets my gaze bravely.

Nonchalantly, I skim my eyes over every surface in the living room. While I walk over and touch the parts of the wall that needs repairing, I survey the space for the alleged cameras. Sure enough, one is mounted high in one corner. The Dean Martin song ends and soon Stephen Tyler is belting out the lyrics to "Crazy." Now this, this I approve of.

"Where else is there damage?" I question, my voice all business.

She motions for me to follow her down the hallway. A quick glance tells me there isn't a camera in here. But as we pass a door with a keypad, I stop and point at it. "What's in there?"

Her head whips around to face me and her eyes widen. "The basement. Dreadful place."

Running my finger along the keypad, I raise an eyebrow at her. "Keeping the monsters out," I question, my voice dropping low, "or in?"

Her face blanches and she swats my hand away from it. "If *only* it kept them out," she mutters, a hint of fear lacing her words. "Now don't touch that again. Not ever." Her gaze becomes hard and it makes me curious. I give her a clipped nod and follow her to a bedroom where the doorframe is splintered and a piece of wood hangs from it. My eyes skim the room and I notice another camera.

I pull out my measuring tape and jot a few things down on my notepad, ignoring her eyes boring into me. Once I've taken a few pictures of the doorway and made my notes, I go back into the hallway. When I walk into the master bedroom, she yells at me.

"Don't go in there!"

Scowling at her, I shrug my shoulders and make my way into the room anyway. A quick glance around tells me there's another camera in here. I slip into the bathroom to take a piss. After I wash my hands, I exit the bathroom to find her glaring at me as she sits on the bed. I smirk at her and let my eyes graze over a locked chest at the end of the bed before stepping back into the hallway. When I'm certain she's on my heels, I turn around abruptly. She lets out a squeak when she runs right into my hard chest.

"No cameras in here?"

She shakes her head and furrows her brows in confusion. "No, why?"

My hands find her curvy waist and I push her gently

against the wall beside the key pad. "Because I should have kissed you yesterday and I've been wanting to do it ever since." Her eyes widen when my mouth descends on hers.

"No," she retorts with a bite to her voice, "I would never—"

But her words are silenced when my nose nudges against hers and I inhale her. She parts her mouth open and lets out a sweet gasp the second my lips brush against hers. I slip a hand into her dark, wavy locks and grip her hair, tilting her to where I can gain better access. A small sound escapes her and it makes my cock thicken in my slacks. Crushing her with my kiss, I plan to take it slow. Tease her with it. Instead, I end up devouring her because she tastes so goddamned delicious.

A few moments later, she places her hands on my chest and pushes me away. Her brown eyes, which swirl like melted chocolate, regard me curiously. When I'm this close to her, she seems like less of a villain and more of something I'd like to conquer for my own selfish male reasons that have nothing to do with my sister. With my lips still wet from our kiss, a haze of confusion briefly clouds my mind.

"Never what, sweet Jayne? Kiss me? Too late," I taunt, a hint of playfulness in my voice. I want to throttle myself for sounding like a pussy but I calmly remember that I'm supposed to be wooing her, not treating her like a fucking asshole.

She starts to argue but my lips are on hers again. Her hot breaths quicken as I thrust my tongue inside of her.

"The video," she squeaks out suddenly and jerks from my grasp.

I frown at her, understanding washing over me, and

saunter down the hallway away from her. She scampers into the bedroom with the splintered doorframe. Licking my lips, I revel in her sweet taste while I measure the wall for the Sheetrock. After several minutes, she comes up beside me and peers at what I'm doing.

"We shouldn't have done that," she whispers.

Shrugging, I turn toward her. "Does it pick up sound?"

"No," she assures me. "I've tested it before."

"So he won't hear if I fuck you against the wall in the hallway?"

She swallows and her eyes dart to mine at my words. A crimson heat darkens her neck. It affects my cock and I grit my teeth to ward off the obvious hard-on. "I guess not," she murmurs. "Care for a drink of water?"

When she motions for the kitchen, I trail after her and look for cameras along the way. The moment I step into the kitchen, I quickly determine there isn't a camera in here either.

"What's with all the cameras?" I wonder aloud as she locates a glass from a cabinet.

Her lips pout into a small frown that has me wanting to suck on her bottom lip. "He's very...protective."

"No," I tell her, clutching her bicep as she turns to face me. "He's a lot more than protective. He's fucking obsessive."

She winces at my gentle grasp and I frown.

"Did he hurt you again?" I demand, anger bubbling in the pit of my stomach. Last time I'd been amused. But this time...this time I'm irritated as fuck.

"No," she breathes, her one word a vicious lie. Her eyes drift away from mine and she fixates them on the floor.

I blink at her in shock. "Then show me."

Snapping her gaze back to mine, she furrows her eyebrows together and shakes her head. "No, Kasper."

With a huff, I grab on to her hips and push her against
the cabinet. I grasp onto the top of her dress and slowly drag
it down over her shoulder. Her eyes snare mine in her brave
gaze. She doesn't try to stop me, even when I pull the material down over her tit that's hidden under a black bra. Once
I can see from her shoulder to her elbow, I inspect the flesh.
Bruises paint her skin, and in some places the flesh is torn,
a fresh scab on top.

A familiar rage, one that's always been pointed her way,
blooms inside of me. But once again, I'm angry *for* her. She's
really messing with my goddamned head.

"That motherfucker did this to you." My eyes go back
to probing hers. For a brief moment, I'm seeing the all too
familiar look. A look Mom gives me when she's trying to
protect Dale. I know abuse. It's been a part of my life for far
too long. My boss, a man who I sort of looked up to and
who I thought I fairly knew, is nothing but a damn dead-
beat. It's a fact now.

She chews on her plump bottom lip. "It's no big deal
and—ah!"

I push the other side of her dress down to look at her
other arm. Gently, I run my thumb along the purple welts
and grit my teeth. A wave of fury surges through me and I
resent it. I hate that I have the urge to protect her.

I'm supposed to be punishing her.

Making her pay for what happened to Kasey.

But all I can do is think about slitting Logan's goddamned throat.

"What happened?" I hiss out, my furious glare meeting

hers.

A single tear darts down her cheek. I swipe it away with my thumb and then suck on the salty flavor.

"He'll be here soon. Please," she begs and tries to wriggle out of my grasp, her full tits all but spilling from her bra. "Let go of me." The fear in her eyes is bone chilling.

"Tell me what the fuck happened and I'll leave you alone," I lie. I'll never leave her alone. My black heart beats only to tarnish hers. She'll never be left alone as far as I'm concerned.

With a shaky sigh, her teary eyes meet mine. "Donovan. He did this last night because of Donovan."

I glare at her, my brows pinching together in confusion. "I don't understand."

"Donovan hugged me. Twice."

She must sense I'm about to fucking blow up because she hastily pulls her dress into place and stands on her toes to meet my gaze.

"Listen to me, Kasper," she says evenly, her face morphing from fear to determination. "I know what I'm doing. I can handle myself."

I blink at her in confusion. What the fuck is she talking about? This isn't the sort of response I was expecting. Mom never acted like this about Dale.

Sliding my fingers into her hair, I tilt her head back so I can peer into her dark orbs. So I can understand what's going on in that head of hers. The way she darts her gaze all around, I know there are a million things going on inside her mind. I don't miss the fact that she's holding something back. Just out of reach.

I will find out what it is.

This time, I kiss her because I fucking want to. Her perfect pouty lips screamed to be caressed by my powerful ones. With every taste I get of this woman, I lose my sense of reason. It quickly becomes evident that she has a way about her—a way that allures every goddamn man she comes into contact with.

I'm not an exception.

She lets out a small moan that has me wanting to push her against the wall and fuck her brains out. Tearing away from our hot kiss, I peer down at her and try to figure out her angle.

"Why stay with him?"

Her eyes blaze with a passionate fury that makes my heart gallop in my chest. This is most definitely not the same fearful way my Mom looks at me when she defends Dale. "You do crazy things for love, Kasper."

Slipping my fingers over her jaw, I run my thumb over her bottom lip. Her words make no sense. I want to shove them back into her mouth and make her chew them up instead.

"You don't love him," I accuse. "He fucking abuses you."

Before she can reply, the front door swings open and slams against the wall in the living room. She pulls away from my grasp and pushes the button on the icemaker to fill the glass. I pull out my notepad from my pocket and peer down at the measurements. A few moments later, Logan storms into the kitchen, his dark eyes ruminating with jealousy.

"Hey Chief," I say and nod my head to him, careful to keep my voice level. "Want to run up to the hardware store with me and we can get a head start on picking the supplies up? I could come over Saturday and get to work."

His chest is heaving and he stalks over to Nadia. I clench my fist when he grabs her ass from behind rather forcefully, causing her to yelp out.

"Oh," she squeaks. "You surprised me. I was getting Ghost here a drink of water."

He pulls her possessively into his arms and makes a great, showy display of kissing her lips—lips I was just tasting—in front of me. Once he's done mauling her like a starved man, he zeroes in on me with a coldness in his eyes I've not ever seen before.

"Why don't you go on ahead and pick up the supplies?" he says with a growl and nips at her neck. "I've missed Nadia today and would like to spend a little quality time with her."

Anger washes over me knowing he's probably going to fucking hurt her again. "Sure. See you tomorrow."

I make it out to my car but not before hearing a bone-chilling scream.

Her scream is one of pain and hate.

A wounded warrior's cry, not a victim.

It doesn't make any fucking sense.

I should run back in and try to help her like I always used to try and help Mom, but something, one of those tiny details I rely on so heavily, tells me she's got this handled.

Eventually, I'm going to find out what's going on in her pretty little head.

And what the fuck is she protecting?

Six

Nadia

S HIT!
   I didn't mean to scream.

Logan's wild eyes meet mine and he's stunned into silence. Both of us stare at the door as if we expect Kasper to come raging back in here. Deep down, I sort of wish he would. I would love for it not to have to be me who has to deal with Logan, just for once. But, I also know that would be the worst possible thing to happen. I've made progress with Logan and I can't fuck that up.

"I'm sorry," I tell him and wipe away the blood trickling from my nose with the back of my hand. "I didn't mean to scream. You surprised me."

His eyes fixate on my blood like a shark in shallow waters. He wants to devour and own me. To decimate my soul.

"Things are slipping out of my control," he hisses and runs his fingers through his dark hair, messing up the gel that had been holding it in place. "You're fucking this all up for me, Nadia."

I wince at his tone and meet his fixed look with a determined one of my own. "Maybe I like provoking you. Maybe I like being punished." My voice wobbles unconvincingly and I hate that I don't have more control over it.

"Is that so?" His eyes travel along my face and over my breasts. I can tell he's thinking up new and depraved ways to abuse me. The evil wheels in his head are turning rapidly.

I bite my lip and nod, this time feeling a bit braver. "Yes. Hurt me, Logan."

Because I can take it.

I'm the only one who can take what Logan so viciously administers.

He takes a step toward me and I prepare for him to hit me. But he doesn't. Instead, he drags a fingertip gently between the swell of my breasts. "Maybe you bore me these days as my fiancée," he tells me coldly. "Maybe I should have some fun in the basement. You know I like it down there."

I swallow and force my terrified heart to slow its thundering beat.

Not the basement.

Not the fucking basement.

"Bring the guillotine up to your room," I tell him fearlessly. "You haven't used it on me in a while and I kind of miss it. Most of your other toys are up here so it makes more sense to do it up here."

He knows I despise that fucking contraption.

But the glimmer in his eyes tells me it excites him too.

"Fine, doll," he says with a predatory grin. "I'll bite at whatever it is you're feeding me. Until then, cook us some dinner. I'd like to eat downstairs tonight before we play."

I press a palm to his cheek and kiss him softly on his

savage lips. "I'll whip up something quick," I say with a hint of sauciness. "Déjame servirte." *Let me serve you.*

His eyes darken at the innuendo. He plants a quick kiss on my forehead and then stalks out of the kitchen, no doubt eager to terrorize my mind and body all night long.

With shaking hands, I pull out the big container of leftover carbonada. I pour some grease into a pan and heat it up while I prep some premade dough for quick carbonada-filled empanadas. At one time, I'd had dreams of cooking professionally. It isn't what I'd gone to college for but it's a great love of mine. Logan can take away a lot of things from me but this is something I secretly hold on to. He doesn't fully realize how much I enjoy it, otherwise he'd probably use it against me as well. Thankfully he is clueless and the man doesn't complain a bit when I try new recipes out on him.

While I cook, and I'm relaxed in my element, I let my mind drift to places that make me happy. I don't let my mind linger on what's to come. That'd be dangerous to my mind. I'm in control here and I need to remember that.

Once I've fried the empanadas to a beautiful golden brown, I serve them up on a plate. The savory scent of meat and vegetables fills the air, reminding me of my mother who is where I learned to cook from. God, I miss that woman.

I climb onto the counter and find a bottle of red wine in the cabinet. Tonight is going to be a doozy. The least I can do is indulge in something to calm my nerves and dull my senses.

Hopping down to the floor, I pop the cork and pour the crimson liquid into two wine glasses. I guzzle down a glass before filling it up a second time. After I've managed to down another full glass, I close my eyes and smile.

"Logan, darling," I call out in a singsong voice. "I'm ready for you."

And I am.

Game on, asshole.

"This fucker weighs a ton," he complains as he wrestles the big wooden contraption into his bedroom.

I chew on my lip as my eyes graze over the dark stained wood. It's solid and heavy. From experience, I know that the part that rests over my neck and wrists is unmovable even without the locks he always fits it with. There's a small step behind it that sticks out just far enough and is just wide enough to put my knees on it, leaving my ass sticking out in the air. The wine from dinner has long left my system as adrenaline chased it from me. A shiver courses through me as I realize I did this to myself. Sometimes I wonder if deep down I really am a masochist. I taunt and tease the most hellish sadist into torturing me on a daily basis.

All so I can keep him out of the basement.

The basement is where he becomes the king of darkness.

Where he's not afraid to crush my soul.

I'll keep him out of there at all costs. At least up here, he's more manageable. Even with all of his torture devices.

He eventually finishes setting it up and stands. For a brief moment, he seems exhausted. A flicker of uncertainty shines in his eyes, almost as if he wonders if he should continue. But when I latch on to that gimmer of humanity and plead with unspoken words via a quivering lip and teary eyes, the flicker is snuffed out. Almost immediately. He clenches his jaw, gives a slight shake of his head, and I watch with mixed awe and horror as any compassion and normalcy and kindness left in him drains away. Those penetrating dark orbs he loves to intimidate me with are on me in a flash and he takes his time running them over my face, searching for weakness. Weakness he can taste through salty tears and devour. He's once more a predator. The predator whose life revolves around stalking me—his favorite prey.

"Naked. Now."

The beast inside him is most certainly starved for me. His mouth is probably watering just thinking about how he'll tear my soul apart.

"I said now," he seethes.

His order jolts me to attention and I quickly tear off my dress. I must still have a small buzz because I stumble a bit. Once I've removed my bra and panties, I step toward him, awaiting his next instruction.

"You know what to do, doll," he says with a growl.

I nod and make my way over to the device. Resting my knees on the step, I wait for him to lift the top half of the mechanism. Eventually I'm settled with the front of my throat on the curved wood and have given my wrists to the contraption as well. I swallow down my anxiety as he lowers the top part over me, effectively trapping me in. He tugs my hair out between the slats and gathers it in a messy ponytail. With quick fingers, he ties it up and out of the way. When he steps away, I close my eyes knowing what comes next. The snap of the padlock clasping into place sends a rush of anxiety galloping through me.

Go to a happier place.

I don't have to see him to know that he's walked around behind me. Rubbing my thighs together, I attempt to turn myself on some in hopes it'll make the whole process easier to endure. When he touches my ass, I squeak out in surprise.

His laugh is cold and cruel. "You act like you've never done this before, doll. And while I appreciate your attempt at feigning innocence, we both know you're well aware of what's about to happen. In fact, I want you to instruct me on what to do."

Tears threaten but I blink them away. "Uh, okay. Well, you need to apply some lube to the anal hook first."

A pop of a cap behind me chills the blood in my veins. His heavy breathing is in cadence with mine. "And then?"

"Insert it into my ass," I say in a whisper. "Dios mío, dame fuerza." *Dear God, give me strength.*

"Remember, your God isn't here, doll." He's surprisingly gentle as he pushes the bulbous head of the hook past the tight rings of my asshole. Once it makes it beyond the opening, my body seems to suck it all the way in. I let out a gasp at which he chuckles.

"Now," I instruct with a wobble to my voice, "attach the chain to the end and bring it over the top of the guillotine to my hair."

The cold, thin chain slinks along my spine and goosebumps rise all over my flesh. He's not as gentle as he ties the chain around the bun in my hair. It tugs not only my hair but at the hook inside of me.

"Ah!" I yelp out and then let out a rush of relieved breath when he releases the chain. "Uh, then, well, what do you want to do with my mouth?"

"Hmmm," he says thoughtfully and rounds the contraption so that he's standing in front of me, still in his work slacks. "I feel like gagging you. What do you want to be gagged with today?"

He starts undressing and I attempt to come up with the least brutalizing answer.

"Your cock. Fuck my face with your cock," I suggest, a little too eagerly.

As if answering me, his thick, proud dick bounces heavily from his boxers as he shoves them down his thighs. Once he's completely naked, he strides over to me. With no warning, he pokes the tip of his cock against my parted lips and then shoves himself all the down my throat.

I gag and fist my hands but I'm helpless against his assault. I'm trying to relax my throat to take his enormous size when he grabs on to the chain in my hair. A scream hums through me around his thick length as he jerks at the chain over and over again. It's not that it necessarily hurts, but I hate the fact that I worry about what sort of damage he could inflict if he pulls too hard.

Instead of focusing on what I can't control, I close my eyes and focus on the past.

Go to him.

To your mental safety net.

"I need to see Donovan." My tone is clipped and cool. Darcy—with her platinum blonde hair, red razor claws, and long legs—is a real irritant. Every time I come to visit him, she has

trouble keeping the plastic smile on her face.

For me, she sneers.

For me, she glares.

For me, she lets the ugliness hiding under the pretty façade show.

She clearly has other thoughts about her boss—my stepfather—besides those that include employee and superior. And it pisses me off more than I care to admit. Not because he belongs to Mamá. Not at all. In fact, I'm quite frustrated with my mother's behavior since her marriage to Donovan. Even though I was shocked at their sudden nuptials, I soon realized he was simply a placeholder. Someone to fill a spot so we wouldn't be lonely. They slept in different bedrooms from the beginning. And while they never argue—they actually seem to like each other, often tag-teaming against me when they think it benefits me to do so—they've not once been intimate or affectionate around me. Mamá's never gotten over my father and quite frankly, I don't think she ever will. That's what's so unfair to Donovan and why I attempt to fill the void of her mental absence.

But even if their marriage was on the fritz, I wouldn't approve of Darcy's blazing red fingernails anywhere near Donovan's firm chest or broad shoulders. Darcy is a bitch with ulterior motives. And my stepfather deserves better. He deserves better than my mother, too, but I'd never voice that one aloud.

"He's in a meeting," Darcy sneers.

Yep, saves all of her catty bitchiness for me and me only.

"I'll wait. It's important. I'm leaving tomorrow and I need to talk to him."

She rolls her eyes and drags her attention to her computer monitor. Her gaudy nails tap away at the keyboard as she ignores me.

Since she chooses to pretend I don't exist, I give her the same treatment and make a beeline for Donovan's office door. "Miss Jayne!" I hear her protesting in my wake, along with the sound of her chair scraping against the marble floors, but she's too slow. I shove through the double doors to his office, abruptly turning and clicking the lock in place behind me.

"—the fucking mountain to its goddamned knees for all I care. The resort is mine, not theirs, Dan," Donovan snarls at the man from across his desk as I enter, interrupting a meeting indeed.

I let out a sigh of relief to see it's his CFO, Dan Reed. Donovan's steely glare snaps to mine and for a moment, I freeze. He appears furious. But as soon as he registers it's me standing in his office, the anger melts away like butter and a smile tugs at his lips.

"Hey," I say with a wave. "I wanted to talk to you before I have to leave tomorrow."

With a small nod, he redirects his attention to Dan and motions to the door. "I'm sorry, man. I don't mean to take it out on you. Figure something out we can work with. We'll continue this later this afternoon when I'm in a better frame of mind."

Dan rises to his feet. He's taller than Donovan, an old high school basketball superstar in our town, which means he's nearly twice as tall as me. The man gives me the creeps but I never let it show. As his pervert eyes skim over my low-cut top, I roll my eyes and storm past him, ending his peep show.

Donovan is glaring after him by the time I reach his desk and sit down. The door slams shut behind us and silence fills the empty air. When his eyes find mine again, a fondness glimmers in them. I chew on my lip and try not to shiver under his gaze.

"Hey, sunshine," he says, his voice low. "Couldn't wait until dinner tonight? Your mamá reserved us a booth at your favorite Italian restaurant on Main Street."

I drop my purse into the floor and thread my fingers together over his desk. When I lean forward, my heavy breasts sit on top of my arms. Unlike Creepy Dan, I actually like when Donovan notices my body.

And boy, does he notice.

Unashamed, his eyes drop to my lips for a brief moment before flicking down to my chest. A hiss of air leaves him before he clears his throat and finds my eyes again.

"I went to The Joint. I thought maybe I could interview some people to see if—" I start, but his fist slamming on the desk startles me and the words freeze in my mouth.

"What have I told you about going there?" he snaps and rises to his feet. "With Dale and all the other goddamned dirtbags in this fucking town? You know my stance on this, Nadia. You're barely eighteen years old, for crying out loud!"

I bristle at his outburst and lean back in my chair. "I'll be nineteen in a few months. Anyway," I seethe, ignoring him, "I started asking around. To see if there were any drifters who could have passed through here last August. I know it's been a year, Donovan, but people don't forget stuff."

His lips press into an irritated firm line but he lets me continue.

Nervously, I dig around in my purse on the floor until I retrieve a packet of gum. Without asking if he wants any, I tear open the foil wrapper, break the cinnamon stick of gum *in half, and offer him the other half. Like always, his powerful fingers brush against mine, sending a jolt of something enticing through my body. This time, my eyes are on his mouth as he tosses the gum into it.*

I shove mine into my mouth and let out a huff. "Mike Hyland. A trucker. They say he's an off again on again resident here. The last time anyone saw him was right before Kasey disappeared."

Donovan chews on his gum, furrowing his brows together in a thoughtful manner. This is one of the reasons why I love him. He's got my back. Whenever I come barging into his office with another fire under my ass to chase a lead I think I have, Donovan always assists me. He has canceled business trips. Postponed meetings. Fought with Mamá. Annoyed the fuck out of the police. Whatever I need, he's there to help.

Unfortunately though, every single one of my leads has come up empty.

Not today, though.

Today I have a good feeling.

"Hmm," he says with a grunt, "I remember Mike. I'm pretty sure Logan's had a few run-ins with him over the years, but I hardly think he's a kidnapper. I could call Logan, though, and have him run a background check. See where the guy's been these days."

I jump from my seat and round his desk. By the time I reach him, he's turned his chair and stood to envelop me in one of his strong hugs. A year ago, I pretty much hated Donovan and choked on his masculine scent anytime he was near.

Now, I inhale him.

Call it sick.

Call it dirty.

But to me, he smells like comfort.

His fingers brush through my hair as he holds me tight, and I let out a small sigh of contentment. I'm going to miss him when I go to LA. My bottom lip quivers and I bite down on it to keep from crying.

"Thank you for always trying, D," I choke out.

Those same fingers brushing my hair grip it, and he tilts my head back. His steely grey-blue eyes find mine and he frowns. "Baby, why are you so upset?"

I try to look away but he won't let me. When Donovan has me on his radar, he sees nothing else. Ever.

"I'm going to miss you," I half sob, half laugh.

He leans forward and presses a soft kiss to my forehead. "I'm going to miss you, too. So fucking much."

I'm once again pulled into his warm embrace. Our relationship is weird, I know. Everyone in town questions it. I've heard their hushed whispers.

"He's practically twice her age, the pervert."

"The pedophile."

"How can he have eyes for his stepdaughter?"

"What a sick family."

They can all go fuck off because it isn't like that.

Donovan is my friend.

I trust him implicitly.

"I want you home for fall break," he says with an authoritative growl that has me giggling.

"And if I'm not?" I taunt as I pull away.

Despite our friendly banter, neither of us is ready for me to go to college.

His eyes caress the naked flesh of my exposed breasts before his lip quirks up into a smug grin that sends shivers run-

ning through me. "Then I'll have to put you over my knee and give you a good bare-assed spanking for disobeying."

Words like these...jokes threaded with truth, are the foundation of our friendship.

One of these days, I wonder if he'll actually make good on his threats.

"Then I better be a good girl," I tell him with a wink before bouncing back over to my purse. "See you at dinner."

Our eyes meet once more before I exit his office. Despite our moment of humor, his are haunted and sad. Mine are an exact reflection.

And then I leave.

The ache in my heart is painful. I'd cry if it weren't for bitchy Darcy eyeballing me as I hurry away. Once I make it into the foyer of the building though, I release the dam and with it a flood of tears.

I don't want to leave him.

"Why are you crying?" Logan taunts, jerking me from my memories. "I thought you wanted this."

I hate dragging myself from Donovan's warm memories and back into the hellish reality that is my life with Logan. With hesitation, I blink my eyes open and try to take stock of my injuries. Everything hurts. My throat especially but also my scalp and my ass. Streaks of fire burn along my spine and I know he's either cut me or whipped me—it's too early to tell.

"I love watching you bleed, doll." *Well, that answers my question.* "So fucking beautiful." His voice is almost loving and I latch on to it. Staying with Donovan inside my head won't help the situation. As much as I'd prefer to be in his office hugging him, I know I have my present hell deal with.

Logan.

"I'm so weak," I whisper. And I am. But I mostly want to draw out his affectionate side. The one that I can pull answers from.

He chuckles, as if I'm cute, and sets to removing the anal hook. Once he's freed me from the metal and untied the chain from my hair, he begins unlocking the padlock. As soon as he lifts the heavy wood that held me in place, I bite back a sob of relief.

So many times I died a little on the guillotine.

So many times I lost a piece of my soul.

But not this time.

This time, I feel stronger.

Satisfied even.

This time I made it through in one piece.

Focus on the end game, Nadia Jayne.

I harden my heart and smile sweetly at Logan as he helps me stand on shaky feet.

I have *to do this.*

Seven

Kasper

LAST NIGHT, I DIDN'T SLEEP A FUCKING WINK. I LAY ON my back and stared at the dark ceiling. For hours. My thoughts were on one person.

Her.

And as much as I craved to find the hate inside and hold on to it, my mind kept replaying our kiss over and over again. Her soft, wet lips. The way she confided in me about Logan hurting her.

All night I tried to summon the anger.

But I couldn't.

She's a heavy drug I want to shove into my vein. *Even though I'll hate myself later for succumbing to using.* To feel the intoxicating bliss as it infiltrates every nerve ending in my entire system. It's darkness feeding darkness—and she's oh-so fucking dark. Sometimes I wonder if I'll ever know light again. But right now, I'm overwhelmed with the need to conquer her. I wouldn't hurt her though—not the way Logan does. When I hurt her, she'll beg me for it. The bruises will be nothing more than love bites—evidence of my desire for her.

My dick rises, lifting the sheet with it, and I grunt in frustration. Whacking off will do nothing to satisfy my craving for her. I'm eager to get to their house and start this job just so I can see her again.

Has she really fucking pickled my brain like she does to all the other men who fall into her web?

Fuck her and then fuck with her life.

A growl rumbles through me as I slide out of bed in search of something to wear. Once I locate the pair of jeans I'd discarded on the way to bed last night, I slide them on and then make my way into my office. I flip on a light and sink down into my desk chair. Her file sits open on my desk. Plucking her picture from the paperclip, I stare at her pretty features. The woman was blessed in the looks department. Her brown eyes are mischievous, almost as if she's got a secret hiding behind them. The smile on her face is broad and infectious. If I hadn't spent so many years hating her, I'd almost smile back.

But I don't.

I need to focus and stop letting my dick have a say in any of this.

Yes, she'll be a great fucking lay.

But she still needs to pay for letting my sister's kidnapper slip through the cracks.

I want to imagine a scenario where her full lips drop into a pouty frown once she realizes she's been literally fucked. When her perfect world crumbles around her. It will be a beautiful vindication, and only then can I move the fuck on with my life. I'll never stop searching for Kasey, but at least I can stop obsessing over Nadia.

My mind flits back to last night.

The bruises and scabs.

Anger rises in my chest causing my fists to involuntarily clench in response. I'm thoroughly confused about how I can go from hating her in one breath, to hating Logan on her behalf in the next. It doesn't make sense to me, this urge to protect her from him. I know I'm a selfish bastard, but this is more than that. Down in my bones, a part of her seems to have linked itself to me. She, in some ways, almost reminds me of Kasey. Talk about fucked up. No matter how hard I want to claw her from my soul, she imbeds herself there.

And as a form of cruel punishment to myself, I like her there.

I like the warmth she brings that bubbles just below the surface, such a dim light flickering in my darkness.

What are you doing to my head, Nadia Jayne?

"Morning," Logan grunts in greeting and waves me inside his fucking lavish estate.

I shoulder past him, toolbox in hand, and make my way over to the biggest hole in the wall. "You going to the station?" I question and eye up his uniform. It's Saturday and he doesn't normally work weekends.

"Yeah, I have some shit to deal with," he grumbles insolently. "I shouldn't be gone long." The warning in his voice is loud and clear.

"Do you have coffee brewing?" I set the toolbox down

and saunter into the kitchen. I'd hoped to see Nadia standing there in a rumpled nightgown with mussed hair and
sleepy eyes, fresh out of bed. Instead, I find nothing but a
vacant kitchen filled with the aroma of coffee.

Logan follows me and locates a mug for me. I pour a
cup and take my time stirring it up.

"Your woman still sleeping? I doubt she'll sleep through
my demoing that wall," I tell him and sip the hot liquid.
My intention is to casually feel out where she is. Part of me
wants to shove him out the front door so I can hunt her
down and find out why she screamed last night. I want to
know if he hurt her again.

"I wore her out," he tells me simply with a shrug. "Girl
likes to fuck. She'll sleep through it."

I grip the handle on my mug and try not to say anything
stupid. He eyes me up for several more minutes before he
starts gathering his keys and wallet on the bar. "You do
realize Nadia was the only witness to your sister's abduc-
tion. She sat in my office and told me nothing. Absolutely
nothing, Kasper. I know you have eyes for her," he says with
a growl. "I'm not fucking stupid. But remember what she
didn't do for you. I know you obsess over that case. How
could you not?"

I glare at him, my jaw clenching, furious he so easily
read me. And here I thought I was a pro at keeping my emotions guarded.

"I fuck her every night. I make love to her, Ghost. And
I've tried to get information out of her. She knows nothing.
If you think getting close to her will help get you clues, you're
mistaken." He smiles at me then and it makes me want to
punch him in his goddamned throat. "Plus, I've knocked

her around one too many times. Poor girl is practically re-tarded. All she's good for is to take a nice ass fucking and to cook my meals. You're barking up the wrong tree, Kasper."

Who is this asshole?

He certainly isn't the same Chief that everyone grav-itates to when he saunters into the station each morning wearing a cheery, easy grin. In his own home, he clearly feels comfortable enough to let his true colors show.

It takes everything in me to swallow down my rage and feign disinterest. "To be honest, it's irritating to have to work in her presence, knowing she can't remember shit. But don't flatter yourself," I tell him with a shrug of my shoulders. "I'm not interested in your property, man. I'm just here to make a little extra cash."

His eyes study mine for a minute before he nods. "Sure. Just wanted to establish some rules before I left." He starts to walk away but stops and turns. "Anything on Donovan?"

"Nothing. He's pissed but business as usual."

He beams at me. "Perfect."

I sip my coffee, my eyes never leaving him, and watch as he punches in some numbers on his phone. "Tell her I'll be back in an hour," he instructs before storming from the kitchen.

"Yep." My voice is disinterested. Uncaring. Yet my skin is crawling and my jaw is clenching hard enough to break my teeth.

Leaning my hip on the counter, I blow at the steamy liquid as if that's my focus. But what I'm absolutely aware of is Logan. The sound of his zipper as he dons his coat in the other room. A jingle of his keys. Heavy thuds through the house. A creak of the front door and then a slam. Flitting my eyes up, I watch him stride out to his car. His phone is still in hand as he intently stares at whatever is on his screen. When he finally shoves it back in his pocket once he's in his vehicle, and starts the car, I let out a breath of relief.

As soon as his car turns out onto the road, I set my coffee down and exit the kitchen. With calculated steps, I make my way over to one of the holes in the wall. My gaze drifts down the hallway and I try not to think about what he did to her last night. If there weren't cameras everywhere, I know I wouldn't be able to hold myself back from going to her. And God only knows the kind of wakeup call I'd end up giving her.

"Nadia?" I call out, knowing the cameras don't pick up sound. "It's about to get loud in here."

No response.

Not a squeak of the wood floors.

Nothing.

With a sigh, I pull on a piece of drywall that is damaged. It doesn't move easy but needs to be replaced. The hammer sits on top of the toolbox. I should get to work but the whole house is oddly too quiet.

"I hope you like ACDC," I call out.

Silence.

And I'll be damned if it doesn't niggle at me. I want to see her. She's a fucked up mystery to me and I like peeling away at her layers like one would fuss over sunburned skin after a few days. I want to pick and pick and pick until she's raw. Exposed and revealed. Mysteries solved.

My eyes flit over to the camera in the corner. I clutch onto the drywall and give it a yank. It tears off with a loud noise that cuts through the quietness.

"For fuck's sake," I complain as I toss the piece of wall into the floor.

Curiosity gets the better of me and I stride quickly down the hall. When I reach the master bedroom, I frown to see it empty. My eyes fall on a wooden, medieval-looking piece that wasn't here yesterday. It has a larger hole cut out in the center and two smaller ones on either side of the hole. A sickness washes over me knowing he probably put her in that thing. Logan seems like one of those fucked-up doms who's into all sort of creepy sexual acts. Probably making up for having a small dick or something, the bastard.

With a grunt, I walk back over to the guest room. The sun shines in through the window and blankets her bare skin. *I knew she'd be naked.* Doesn't seem like the kind of girl who sleeps in pajamas, not that Logan is the kind of guy who would let her. But what confuses is me is why she's sleeping in the guest room.

"Trouble on the home front?" I bark out.

She jerks in bed and sits up, drawing the covers to her chin, further denying me a view of her perky breasts. "What are you doing here?"

Her dark hair is wild and messy. My fingers twitch to smooth it out. Gritting my teeth, I motion toward the splintered door frame. "Gaping holes in your walls? Ring any bells? The hardware store will be delivering some Sheetrock and two-by-fours later this afternoon. Until then, I'm going to tear down the old stuff."

She nods and her eyes dart behind me in a frantic way. "Where's Logan?"

I flash her a wicked smile. "He left…about ten minutes ago. We're all alone."

Her eyes widen and she waves me away. "I need to get dressed. Did he say anything?"

"Said he'd be back in an hour."

She shrieks and sits up on her knees. "Go! I need to hurry."

Frowning, I turn from her and leave the room. But as soon as I hear the bed squeaking, I peek my head back inside.

Big mistake.

She bares her big round ass to me on the way to the bathroom. Long, dark hair hangs in disheveled waves about halfway down her back. When my eyes decide to leave her ass, I notice the marks all over her backside.

Tons of them.

Small cuts have been sliced into her flesh all over. I'm still gaping when she shuts the bathroom door, effectively cutting off my view. With a huff, I run my fingers through my hair and pace the hallway for a minute to compose myself.

What the fuck does he do to her?

Why in the hell does she endure it?

I stalk back toward the living room and let the rage flood me. Once I've turned on some Aerosmith and laid out some protective sheeting on the floor, I begin my demo and let the screams of the lyrics fuel me on. Picking up my hammer, I start smashing the already ruined Sheetrock and yanking it from the studs. It feels good to take my anger out on the wall but it would feel fucking satisfying as hell to take it out on Logan's face instead. I'm lost in my haze of fury, so when she passes by in a nervous rush, I don't even glance up. It isn't until the heavenly scent of something fucking delicious fills the air, that I wipe the sweat from my brow with the back of my hand and set down my hammer.

Dust fills the living room and broken pieces of Sheetrock are all over the plastic sheet. My heart still thumps angrily but I'm calming down. I'm about to go demand answers from Nadia when something beyond the studs has me halting.

"What the fuck?" I mutter as I reach inside the wall and touch a huge-ass pipe.

I've been remodeling houses ever since college, despite having joined the force. I have brought them down to the studs and then worked my magic, recreating something better. Not once have I seen something like this.

I run my fingers over the dark grey pipe. It's icy cold to the touch. Biggest fucking pipe I've ever seen. Instead of the typical PVC pipes in every home I've ever worked in, this thing is thick, corrugated galvanized steel. They don't even sell this shit in the hardware stores. It has to be twenty inches in diameter.

Who the hell needs a pipe that fucking big?

And for what?

I wipe the dust from my fingers on my jeans and follow my nose into the kitchen. Nadia looks normal and composed in a fitted pair of jeans and T-shirt. She's always dressed nicely but today she seems comfortable. She's piled her hair up on top of her head in one of those messy buns and her ass jiggles every time she stirs the pot on the stove. Her head bobs to the music that's playing in the living room and I can't help but smile. One of her only redeeming qualities is she shares a love for seventies rock like me. Looks like Donovan did something right in raising her. Forced his music on her like he used to force on me all those years ago. But with thoughts of Donovan, other depressing memories press at me. I shake my head and focus on why I'm here, chasing away sadness that eats at my black heart.

"What happened to your back?" I question, leaning my hip against the counter beside the stove where she's cooking.

Her eyes briefly flit to mine and they're almost black. She flips her wrist to check the time and continues stirring. "I don't know what you mean."

I raise an eyebrow at her and close the distance between us. Her attention is still on the cooking meal, and I gently run my fingers down her spine. When she winces, I pull my fingers away. "This is what I mean," I tell her with a grumble. "Tell me."

She shudders for a moment. But then, she squares her shoulders and turns to face me. Her dark brows furrow and she frowns.

"No te metas en lo que no te importa," she snaps.

My eyes fall to her lips. "Huh?"

She rolls her eyes and starts to turn away, but I grab her by the wrist and don't let go.

"Tell me, sweet Jayne."

"Stop calling me that." The anger in her eyes fades and she bites on her lower lip. "What, you need me to spell it out for you? He's kinky. What can I say?"

I slide my hand around the side of her throat and draw her to me. She's snared in my heated gaze as I bring my lips close to hers. The intensity in her eyes has alerted my cock and I'm craving more than breakfast right now.

"He's beyond kinky. Logan is abusive," I remind her, my

hot breath tickling her lips. "Is he ever *not* an asshole to you?"

She starts to speak, probably in his defense, but I silence her by sliding my tongue in her mouth. Her fingers are fisted in my T-shirt and I can't tell if she is about to push me away or pull me closer. Quite frankly, I don't care which it is. Our kiss is brought to an abrupt halt, though, when my phone rings. With a groan, I pull away from her and take the call.

"What are you doing?" Logan's voice demands.

I roll my eyes and grab a Coke from the refrigerator. "Getting a drink and trying to figure out what the fuck Nadia is cooking," I say truthfully as I peer over her shoulder. It smells awesome but it doesn't look like anything I've ever tasted before. "Why?" I purposefully walk slowly out of the kitchen and back over to where I was tearing out the wall.

"No reason."

"Do you need to speak to her?"

"No," he clips out. "I'll be there in less than ten minutes. See you soon."

I shrug my shoulders as if I'm confused by his call, for his camera viewing benefit, but seethe with rage. He's all-out unleashed when it comes to Nadia, unabashedly so. I've never seen Chief act this way before. Back when Taylor and I used to hang out at his house as teens, I'd sometimes see Logan there with Donovan. His behavior had always seemed a little erratic, even back then, before he was well off. He was good looking, cocky, and confident. All things that I was *not*, so I just chalked it up to that and the sense of superiority that it surely brought with it. Taylor liked him, so I put up with him for my best friend's benefit. Then, after

I began working at the precinct, I'd actually been impressed with his police skills. He runs the police department like a well-oiled machine. It's admirable and I'd looked up to him.

But now that I have an inside peek into his life as an adult, I know the superior exterior is just that—a cover. The monster who's marrying Nadia has been putting on a pretty damn good show for everyone. He's not just an incredibly jealous motherfucker. He's more.

"Nadia," I call out, my back to the camera as I pretend to measure the space. "Logan's a fucking lunatic. I'll figure out what the fuck's going on around here."

Something clatters in the kitchen and she curses up a storm in Spanish. She doesn't respond but instead hurries to finish breakfast. I narrow my eyes at the thick pipe once more and scratch the scruff growing in on my jawline with the end of my tape measurer.

I will find out what the fuck is going around here.

With her help or not.

"She must really feel bad about that haircut," Rhodes snickers as he sips on the shitty draft beer at The Joint. "My wife hardly ever lets me get a beer with the guys."

And by guys, he means me. Ashley has Jason Rhodes' balls in an iron vise. Sometimes she plays the nice wife and releases her clutch on him. Other times, guilt motivates her. Based on the shitty haircut she gave me earlier at their place, I'd say she's feeling really fucking guilty. Looks like I'll have to let Regina suck my cock after all just so she'll make me look halfway decent again.

"You're pussy-whipped, Rhodes."

He chuckles and clinks his glass to mine. "I've been called worse. Speaking of worse, did you hear that Chief canned Stokes today? Lena said it got ugly as hell. She texted Ashley and said Stokes was pissed. Said everyone thought he was going to get himself arrested by the way he raged around the precinct like a bull."

I frown and let my gaze flit past him to my mother dancing beside the jukebox. Dale, grinds against her from behind, causing my stomach to roil with disgust. Jerking my gaze from the horror show, I meet Rhodes's twinkling stare. The man truly is happy to leave his pregnant wife for a few hours.

"Lena is a shit stirrer. She probably exaggerated."

He shrugs his shoulders. "She said someone told him he'd been checking out his fiancée. Of course Chief fired him for some shit that would actually stick—like the countless cases he's fucked up on lately—but I can't help but wonder if there wasn't truth to her words. Logan acted like"—*a psychotic, possessive lunatic*—"a jealous teenager when he showed off his best friend's daughter. How do you think that's going anyway?"

I roll my neck along my shoulders as I try to work out the kink from working all afternoon. Logan had shown up not long after his call and hovered around Nadia like she might poof into thin air. It irritated me but it left me alone to work. I'd chosen not to ask about the thick pipe but instead took a discreet photo while he was in the kitchen, bitching about the color of the toast, to investigate later when I was back home.

"Knowing Donovan, he's probably pissed. You know he

thinks everything he touches turns to gold and suddenly becomes his," I say with a growl and bring the cheap beer to my lips. My eyes flit back over to Mom. Her once pretty blonde hair is now dulled and frizzy. Jade-colored eyes that matched mine at one time are now a sickly green that only flicker to life when Dale brings her another overfilled tumbler of Jack and Coke. Alcohol and Dale have turned her into a fucking animated corpse.

"It's hard to believe Taylor and him were bro—"

"Stop," I snap and slam my glass down, letting the warm liquid slosh over my knuckles. "I don't want to talk about Taylor."

Rhodes's eyes flicker with sympathy and he nods. "Okay, man. Shit, you're on edge today."

Shrugging my shoulders, I dive my hand into my jeans and find some coins. I leave my chatty friend to stalk over to the jukebox. When Dale's gaze meets mine, his eyes flicker with hate but he wisely breaks free of my mother and heads to the bar, surely to order them another drink. I push the coins into machine and flip through the endless pages until I find what I'm looking for. Soon, "Sweet Jane" by Cowboy Junkies fills the bar and several old men complain for having changed it from their stupid country shit music. I ignore them and then stalk over to my mom.

"Hey, baby boy," she purrs, the slur in her voice ever present as she sets her glass down on a table.

Her thin arms wrap around my middle and she lays her cheek on my chest. My mom, who at one time when Kase and I were kids smelled like sweet florals and home baked cookies, now reeks of stale smoke and Dale's body odor that lingers like a cloying fog. I sigh but wrap my arms around her. Together, my mom and I slow dance to a song that reminds me of the real sweet Jayne.

Dark, wide eyes full of mystery and intrigue.

A brave woman with ulterior motives.

An ass that could make a Kardashian jealous.

"How's my son?" Mom questions, lifting her head to look up at me. "How you been, sugar?"

I clench my teeth but force a smile. "Fine. Working long hours. Is Dale being good to you?"

Shame makes her look away and she once again rests her head against my chest. "Oh," she says with a tired sigh, "you know how Dale is. Dale's Dale. A little rough around the edges for everyone else but he always shows me his sweet side."

I glare over her head at Dale who's flirting with some hag at least a decade older than my mom and with twice as many wrinkles. Her cackles fill the air but thankfully the song drowns them out.

Bet she won't cackle that first time Dale cracks his knuckles across her cheekbone. My mother certainly doesn't laugh anymore and that's been the case since well before Kasey was stolen from us. Dale stole my mother's light long before that. And though I can find nothing to confirm my lingering thoughts, I still feel like Dale has some hand in what happened to Kasey. The dumb fuck, though, if he were really guilty, would have already slipped up. Dale's an idiot who can't keep his mouth shut. If he had anything to do with it, I'm sure I would have figured it out. Besides, I'd already been through their shitty trailer with a fine-tooth comb one day and got annoyed as fuck having to dig through their piles of clutter. There was no way he'd have the foresight to keep records of his past, much less to hide them effectively. There was nothing to be found where Dale was concerned.

The song ends and I let out a sigh. Mom and I will always have a strained relationship but it doesn't mean I don't stop trying. She's all I have left after losing Kase. I won't let her slip through my fingers too. I may be an asshole but my heart is still linked to my flesh and blood.

When a country song starts screeching on the jukebox, I cringe and step away from Mom. I frown as she smiles at me.

"You're so handsome, Kasper. One of these days, you'll find you a good girl and make me a grandma."

I smirk at her. "Maybe I don't want a good girl."

You're certainly fucking obsessed with a bad girl, Kasper Grant.

She laughs and it's musical. My heart aches in my chest to hear the sweet sound that reminds me of my younger sister. "A good girl is going to want you. Trust me, sugar. A momma knows these things."

"My turn for a dance, Karla," Dale snaps as he thrusts a glass full of amber liquid in her face. It sloshes out and splashes her shirt but she doesn't flinch. Instead, she takes the glass from him and averts her gaze.

I'm about to leave them when he grabs on to her bicep hard enough to make her yelp. I have self-control when it comes to a lot of things. But when Dale is involved, I lose my shit every goddamned time.

"You think knocking around a woman makes you a badass?" I bellow and fist my hand. Truly, the loser isn't even worth bloodying up my knuckles. But tonight...tonight I need to blow off some steam.

"Mind your own business," Dale sneers. "*Officer*, I've got this handled."

Before I change my mind, I charge for him and seize his throat in my brutal grip. He hisses when I back him against the wall easily with one hand. His dulled eyes have sparked to life—fear dwells in them. Good, he should be afraid. My mother wears the same look every goddamned time he raises his hand at her. Hell, Nadia's isn't much different when she's fretting over Logan.

"Why don't you try your fists on a man?" I grit out as I squeeze his neck. His eyes bulge out and he claws at my wrists as his face becomes eggplant purple. "Only pussies hurt small, defenseless women." *If only I could say that to my boss as well.*

The country song drones on and Mom's sobs fit right in with it. I'd love nothing more than to bash Dale's head into the wall for every time he's laid a hand on her and made her cry. But when he grows limp and stops struggling, I blink away the furious haze that has wrapped its red claws around my head. Releasing him, I snatch my hand away as if he's diseased. For Mom's sake, I hope to hell not. The stupid fuck wobbles for a minute before collapsing. I watch with sick satisfaction as he crashes to the dirty-ass bar floor.

"Okay, buddy," Rhodes grunts from behind me and pulls me by the back of my jacket toward the door. "Time to go home."

I cast one last glare of disgust Dale's way and a quick apologetic glance at my mom before striding away.

I'm tired of standing by while all the dickheads around me hurt the women in my life. Dale better watch his ass. Hell, Logan better watch his too.

Eight

Nadia

ACHES.

And darkness.

I moan and try to make sense of where I'm at. The chill that snakes its way around my ribs and up my spine tells me what I loathe to know. I keep my eyes pressed shut because opening them would confirm my fears.

I'm in the fucking basement.

I failed.

With the realization of failure, comes the urge to cry. Bottling up all of my emotions is exhausting. Tears of defeat slide from the corners of my eyes.

God, everything hurts. The moment Kasper left after a long afternoon of repairing the walls, Logan let me have it.

There was no consoling him or explaining to him that I hadn't spoken about us to Kasper. He doesn't believe that I was simply being hospitable. But I couldn't bring myself to admit that his employee knows he beats the shit out of me. Instead, I clung to my lies like a sinking raft in a stormy sea.

It wasn't working but it was all I had.

"I'm sorry," I murmur, my voice a hoarse whisper.

Fingertips brush my hair from my eyes and soft lips kiss my forehead. Even when Logan punishes me, I still find solace. I find peace.

Another form of peace threatens to rip my chest open as unconsciousness threatens to steal me from the concrete hell. In my mind, I search out grey-blue eyes. Always there for me—always saving me.

"Shhhh."

I let the soft, murmured assurances wash over me as I flee into the darkness of my mind. With open arms, I run back to Donovan.

Always Donovan.

"Where's Mamá?"

Donovan swivels in his office chair and gapes at me. His dark hair is slicked back and styled in its usual perfection while his suit is unwrinkled and smooth. It's been months since I last saw him. Our Skype conversations had been few and far between around final exam time, and my last visit had been at Christmas. He'd wanted me home for spring break but my job—a job Donovan fought tooth and nail for me not to have at the police dispatch call center—hadn't allowed me to leave until now. After eight months of working there for barely over minimum wage, I'd been granted a few days off for the summer.

He launches from his seat and strides over to me, his long legs bringing him in front of me within seconds. I let out a relieved breath when he scoops me into his arms. A squeal echoes around us when he lifts me off my feet and spins with me in his arms.

"Jesus Christ, I've missed that laugh."

His words warm me to my core and I shake away the fact that five minutes ago I'd been texting my boyfriend and now, if you were to ask me, I couldn't even recall his name.

That's what Donovan does to me.

He makes me the center of his world and I don't care about anything other than being that for him.

"Where's Mamá?" I say with another laugh for his benefit.

He groans and tugs away from me. His dark eyebrows furrow together angrily. "Your mother went to Venice."

I blink at him and frown in confusion. "She didn't tell me that when I'd texted her on Monday."

His lips purse into a line. Practiced indifference is the mask he wears. "She didn't tell me either. Just left a note."

"Well, we can still have fun. I'll be here for five days. Maybe Mamá will be back in a couple of days," I say with false cheer, hoping to lift his mood.

He shakes his head and regards me with a sad expression. Not sad for himself but instead sad for me. It's always about me with him.

"Selene needed to get away."

I snort and shrug my shoulders. "That's stupid. Since when does she ever care about getting away? She likes it here."

"Does she?" He cracks his neck and meets me with a level stare. "Truth is, she wanted some space from me."

Blinking at him, I search his gaze for humor. He's not amused. His jaw clenches and his cheeks turn slightly pink with embarrassment.

I'm going to kill her for hurting him.

"Are you guys okay? Is she having an affair?" My voice is

a shriek that will no doubt have bitch Darcy peeking her head in at any time.

He storms past me and locks his office door, anticipating Darcy's nosy antics before she even reaches his office. Then, he stalks over to me and places his warm hands on my shoulders. His knees bend so he can gaze right into my eyes. I get lost in the way flecks of silver sparkle like shards of glass in his icy irises.

"She's not in love with me, sunshine. I know *you see that. I'm going to stay at the Penthouse here at the resort until…"*

I scrunch my nose up and arch an eyebrow up in question. "Until what?"

He sighs and runs his fingers through his gelled hair, messing it up. I want to run my fingers through it too. "I thought I'd stay here until…" A groan of frustration. "We're getting a divorce."

Tears well in my eyes. Selfish fucking tears.

"But you're my…you're my…" I can't finish my statement before I burst into tears.

His warm, strong arms are once again around me and he hugs me to him. Long, capable fingers dig into my sides and I want them to forever latch themselves to me. If they divorce, where will that leave us?

"Listen to me," he murmurs against my hair, his breath hot. "You'll always be my Nadia Jayne. Mine. Okay?"

I nod as my tears soak the front of his neat suit.

"You share my last name. You're my family. Nobody can take that away. Got it, baby?"

My palms find his chest and I hug him under his suit jacket, my fingertips skimming across each of his firm muscles on his back. I want him to keep me cocooned in his embrace and never let me go. Here, I don't worry about all the leads on Kasey that go nowhere. My mamá's sudden need to push away her husband. And I certainly don't worry about my job, my college courses, or that boyfriend—whatever his name was. All I care about is this man.

"You look beautiful today. Every day more so than the last."

I sigh against his chest and hook my thumbs into the back of his slacks over his belt. My boyfriend—he's definitely my ex now—would tell me I had a nice rack or a nice ass.

But Donovan?

He knows how to make a woman melt with a compliment.

As he rubs circles on my back, he gets lower and lower until his fingertips stop just above my ass. Neither of us say a word—we just hold each other. I let out a tiny sigh of disappointment that he doesn't slide his hands any lower. If I were braver, I'd do something about it, like push them down for him.

Yet, if he, for some reason rejected me, I'd be crushed.

I'll cling onto the closeness we have without trying to wreck it with my weird womanly hormones.

"Te amo, Donovan."

His chuckle fills my soul with joy and I smile. He presses a kiss to my hair. "My sweet Jayne. I love you too, baby."

A pounding on his office door makes us break apart.

Pounding and pounding.

It takes me a moment to realize that the pounding is inside my head. The memory of Donovan disappears as my recollection of what happened with Logan thunders into my mind. After Kasper had left, Logan hit me.

In his rage, he'd waved around a fucking two by four.

Threatened to hit me over the damn head with it.

Logan's too smart for that, though. He would have had to deal with a corpse then. And that's simply not his style. So at the last minute, he tossed the wood and opted for his fist instead. And then he dragged me down to his hellhole and left me.

For a fleeting second, I wish he'd have finished the job. That he had the balls to use that plank of wood instead of his powerful fist. Because sometimes this—*all of this*—is too hard. An easy way out, at times, seems preferable.

But then I *always* remember my reason.

Then my situation isn't so tough after all.

"Jesus," I groan as I sit up.

"Shhhh."

"God, I fucked up," I hiss as I crawl off of the sofa. I purposely avoid the door by the stairwell and clumsily make my way over to the steps. If I open that door, I can kiss all of this goodbye. All progress will be lost. I'll be back to square one. "I'll fix this."

Clambering up the steps, I blink away a wave of dizziness before I climb the rest of the way up. Once my palm finds the cold steel door, I slap at it.

"Logan!" I hiss and clutch onto the knob. "Let me out!"

My fingers fly over the pad, finally getting a chance to try out some number combinations I'd hoped would work. Birthdates. Alarm codes. Addresses. But each one beeps its decline.

Don't give up, Nadia.

I wake to hot, powerful arms peeling me from the top step and freeing me from my prison. I'm not sure how long I clawed and pounded at the door but eventually, he had mercy on my poor soul. And now, sometime in the early hours of dawn on Sunday, Logan carries my broken and blood-crusted body to his bedroom. He sits me on the bed, gently, and then disappears into the bathroom. The room is dark so I can't take stock of my injuries. Not that I even care. My biggest wound is to my heart.

A short time in the basement was enough to slice it to bits.

"Come on, Nadia. Time to clean you up."

With gentle movements, he tugs my dress down off my shoulders. I let him guide me to my shaky feet where he can finish removing my undergarments. I'm trying to remain strong—to remember my ambition—but it's difficult when all I want to do is sleep for a week.

He guides me into the steaming hot bathroom to where he quickly sheds his clothes. Together, we step into the slate-tiled walk-in shower and the heated bliss cloaks me almost instantly. I'm not sure why Logan is showing me kindness and I'm sure there's an ulterior motive—but just this once, I cling on to it and pray that it's genuine.

I wince when he begins massaging shampoo onto my sore scalp but remain immobile. Logan does what he wants. And right now, he wants to take care of me for some reason. So I'll let him.

"That's a nasty bruise on your cheek. Kasper will have to be more careful where he leaves his tools and supplies. My clumsy fiancée just tripped right over that board and hit her face." He clucks his tongue as if he really believes his words.

I shudder, the chill that always emanates from him gripping me in its clutches. "I can cover it with makeup."

Our eyes meet and I am too frozen in his gaze to break from his heated glare. But it isn't a hate-filled glint in his eyes, it's something different. Something foreign. Something I cling on to desperately.

It's the brilliant shimmering glint of progress.

"I love you," he says in a whisper, almost as if he hates saying the words out loud.

I smile and slide my fingertips up his firm tattooed chest. "I love you too, D"—my heart plummets to the floor but I quickly fix my mistake—"d-d-darling."

The growl of anger softens as his mouth descends upon mine. Our kiss is intense. I throw everything I have into it. His rough, masculine hands grip my ass and he lifts me. I hook my legs around his waist and hiss out in shock when the icy cold tile hits my back. He pushes his cock into me but he's not rough—he's needy almost. Greedy for me. I'm not sure what to make of his unusual behavior.

"You're mine," he says with a possessive growl as he thrusts into me. "All mine."

As he fucks me with a gentle eagerness that's never been there before, I let my mind slip. This is too much—too kind. In some ways, it's worse than when he's awful to me.

"How's school?"

I let out a sigh and stretch along my bed in my dorm room. "Fine."

He remains quiet for a moment. "Just fine? What's going

on, baby? I can hear it in your voice."

Chewing on my lip, I blink away the tears in my eyes. I can't tell him that I feel lost all the way out here in California. That I haven't made many friends despite being in my second year of school here. That, no matter how many trails I follow, none of them lead back to Kasey. And most of all, I can't tell him that I miss him so fucking much.

It's not right.

Grossly inappropriate.

But I do miss him with every cell in my body.

"I broke up with Jake yesterday." Another boyfriend in a long list of forgettable ones.

Donovan lets out a grunt on the other end of the line and it charges my nerve endings to life.

"Good."

Of course I tell Donovan everything. He knows every single detail in my life. We both like it that way.

"What are you doing?" I question, trying to change the subject.

"Just got out of the shower. Today was quad day."

A mental picture of Donovan, wet and sculpted, in nothing but a towel sends curls of pleasure straight to my core. I'm twisted because I'm pretty sure I'm in love with my stepdad. As his deep voice rambles on about a new property he'd put a bid on, I tug at my nightgown and bring it up over my hips. Shame makes my neck and cheeks heat but it doesn't stop me from dragging my index finger over my clit through my panties. I jolt from the touch and let out a small gasp.

"You okay?"

"Mmmhhhm. Just tell me more about your day," I breathe, "Mi querido amigo." My dear friend.

He groans, always an animalistic growl when I murmur Spanish endearments to him, and launches into how he found out Darcy and Dan have been fucking on the side. Even though I hate her, I still want Donovan to tell me about it.

"It's a problem," he says, his voice sad almost.

My heart catches in my throat and my fingers stop their assault on my sex. Does he like her? The thought is a terrifying one. "Why is it a problem?"

He lets out a breath into the phone that makes me shiver. "Well, for one, it's a conflict of interest."

At least he didn't say because he wants her or something. I'm not sure I could have handled that kind of information coming from his handsome mouth.

"Why? Because she works for the execs? Can't you just transfer her to a different department?" I question. I'm not sure why I'm advocating for Darcy's sex life but I feel like Donovan's not telling me everything. Something tells me to fight for her.

His silence is unnerving. I can hear him breathing and I can almost imagine him tugging at his dark hair in frustration. But why? Why is something so trivial as an inner office affair upsetting him?

"Tell me," I prod, my voice a whispered plea.

"It's more than that actually." The painful way he says his words makes me want to reach through the phone, wrap my arms around him, and curl up in his lap. To promise him whatever he's worrying about is just another obstacle. The great Donovan Jayne doesn't feel guilty. He fucking conquers!

My heart ceases to beat, though, when he lets out a resigned sigh and speaks his next words.

"He's a superior in the company," he says carefully. "It

could be argued that he abused his position of authority. That she wouldn't have ended up in bed with him had they met under regular circumstances." I hear it. Shame. Embarrassment. His words have nothing to do with Darcy and Dan. They have everything to do with us. And that makes my heart jumpstart back to life.

"What if Darcy loves him? That should be the only thing that matters," I argue, a little too enthusiastically.

"She'd be risking so much. He's taking advantage of her."

Emotion chokes me as I say my next words. "Maybe he's worth the risk to her. Maybe she'd give up everything and everyone just to be with him."

"Nadia, you don't understand the ways of the world. What people would think..."

"I understand. But you don't hear me when I say that I do," I argue, my voice a desperate whisper.

His breathing is the only indication he's still on the line. "I always hear you, baby. Always. Even when I don't know what the fuck you're saying and even when you don't actually say anything. I. Always. Hear. You."

The line goes quiet.

Things are tense.

And then they're not. It's as though whatever was bugging Donovan has been cut free. I can feel him smiling into the phone, even if I can't see him. He calls me sunshine some of the time but I'm the one basking in his warmth all of the time.

"I thought you hated, Darcy," he teases.

"I do hate her," I say with a laugh. We both know this conversation was not about those two. "Do you think he is awful to her?"

Donovan laughs and it's rich. Perfect. Soul warming.

"*Probably. Dan is awful to everyone.*"

"*Do you think they do it in the conference room? What you think they do?*" *I urge and start moving my hand between my legs again, now that we've navigated into better territory.*

"*Hmmm,*" *he ponders aloud, his deep voice delicious enough to make love to.* "*He probably fucks her in the ass over his desk and then comes all over her face.*"

His words have their desired effect and I massage myself more quickly. The need to come is overwhelming. Donovan would feel so much better than my own finger. Will I ever have the courage to instigate something between us? I'd die though if he laughed me off.

"*What are you doing, pretty girl? You're breathing heavily.*"

I try not to moan the closer I get to my climax. My fingers don't stop and suddenly the panties are too much. I quickly shove them down and off of me so I can spread my legs. When I push a finger into my hot center, I do let out a small moan.

"*N-n-nothing,*" *I lie.* "*Just relaxing.*"

I push deep into myself and when my finger grazes my G-spot, my eyes roll into the back of my head. So close.

"*I want to see you.*"

More heat floods through me. I want to see him too. If I angle the camera on my face, he'll never see what I'm doing. The thought thrills me.

"*Okay.*" *I mash the Facetime button and his narrowed silvery eyes fill the screen.*

"*Jesus Christ, baby,*" *he groans.* "*Are you feeling okay? You look flushed.*"

I attempt to keep my face expressionless as I finger myself. What would he do if I "accidentally" turned the camera?

Would he hang up on me? Would he talk dirty to me?

"I'm fine. Tell me more about Dumb Darcy and Dirty Dan." I smirk.

His eyes are all over me as he assesses me. Dark eyebrows knit together with confusion. I can see him trying to read me. He's really good at it. Too good. And, right now, I kind of wish he knew what I was doing.

"I don't want to talk about them," he says, his voice low and gravelly. "I want to talk about us."

My eyes fly to his on the small screen and I bite down on my lip. I can see his bare shoulders and collar bone. He's probably in nothing but a towel, just like I imagined. Dear God, I can't get that image out of my head.

"What about us?" I whisper as I drag a finger back along my slit, the juices from inside me making the path to my clit come alive with fiery need.

"You make everything bearable when you're around. Lately, I'm so fucking lonely. When do you come home for another break? I need to see you."

His words make me close my eyes and I smile. "I miss you too. You have no idea how much, Donovan. I'll be home soon."

Our conversations always teeter the line between friendship and something else. Now that his divorce to my mother is finalized, I don't feel as bad about how close we are.

"Sunshine, tell me what you're doing. Don't be shy. I can tell you're up to something. Seems like you're having trouble. Can I help you?"

Oh God.

"Umm…"

Put your cock inside of me, please.

"Tell me." His voice is demanding. A needy growl.

"I'm too embarrassed."

He grunts and I imagine him fisting his beautiful cock. I've never seen it but I can only imagine it's thick and long. And how wonderful it would feel to take him inside me.

"I love you, sweet Jayne. Nothing you could ever say would make me think less of you."

I tense up. The words feel awkward on my tongue but what if…what if… "If I show you, do you promise not to get mad at me? Promise me, Donovan."

He chuckles. "There's no way in hell I could ever get mad at you. Please show me before you drive me crazy."

And I do.

Slowly, I let the camera leave my face and drag it along my heaving breasts. I point it right where he can see exactly what it is I'm up to between my legs. My fingers tease my pussy for a minute before I bring the camera back to my face.

He's pissed.

Shit!

His jaw clenches in an angry manner and his eyebrows are furled together. Those full, perfect lips of his are pressed into a firm line.

"I knew you'd be mad," I say in disappointment.

He shakes his head and lets out a huff. "Baby, I am far from fucking mad. If you only knew what you just did to me. You're fucking with my head, Nadia, and I'm not just talking about the one on my shoulders."

My eyes widen and his lips twitch with amusement.

"You need help, right? Well, I'm going to help you. I want that camera back where I can see that pretty pussy. You're going to spread yourself open and show me everything. Then,

I'll tell you exactly how to touch yourself so you can get off. Sound good, baby?"

I nod and do as he says. My heart is thundering in my chest. He didn't reject me or laugh at me. No, he looks like he wants to devour me. And I love it.

"Jesus," he groans from the speaker when I position the camera for him to see my pussy. "Push two fingers into yourself. I want to watch you fuck yourself with your hand. Show me how wet you are."

His words light a match to my soul and I nearly come. A light sheen of sweat breaks out over my flesh. I'm craving him with every bone in my body.

"Like this?" I push my fingers inside of me and thrust them in and out several times before pulling them back out. They glisten with my arousal.

He growls and it sends a shiver through me. "Exactly like that. Now suck on them. I want to watch you taste yourself."

"Will it be gross?" I question as I bring both the camera and my wet fingers back to my face.

His features are tight and serious. "Not gross at all. If I were there, I'd taste them for you and let you know before making you suck on them. But I'm not so you have to be a big girl and taste them for me."

Nodding, I bring my fingers to my mouth and slip them between my lips. The musky taste isn't unpleasant…just different. I lick between the two fingers to make sure I don't miss any.

"Good girl," he breathes. "Such a fucking good girl."

I beam at his praise and my pussy aches for more touch. "Now what?"

The next few minutes are a blur of my frantic massag-

es and his growled orders. Everything spins and fades out as
Donovan, via Facetime, gives me my best orgasm I've had to
date. My moans probably woke the girls in the neighboring
dorm rooms but I don't care. This was perfection.

"Now I need another shower," he says with a small laugh.

"Why?" My voice is a soft purr like a kitten. "You're not
the dirty one here."

"It seems I made a little mess actually," he chuckles. "A
mess that you'd be cleaning up if you were here, since it's all
your fault."

Images of Donovan with cum all over his bare belly are
enough to nearly have me climaxing again.

"What we just did," I say slowly, "was that wrong?"

His lips draw down into a frown and I curse myself for
souring his mood. "It didn't feel wrong to me. But maybe we
shouldn't ever do it again." He doesn't look convinced though.

Tears well in my eyes and I nod. "Okay. I have to go. I'm
sleepy now."

"I love you, baby."

Te amo, Donovan.

"Goodnight, Donovan. I'm sorry."

Not waiting for his response, I hang up and then let out a
sob. A short brief, sexual moment with Donovan was worth
the strain I just put on our relationship. He might not want us
to do it again, but I'll not settle until it does.

This will happen again.

And soon.

"Fucking hell!" Logan grunts as he comes inside of me.

His heat pours into me which sends my body into an orgasmic shudder. With Donovan still on my mind, I climax hard and without abandon. When I finally come down from my high, Logan laughs. His laugh is warm and unusual. It should make me happy for the progress I've made but instead, it coils its way into the pit of my belly like a snake.

"I've never seen you come like that before. After all this time, and it's a first." He pulls out and sets me back to my feet. My legs shake but he keeps a grip on my biceps to keep me from falling. "Maybe you like it when I'm sweet."

I smile at him and nod despite the raging headache thundering in my skull from where he hit me. "Maybe I do."

Nine

Kasper

I SIT IN MY CAMARO IN THE PARKING LOT OF DONOVAN Jayne's resort and stare up at the monstrosity through my windshield while listening to The Eagles. Once again, Logan has me on babysitting duty. I glance down at my knuckles and groan. They're still bruised from when I punched the brick wall outside of The Lounge after nearly choking Dale to death. If it didn't earn me a straight ticket to prison, and hell for that matter, I'd have already put a bullet in Dale's head.

A few snowflakes swirl around the windshield, and I fixate my gaze on them. I wonder if Nadia is wearing another one of her signature dresses that are all too inappropriate for a Colorado fall. Yesterday, when I'd gone to work on the walls some more, she'd been nowhere in sight. Logan mentioned she had a migraine and she spent the entire time in bed with the door closed. He drank beer and shot the shit with me while I worked. It had driven me crazy not to see her again.

I've been obsessing over where the hell she's really been ever since. Something in his smug grins told me he put his hands on her again. It's not natural for me to care about her—fucked up is what it is. But I can't help it. She reminds me of Kase sometimes and that really scrambles my damn head up. As a result though, it makes me protective over her. It makes me want to throw her over my shoulder and get her the hell out of there.

Before I left Logan's yesterday, I almost did just that. Pure fucking insanity is what it is. Me trying to save someone I've hated for so long. Yet, I still went into the guest bathroom and contemplated how I could sneak into the master bedroom. We could have easily slipped out the back door undetected. She would have been in the safety of her stepfather's arms by the next morning. But just before I made the decision to kidnap Logan's fiancée, I shook my head in frustration and left. He'd have thwarted a rescue before I even made it to her bedside. The prick has cameras everywhere and would probably punish her somehow for my trying to help her. While her punishment used to arouse me, now it only infuriates me.

Shit is way too fucking complicated right now.

Needing some cold air, I press the button to the window and nearly sigh aloud when a blast of icy air rushes in around me. Snowflakes stick to my flesh and cool me off almost immediately.

"Is there a reason you're following me?"

I jolt in surprise to see Donovan Jayne standing before me, peering into my car. Bristling at his words, I quickly recover and shoot him an uninterested smirk. "Logan asked me to."

He frowns and rounds the car without another word. Then the passenger door opens and he plops down beside me. Once he slams the door shut, he turns to glare at me.

"Why did he ask you to?" he seethes. "*I* have done *nothing* wrong."

I meet his stare and shrug my shoulders. "Just taking orders. Besides, I hardly call assaulting the police chief in his own home and pulling a gun on him nothing. In fact, that's some pretty serious shit, Donovan."

He huffs out a breath of air and runs his fingers through his hair before resting his elbows on his knees. His gaze is on his massive building in front of us. "Cut the crap, Kasper. We go way back. Be straight with me," he says, sounding oddly like Taylor. "I've never given you any reason not to."

My mind flits back to the day I found his brother. We were supposed to go play some basketball with some of our friends at the rec center. But, when I'd gone across the street to catch a ride with him, I found his dead body instead.

Blood splatter was all over their white leather couch which cost more than everything combined in the shitty-ass trailer I lived in with my family. The shotgun was still wedged between his thighs and his thumb was twisted inside the trigger guard. I'd thrown up all over the late Frank Jayne's marble floors that day.

My best friend left me for no fucking reason.

Well, Donovan knows the reason *I think.*

A single envelope with Donovan's name scrawled across the top in Taylor's messy handwriting had been lying on the coffee table. Every cell in me begged to tear it open and demand answers—not only for me but for Kasey. Those two were in love. Having to tell her Taylor took his life was the hardest thing I've ever had to do. She'd already been suffering a bout of severe depression. I'd assumed it had something to do with Dale at the time. Now, I wonder if she knew Taylor was unhappy. Regardless, she spun deeper into her own head after that. Withdrew from everything and everyone. Started dressing all gothic. I had just started seeing her smiles again nearly three years later during my summer break of college, right before she was taken.

"In case you missed it, your good buddy Logan is obsessed with your stepdaughter—says he's in love with her. That's why I'm here. To keep you away from her." I shouldn't be telling Donovan any of this. He went from a semi friend to enemy the day his stepdaughter became a witness to a crime involving my sister. I'm still curious, though, about what his take is on the whole ordeal.

He fists both hands and his glare becomes murderous. "She doesn't love him," he seethes in a tone not to be fucked with.

My eyebrows pinch together in irritation and the familiar ache in my shoulders presents itself. I'm always tense when the subject goes to Nadia. I hate the fact Logan controls her every move. That he puts his hands on her. He's no better than Dale. "They're getting married. She lives with him. Sure seems like love," I taunt. I know better, but does he?

He curses and loosens the knot on his tie. "She's been gone for three years, kid. Three fucking years. And now, suddenly she's back and…involved with that slimy bastard. You're the cop—does that add up to you?"

"I thought you and Logan were close. Maybe she's doing it to piss her 'ol stepdaddy off," I muse. "What'd you do to her? Seems like if she has an agenda, it involves you."

His hand is at my throat before I can stop him and he clutches a fistful of my collar. "*He's* nothing to me any-more—*she* is my everything!" he snaps. "I *love* her. So don't ever say that shit to my face again."

I swat his arm away and he leans back in his seat huffing. He's no better than Logan with the possessive love crap.

"Get out of my car."

He frowns and runs his fingers back through his hair. "Jesus! I'm sorry, okay?" he mutters. "You know me, man. At one time you were practically a kid brother to me. You bailed after what happened with Taylor. I get it—it screwed me up too. Trust me. And then with your sister getting kidnapped... You've every right to be angry about the whole damn situation. But blaming Nadia for all of this is blinding you to the truth. Take yourself out of the situation. What if the roles were reversed? If someone you loved were in trouble, you know I'd try and help. I *did* help. Think about it. You can't act like I wasn't at that damn station every week after Kasey went missing." His tortured expression meets mine and I have to close my eyes for a brief moment. Donovan and Taylor always looked so similar. Seeing him so vulnerable is a painful reminder of just that. I often wonder if Taylor would have ended up just like his brother, running multiple lodges and resorts.

"You were there because of *her*. Not my sister. *Nadia*." My argument is weak and I don't feel strengthened by my anger anymore. What if he's right? What if I am fucking blinded? "You came to the station to help *your* family. Not mine."

He sighs. "You were always family because of your

friendship with my brother. And *my family* has done nothing but try to get her back since day one. Open your eyes,
Kasper."

It annoys me that he's lost his glossy façade and is struggling. Donovan is always composed. The fact that he's coming apart at the seams has my nerves on edge. I don't want
to trust him. My familiar anger reminds me of this. But the
investigative part of me—the bloodhound cop who drives
me forward—tells me he's not all bad and that there's truth
to his story. Never once was Donovan cruel to me or my
family. It was me who pushed away, not him. And once Nadia got involved, I truly did become blind with hate.

There's most definitely something strange going on between Logan and Nadia. He's absolutely right. It drives me
a little fucking insane that I can't figure out exactly what,
though. All the puzzle pieces seem to be hanging in the air,
waiting for me to snatch them up and put them together. It
has to do with Donovan too—I'm sure of it—which is why
I'm not too eager to buddy up to him. Something drove a
wedge between those two guys. When Taylor and I were
friends as teens, I'd seen how Donovan strutted around
this goddamned town like he owned it. It only got worse
when his father passed away, leaving him as the sole heir to
an empire. Logan was always at his side like a loyal puppy.
They were every bit as close as Taylor and I were.

So what happened?

When did the two kings of Aspen go their separate
ways?

He shifts his body toward me, his movements jerky.
"You have to help me see her, man. That's all I'm asking. I
haven't spoken to her properly in three years. There's a rea-

son for that and I intend on uncovering that reason. Everything was perfect and then she just fucking vanished with
nothing more than a stupid letter sent to me not long after she left, only to turn up engaged to that motherfucker.
Something isn't right. Can't you use your police skills and
just help me find out what the hell is going on around here?"

I rap my sore knuckles on the steering wheel, anger
surging through me, eager to use them again. Maybe the
next time I'll use them on Logan's face. "I've spent the last
decade using my 'police skills' to find my fucking sister and
look how that's turned out," I snap and scowl at him. "Your
stepdaughter has been a thorn in my side since day one. She
never cared about what happened to my sister back then so
why the hell should I care about what happens to her now?"

"She was a minor at the time. I had to protect her from
the media." He stares at me like *I'm* the moron here. "But
Jesus, you're an idiot for not seeing past your anger. If you
would have, you'd have seen she spent every single extra
ounce of her energy looking for your sister. I funded every one of her endeavors. You don't think she feels guilt for
what happened? Why the fuck do you think she went to
college for criminal justice? She wanted to join the damn
police academy for crying out loud!" he bellows from beside me. "Open your fucking eyes, Lieutenant. Nadia is a
good person and doesn't deserve this."

I cock a brow at him. It's news to me that Nadia was actually searching for my sister. All I ever saw was Donovan's
formidable presence shielding her from everyone. I mean,
sure, I saw her come to the station from time to time but
nothing ever useful came from it. Not that it really changes
the fact that she let her slip away in the first place. Why

didn't she attack that bastard? Remember one incriminating clue the police could use? Memorize a fucking license plate for crying out loud? She gave them nothing and trying to soothe her guilty conscience years after the fact is a joke. If I can't find Kase, nobody can.

"Logan is a damn psycho," he mutters. "She's not safe with him. You don't know the half of it."

At this, I'm intrigued. One of those puzzle pieces locking into place. "Why do you say he's a psycho?" I question, avoiding his small but desperate voice in my head urging me to ignore the years of blame I've placed on his stepdaughter.

He shrugs and lets out a bitter laugh. "I've known him for a long time. He's never been one to date much, but when he does, he's a prick to whichever chick he's putting his dick into."

"If he's so psychotic like you say, why doesn't she just leave?"

His eyes cut over to mine, cold and flashing with hate. "I know her and it was almost like she was imprisoned by him when I saw her. Her eyes told a different story than the words that came out of her mouth. Maybe not a physical prisoner, but definitely a mental one. There's a reason she is *choosing* to stay there. Nadia is stubborn as hell and oftentimes takes dangerous chances if she thinks it will get her what she wants."

I scoff at him. "So she uses people. She wants him for his money? Is that it?"

Another look. Just like before. Like I'm a fucking idiot. "Don't be ridiculous. She has access to a shitload of money—far more than Logan could ever dream to make on his police chief's salary. If she's embedding herself into his life, she must think he will help her somehow."

"Help her what?" I'm growing impatient with his talking in circles.

He shakes his head and gapes at me in astonishment. "She must think he can help her find Kasey. It's the only logical explanation—the only reason I've been keeping my distance. And my patience with the entire situation is wearing incredibly thin. So are you going to help me or not?"

I mean, I still plan on pulling any answers I can glean from Nadia, but I'm not really interested in destroying her any longer.

"I'll see what I can do."

I lean back on the leather sofa and stare up at the ceiling. It irritates me that Nadia has been hunting for my sister all of these years. The glowing burn of hatred has begun to flicker and die out. Without that fueling me, I'm lost.

Why does she think Logan can help her? How?

"Thought you had to work on that wall or some shit, Ghost," Rhodes says as he sips his Heineken. Mine remains untouched on his coffee table. I'm not in the mood to drink at the moment. I want my head clear so I can figure this shit out.

"Logan said he was taking Nadia to dinner or something and to come back tomorrow after work." I'd been annoyed when he popped into my office to mention it earlier this afternoon long after I'd been to see Donovan. I didn't miss the way Logan's eyes didn't meet mine when he'd told me the change in plans. He just didn't fucking want me there for some reason.

"I still don't understand what she sees in Chief. The guy can be…"

"A prick?" I quip.

He chuckles. "You said it. Not me."

Ashley comes waddling into the living room carrying a big purse and interrupts our exchange. "Babe, I'm going to go pick up Ames. Her flight will arrive within the hour."

"I can leave," I state as I stand.

She waves me off and grins. "No, stay. Jason hovers too much as it is with this pregnancy. It'll do him good to have some time to relax. Besides," she tells me with a mischievous grin, "Ames and I have to gossip, which is never much fun when your husband is around."

Jason grunts and saunters over to her. She squeals when he pulls her into a tight embrace and sucks on her neck.

"Be careful, beautiful. And tell Ames she's not allowed to hit on my friend."

She giggles. "I won't let her go for Kasper anyway. He's too…"

"I'm right here. I can hear you," I groan with faux annoyance. "I'm too what? Too much of an asshole?"

Ashley walks over and swats at my shoulder. "No, punk. You're too serious and she's too…bubbly. You'll just break her with your broody, grumpy self. Amethyst loves a project. And you, my friend, are a broken project she'll want to fix."

I frown but nod. "I'm not going to hit on your sister."

She bends down and kisses the top of my head. "You can hit on her. Just don't sleep with her. She's better than a weekend fling."

Shrugging my shoulders, I lean back against the sofa. "Sure, Ash. But I can't promise I won't look after her. If she's your family, then she's my family too."

Ashley beams at me and I can't help but crack a smile when Rhodes kisses her belly before she leaves.

"Have you thought of names yet?"

"Aiden for a boy," he says as he sits back down, "and Arden for a girl."

We chat and a couple of beers later, I'm relaxed after a stressful as fuck day.

"Another cold one?" he asks as he stands to toss out our empty ones.

"Nah, I'm about to head out here in a second. But, hey, does your dad ever do any commercial plumbing projects?" I ask and pull out my phone.

"On occasion, why? Are you going to take on a bigger project?"

I shake my head and locate the picture of the pipe from Logan's. "Do you know why this size pipe would be in a residential home?"

He inspects the picture for a moment. "No, but if you'll text it to me, I'll send it to Dad and ask him about it. Why you want to know?"

"Between us," I say carefully. "This was behind the wall at Logan's. I'm curious to know why."

His eyes narrow at me. "And you didn't just ask Chief?"

Clenching my jaw, I shake my head. "He and I aren't exactly best buds at the moment. Ever since his engagement became known, he's been acting strange. I'd rather just find this out on my own. It's weird and I want to know why he'd have a pipe that size in his home."

"Whatever, man. I'm not getting in the middle of anything between you and our boss but I'll ask Dad. Did you ever—"

My phone rings and, speak of the devil, it's Logan calling. I have a good mind not to answer it but he is still my boss.

"Yep," I bark out in a gruff tone while Rhodes saunters off to fetch another beer.

"Kasper," Logan bites out with equal annoyance, "I need you out on highway 82 at the Owl Creek Road exit. Now."

"Out by the airport? What's happened?"

"There's been a fatality," he says in a grim tone. "And I'm sorry but I think it was Dale's truck. Your mom is still at The Lounge. I double checked before I called you."

I don't normally handle traffic accidents but this one involves my stepfather and I'm grateful for Logan calling me to it.

"I'll be right there."

My stepfather dying would be a blessing. Mom could be free of that prick once and for all. I don't even feel like an asshole when I send up a quick prayer wishing that he suffered a little before he died.

As soon as I climb out of my car at the scene, my stomach flops. Dale's beat up truck is barely damaged. But the silver Honda is completely smashed in the front. If that motherfucker hurt someone else, there'll be hell to pay.

"Ghost," Logan calls out and waves me over to his Tahoe. "We've got a big fucking problem."

I frown and stalk over to him. "What is it?"

He shakes his head and waves at his vehicle in disgust. I can see Dale's glazed over eyes in the backseat.

"The woman he had in the truck with him was dead on arrival. Apparently he was going the wrong way on the exit ramp when he collided head on with the other vehicle. His headlights weren't on, which could have prevented the collision if they had been on. An officer already made note of that when processing the scene."

"The woman with him wasn't Mom?" I know he said she was still at the bar, but my stomach remains twisted up.

"No. She's fine. But," he murmurs and slams his fist on the hood of his Tahoe. "It's the other vehicle that is the issue."

"Why?" I croak.

His brows furrow and I can tell it pains him to say it. "It was Ashley Rhodes."

I double over and suck in a deep breath of air. "Is she okay? Has she been sent to the hospital? She's fucking pregnant, Chief!"

He scowls and nods. "I know. They rushed her off in an ambulance right before you got here. I'm not going to sugar coat it, Kasper. She was in bad shape. The paramedic wouldn't say but I think her neck might've been broken."

"Shit! What about Rhodes? Why didn't you tell me who it was? I was at his house."

He lets out a sigh. "I sent a uni to his house to take him to the hospital. I needed you here because it was Dale who caused the accident and I wanted someone else to make sure he was okay, besides you."

Red rage blinds me and I shoulder past Logan to get to

the backseat of his Tahoe. I ignore his bellows ordering me to stop. Instead, I drag Dale's wormy ass out by his throat and tackle him to the pavement. I've managed to smash my fist into his nose at least six brutal times before Logan and another officer wrangle me off him.

"I'll kill you!" I scream at him. "I will kill you!"

Logan grips my bicep painfully. "He'll get his justice. Slam dunk case. But get your shit together. Get to the hospital to be with your friend."

I run my fingers through my hair and curse at the sky. When I've calmed, marginally so, I turn to him. "Was Ashley the only victim in the car? She was on her way to get her sister. Was there another woman in the vehicle?"

He shakes his head. "No, there wasn't. The vehicle was headed westbound, toward the airport. Guess you better go get her and take her on your way."

I'm already stalking back to my car before he even gets the words out.

Ten

Nadia

AFTER DINNER, LOGAN GOT CALLED OUT ON AN emergency. He's been gone for an hour but thankfully took my call when I reminded him to do what needed to be done. Now that I've bought myself another hour, I've been aimlessly pacing the hallway. Sometimes he doesn't set his stupid timer on his phone. Those days, I can breathe easier and my muscles don't stay knotted up. But I think he knows, deep down, that he's the most vulnerable when he doesn't set it. One of these days, it'll be the right time when he forgets and I'll strike.

I let out a sigh and tenderly touch the bruise on my face. Today was a frustrating day. My body ached from his abuse the day before but I couldn't seem to shut off my mind. It kept wanting to flit *there*. Of course, my mind is one of the parts of me I have control over. I was able to shut it off and focus on housework. Logan was extra needy throughout the day, calling me often to check up on me. He even came home for lunch and gave me a quickie over the back of the living room sofa. Everything about him today is different. It puts me on edge. Logan is never nice or caring. He's never the adoring one. So when this afternoon I received red roses from him, I nearly had a panic attack.

Either, he's on to me and is playing games.

Or I've managed to crack him and I'm one step closer to the end.

But since I don't know which it is, I'm stuck teetering on the edge of sanity until I have more of an idea of what's going on in his head.

A bang on the door startles me from finishing up the dinner dishes and I quickly dry my hands on a towel. Fear threatens to swallow me up alive. If it's Kasper, here against Logan's wishes, I'll have a meltdown. I have a good mind not to even answer the door.

The banging is relentless and irritation courses through me. "¡Calmate!"

Of course whoever it is, won't hold their fucking horses and continues their beat down of the door. When I finally wrench it open, my whole world crashes down on top of me.

"My baby."

The lonely ache in my chest is soothed upon seeing him. The ever present grip on my heart loosens and I let out a choked exhalation.

His hardened features light up as he assess me. Like every time I would come bounding into his presence. Making sure I'm okay. Studying my smiles and my frowns as if they unlock the mysteries inside my head. He's always been able to read me better than anyone in the entire world. While he's staring at me as if I'm a mist that might suddenly dissipate, I'm drinking up his handsome face and inhaling his familiar masculine scent. The other day I hadn't looked at him properly. Everything was a blur. It was too risky. But tonight, I want to freeze time so I can simply stare. So I can make up for three years lost.

He's regarding me as if I'm his entire world. As if no time has passed at all. It's heartbreaking and relieving all at once. Donovan Jayne hasn't changed a bit. And thank God for that.

"Donovan," I gasp, "what are you doing here?"

"I'm here to get you the hell out of this place, sunshine."

He takes a step toward me but I hold up both hands. Reality snatches me from my frozen dream world and a shiver of fear courses through me. "Please do not come any farther."

His silvery blue eyes are narrowed as he assesses my face, his gaze lingering for a moment on my lips. It twists up my mind and starts to pull at the thread that's keeping my sanity tied together. "Then come out here."

I cast a quick glance over my shoulder to the camera and then turn back to him. "Just one moment, Donovan. You have one minute with me."

His sigh of relief crushes me. "No amount of time will ever be enough."

I step out and close the door behind me. My lip quivers as I attempt to keep my emotions in check. As soon as I've come onto the porch, he pulls me into a forceful hug. Being crushed in his loving embrace is painful both to my broken body and my broken spirit.

"Come home with me," he begs against my hair as he strokes my back with firm circles.

Oh God, how I wish.

I suck in a comforting breath of his scent, wondering if I can keep it in my lungs forever, and shake my head. "I can't."

He growls at my answer but doesn't release me. "Don't you miss this? Don't you miss us? What's really going on?"

I have answers but I'm not ready for him to hear them yet. "Shhh, can you just trust that I know what I'm doing?"

With a huff, he pulls away to stare down at me. His hands cradle my face and he runs his thumb over my wobbling lip. I'm glad for the darkness on the porch hiding my secrets from him. I can't have him peeling apart the edges when I'm so close to my goal. Just this once, I need him to let *me* take care of things.

"I trust that you still love me," he says with his air of confidence I so love.

"You always were good at trusting your gut," I chuckle and poke his hard stomach.

He smiles at me but it quickly fades. It's then I notice he's not the usual unflappable man I know. His shirt is wrinkly. He's slightly scruffy as if he hasn't shaved in days. Completely disheveled and not at all like him. It kills me knowing he's like this because of me.

"I tried to stay away, *for you*. To let you follow whatever it was you were after. But…" he trails off and flicks his tortured eyes to meet mine. "I couldn't not come see you again once I knew you were here. You're so close, yet still so far away. I'm selfish and I want you back where you belong. With me."

He smiles again before his lips descend upon mine. The air is stolen right from my mouth as he kisses me passionately. Donovan Jayne owns my mouth with the possession of a man who's been starved for three long years. He marks me with his scent and taste. And all I can do is try not to float away. I'm reminded of what I've lost. Of what I may not have ever again if I don't see this plan to fruition. I'm terrified this kiss may be our last.

"Do you remember Vegas? That first time, baby?" he says, his words poking holes in my heart, before his lips trail along my cheek and down my throat.

I tangle my fingers into his hair as he places soft kisses near my ear. A small moan escapes me and I close my eyes.

"I remember it fondly."

"I'm going to take a quick shower," Donovan says as he works the knot on his tie. "When I get out, let's talk about what happened today. I want to help you remember."

I nod and he disappears into the bathroom. Today was mentally taxing. It's been years since Kasey was taken but not one single day goes by when I don't think about her. Not one second passes when I don't try to find clues as to who could have stolen her. Donovan has come through for me considerably. He's become just as obsessed as I am about finding her.

Mamá still lives in the house but he's long since moved into one of the fancy suites at his lodge. The divorce wasn't messy at all despite my mother's unusual behavior and desire to end the marriage. It was almost as if both of them knew it was inevitable. She never loved Donovan like she loved my father. I think deep down she seems satisfied that she's given me this opportunity.

By opportunity, she means someone to take care of me. A father figure.

But I don't need anyone to take care of me. Not in the way you'd think. I want him to use his resources to help me find the seventeen-year-old girl from my past. He tells me he has his own reasons for helping me and I am forever grateful.

While Donovan showers, I stride over to my suitcase to hunt for something to sleep in. We'd flown to Vegas to see the country's best hypnotherapist. It had cost Donovan thousands of dollars for her services on a whim and he didn't bat an eye when he handed over the stack of hundreds to the greedy old lady. And while she attempted to hypnotize me so I could search for answers that my brain had somehow locked up, he sat beside me and held my hand firmly.

His support has meant everything to me.

At twenty-three-years old, I don't feel much like his step-daughter. More like his partner. When I was in college, we Skyped nearly every day. And now that I'm moved back to Aspen, we see each other all the time. I see and speak to him more than anybody else.

I frown as I dig through my suitcase. I'd thought I'd packed some pajamas, but apparently in my haste to meet with the hypnotherapist, I hadn't packed properly. With a huff, I peel off my jeans and sweater, tossing them into my suitcase. Next, I free my heavy breasts from my bra and then make my way over to Donovan's suitcase to steal something of his. I find a white sleeveless undershirt and pull it on. Since he's so gigantic, it fits like a dress hitting me mid-thigh. Once I'm dressed, I crawl back onto one of the queen beds and lie back. Closing my eyes, I attempt to bring back that day. As each day passes, it seems as if the past becomes darker and less clear. Nothing sticks out to me.

"I was thinking tomorrow we could do a little gambling. I know we came here on business but we can still find time for pleasure," he says in an absent tone as he saunters out of the bathroom.

My eyes pop open. He's looking at his phone as he talks to me. I've known Donovan since I was seventeen and have never really seen him in anything except business attire. In fact, I tease him that his suits are physically attached to him. Even when he "dresses down" he wears a button-up, crisp, long-sleeved shirt. I've never seen him in anything less than professional.

So that's why now, I'm having trouble breathing.

More of those foreign thoughts enter my brain as I greedily drink him up. He's turned to the side reading an email or something, wearing nothing but a white hotel towel tied low and loose on his hips. The swell of his ass is perfection and I bite my lip to keep from letting an appreciative groan escape me. His body is all chiseled curves and definition from many years of working out. And his smooth dark hair, for once, is a wild, wet mess on top of his head. Water rivulets drip from his hair and roll down the flesh of his chest in such a way that has me thirsty—so damn thirsty.

He may have tried to put a wedge between us after our whole phone sex fiasco, but I wouldn't let him. Nothing like that has happened since and I don't mention it ever. Instead, I behave as if it never occurred because I can't afford to lose my best friend that way. Together, we slipped right back into being comfortable around one another. Well, I still crave more from him but never try.

I sit up on my elbows to take a better look, despite the

trouble I know it'll bring. My heart gallops in my chest as a million perverted thoughts run through my head. I'm still lusting after him when suddenly, his inner forearm is revealed to me. All thoughts of dirty sex with my stepfather drain from me as the tattoo unlocks something in my head. Scrambling from off the bed, I all but run to him. His eyes widen in shock when I grab his wrist and pull his arm to where I can look at it properly.

"Nadia," he murmurs, his voice sounding pained. "What the fuck are you wearing?"

I tear my gaze from his flesh to meet his heated stare. His pupils are dilated and I like what's reflected in them. Hunger and desire.

"I didn't think you'd mind," I tell him and a shiver ripples through me as his eyes fall to my lips. "Do you?"

He steps closer to me, almost as if he can't help himself, and I'm enveloped by his clean scent. "I, uh…" he trails off and tosses his phone into his suitcase. "No, I don't mind."

I flash him a grateful smile and then go back to inspecting his tattoo—a tattoo that I never knew he even had. My thumb skims over the name. "Who's Taylor?"

His swallow is audible and I drag my gaze back up to his face. He frowns at me, sadness morphing his features into something heartbreaking. Needing to comfort him, I slip a hand to his cheek and run my thumb along his recently shaven flesh.

"He was my brother."

The sadness takes years off his age and it causes an ache in my chest.

"How did he die? How come you've never mentioned him to me before?" I question.

His hand finds my wrist and he tugs it from his face. "It's a long story," he says dejectedly.

I blink up at him in confusion. "So tell me. He was your brother and I'm just now finding out about this. I thought we talked to each other about everything."

He closes his eyes and groans. "I know, honey. I'm sorry. I don't talk about him to anyone."

"Talk to me," I say softly and step closer to him, wrapping my arms around his waist. "Please."

He stiffens at first but soon, his strong arms gather me to him. His nose is in my hair as he inhales me. "Jesus, Nadia," he says with a grumble. "You make my life really fucking difficult, you know that?"

I laugh and tilt my head to look up at him. His cock hardens between us and I try not to shiver. Instead, I pretend that I don't notice. "I like being difficult. It keeps you on your toes. Now tell me."

He lets out a sigh but absently begins stroking my hair as his eyes dance away from me as if he's getting lost in a memory. "He loved her. Kasey."

A memory of her telling me I reminded her of Taylor surfaces in my mind. "Your Taylor was her Taylor?" I ask in astonishment. "I had no idea."

"They were in love. Hell, I'm pretty sure he took her virginity when she was just fourteen," he says with a rueful smile. "Of course he was eighteen and that was stupid, but my brother did what he wanted to, especially when it came to Kasey."

I let out a laugh. "I wonder who he got that from," I mutter sarcastically.

He tugs at my hair and grins down at me. For once, I

don't see Donovan, the powerful hotel and resort tycoon. No, I see a boyish, happy man. A man who loved his brother and loves hard. I like seeing him this way. But as soon as the smile arrives, he quickly wipes it away. "He killed himself."

The ache in my chest threatens to rip me in half. "What? Why? They were in love!"

He tries to pull away but I tighten my grip. His fierce eyes flicker with anger and his jaw clenches. "There's more to the story, Nadia."

I nod and wait for him to continue. His eyes close and he shakes his head as if he doesn't want to think about it.

Finally, his hardened glare meets mine. "Her stepfather Dale owed my father. Those two were always up to deviant business dealings. When Dale finally couldn't pay one of his debts, my father asked for something—someone. He wanted Kasey."

My eyes widen in horror. "Your father wanted to sleep with her?"

His cheeks blaze red at my comment and he tears away from me. I watch him as he stalks along the foot of each bed back and forth until I'm pretty sure he'll wear a hole in the carpet.

"Donovan. Out with it."

He runs his fingers through his drying hair and his biceps bulge with the action. I bite my lip to keep from doing any-thing stupid like biting the flesh there on him.

"Well, Dale gave my father the okay. Said she was sleep-ing around anyway so it didn't fucking matter. Handed him the key to their trailer and they left. Her mother and stepfa-ther went to the bar, leaving my dad to collect his debt."

I gape at him in horror. "No…"

He grits his teeth and crosses his arms over his bare chest to glare at me. "Yes. And he took and took until his old dick wouldn't work anymore."

Tears well in my eyes and I shake my head. "That's so terrible."

Donovan stalks over to me and slides his fingers into my hair. His eyes are fiery when he looks down at me. For a moment, I think he might kiss me. And if it weren't for the skeletons being aired into the room, I would want him to.

"Listen to me, Nadia. If I tell you something, you must take it to your grave. I trust you more than anyone. So promise me."

My mouth pops open and I growl at him. "Cómo tu te atreves—" I start in Spanish but quickly flip back to English. "How dare you even think for one second I'd take for granted everything you've done for me and betray your trust? Don't you know me better than that? Haven't I always been loyal to you?"

He drops his forehead to mine and the connection sends electric currents pulsating through me. "I'm sorry," he murmurs, and strokes both of my cheeks with his thumbs. "I do know you better than that." His nose nuzzles against mine and his hot breath tickles my lip. "Taylor found out. He'd been in a rage over what happened and went straight for our father. My brother...he—he smothered him in his sleep."

"Oh no..."

His brows draw together and his Adam's apple bobs in his throat, revealing the pain he's just barely keeping contained. "When he called me crying, I had Logan come over with me since he was a detective at the time. Logan and I carried Dad's body to his car after we dressed him, drove him to the railroad tracks on a vacant road, and placed him in the driver's seat. The next train smashed his body to bits and the cops, thanks to Logan, never pursued the case as anything other than an accident."

His lips hover over mine and I let out an eager gasp. "Then what?"

"Taylor couldn't handle the guilt. Our dad was an asshole but my brother wasn't. He had nightmares and couldn't cope with what he'd done. In the end, he killed himself."

"I'm so sorry," I tell him in a devastated whisper.

He swipes my bottom lip with his thumb. "That's why I have the tattoo. Why Logan and I both have the tattoo. As a reminder of what happened and the loyalty we have to one another about the crime we covered up for my brother."

"How tragic."

His breath lets out and it smells minty from his toothpaste. I crave to taste him.

"So, I feel like I owe my friend. I donate to the police department and send Logan frequent deposits because he deserves it for helping me protect my brother."

"Thank you for confiding in me. I swear nobody will ever know."

We both remain still, our heavy breathing the only sound filling the hotel room. I'm frozen in his solid grasp and I like it. It feels right here. Another satisfying shiver jolts through me.

"Donovan," I whisper, tilting my head up slightly. "I love you. I need..."

As if to chase my words, his lips brush against mine. So soft. So gentle. A long, second of hesitation stills the air between us. Each of us giving the other one last opportunity to *state their argument as to why this is a very bad idea.*

Turns out, we're not worried about considering the repercussions of our actions because as soon as that second is over, his tongue is in my mouth.

Oh, God.

Donovan's perfect mouth is crushing mine. Invading me. Owning me. And I'm desperate for more. My fingers claw at his chest as if I could magically climb him and latch myself to him forever. When a pleasure-filled moan escapes him and spills into my throat, I lose it. With greedy, deft fingers, I tug at his towel.

The moment it hits the floor with a soft thud, our thin string of self-control snaps unapologetically. His hands slide down to my ass and he grips me tight, lifting me closer to him. Doing what feels natural, I hook my legs around his waist and cry out in pleasure to feel his thick, hard cock pressed against my sweet spot.

I'm too wrapped up in our kiss to notice what's going on around me, but when he lowers me to the bed, I whimper with need. Our eyes meet when he pulls away to tug at my panties. He hastily slips them down my legs while I rip off my top.

I want him naked and pressed against me.

On me.

Inside of me.

Taking me.

"Please, Donovan," I beg. "I've wanted this for so long."

His possessive growl makes me wet and I squirm with desire to touch myself in an effort to relieve the ache between my legs.

"Have you ever?" he questions in a low tone.

"No. I've been saving myself for you."

"Thank fuck," he mutters as his fingertips dance along my inner thighs. "There's so much I want to do to you. You make me crazy, Nadia."

I spread my legs apart and my heart rate quickens when his gaze falls there. "So do it. Make me feel good. Make love to me."

He flashes me a possessive grin before lowering himself to my pussy. I've had a couple of boyfriends go down on me before and it was always kind of bori— "Shiiiit!" I screech the second his tongue begins lapping at me.

I latch my fingers into his wet hair and let out an embarrassing moan. Donovan is extremely skilled with his tongue. Every movement he makes is exactly what I didn't know I was craving.

"Oh, God! This feels so—"

His hot breath tickles me as he all but devours me. Slurping and sucking echo in the room. All I can do is ride his face while he eats me as though he's starved for me.

I'll feed him all day, every day.

A sharp bite of pain shocks through me as he sucks hard on my clit. But just as I'm about to yelp out, he massages away the hurt with his tongue until I'm bucking against him. Over and over he assaults me with his delicious madness until I'm splitting the earth with my screams.

My body is still jolting and shuddering from my orgasm when he presses a soft kiss to my clit. I jump because I'm still sensitive there and meet his hungry stare. His hand is covering his beautiful cock as he strokes it slowly up and down. When his eyes close and his eyebrows pinch together in frustration, I wonder if I've done something wrong.

"What is it?" I demand.

His eyes reopen. "We can't do this."

As if he's slapped me, I swallow down my emotion and search his eyes for answers. "But you love me." Tears well in my eyes but don't spill over.

And I know this with every part of my soul. So why is he fighting what we both want?

He pounces on me and his tongue is in my mouth a second later. The kiss is an entire unspoken monologue. I can feel his love and desire and need rolled into one sweet kiss. His cock rests between us but I want it inside of me—linking my soul to his.

"Baby," he coos against my lips. "I love you more than anything. I just don't have a goddamned condom."

My tears turn into giggles and soon we're both laughing.

"Oh," I say, a slight pout on my lips.

"Yeah, oh." His grumble makes me giggle some more.

"But I really wanted you inside of me," I tell him with a sigh. "I wanted to feel completely owned and loved by you. Just once. What happens if you just do it for a little bit? Just so we can see what it feels like to be together?" I know I'm driving him crazy and that's my intention. I may not know how to seduce a man like the great Donovan Jayne but I can tell the innocence drives him wild. The fire in his eyes tells me so. Everything in me begs for him to cave, just this once.

He groans but begins sliding his cock against my stomach lower and lower until each thrust slides between the lips of my sensitive pussy. "Just for a minute," he concedes with a conspiratorial grin.

I nod as he continues his slow teases with his body rubbing against mine. When the tip of his cock pokes at my en-

trance, I hold my breath and spread my legs as far as they'll go, hoping he'll do it finally.

"God," he mutters, "I don't want to hurt you."

Shaking my head, I speak with conviction. "You're hurting me by teasing me. Take me. I'm yours, Donovan."

With one powerful thrust, he drives deep inside of me. Hard. He's so hard inside of me. Having him connect with me physically like this is the last part of our souls that needed linking. Now, we'll never sever these ties.

"I'm so sorry if I hurt you," he mutters against my lips as he bucks into me slowly. "Jesus, you're so fucking perfect."

"Don't stop."

And he doesn't. We make love. There's no other way to describe it. Our groans and whimpers and moans are a soundtrack to our bodies uniting. With his thumb on my clit while he thrusts into me, he draws out another earth-shattering orgasm from me. This time, he comes with me, though. The heat from his first burst of semen stings my sore insides before he pulls out and shoots the rest of it just below my belly button.

He collapses on me and buries his face against my neck. We're wet and sticky but I don't ever want him leaving my arms. I want to stay locked up in this moment for as long as I can.

"Te amo."

"My sweet Jayne." I can feel his warm smile against my flesh. "I love you too, baby."

That night, everything changed.

That night, I slept with my stepfather.

That night when he took my virginity, I fell hopelessly in love with the man who is now nibbling on my earlobe.

"We can have that again, sweet Jayne," he breathes against my wet flesh, causing me to shiver. "Let me give you a life much better than this one. I don't understand your motives for running off with him. From running away from me. But we can fix this."

Reality splashes over me like a cold rain and I try to wriggle from his grasp. "I can't do this right now, Donovan. In fact, I absolutely need to get back inside. I've been out here too long."

He pulls away and a murderous glare paints his features into something scary. After such a long spell with Logan, I can't help but cower away from his rage that seems to pulsate from him. When he notices my fear, his gaze softens.

"Baby, I…"

My bottom lip quivers and I close my eyes when his hand strokes my cheek ever so gently. I wish we had more time. But the crushing reality is I've already been out here for far too long.

"Hold on a second," I blurt out. "I'll be right back and then you need to leave. I promise I'll find you again when I can talk. But now's not the time. Donovan, I swear to you it'll be soon. Trust me."

The hardened expression on his face, though, isn't aimed at me. He's angry for me. If he only knew all the reasons to be angry, he'd toss me over his shoulder kicking and screaming to take me far, far away from this hellhole.

For one brief second, I almost beg him to.

But one glance into his shimmering blue eyes, I am reminded that I cannot.

This is my path. For now.

He groans when I run into the house to grab a couple of eggs. I can explain away my absence to Logan if I tell him a chatty neighbor stopped by to borrow some eggs. Once I'm back outside, Donovan wastes no time finding my lips and smashing me against the wall with his undying love.

"I love you, baby. I fucking love you so much."

My body craves to connect with his. To prolong our moment together. To freeze time and make love to him right here on this porch.

"You know I love you," I assure him. I want to make him understand. I want to pick up the pieces that belong to my heart and run off with Donovan Jayne. But I can't. "We're not together anymore though. I'm with Logan."

He jerks away as if I've slapped him and his lip curls up. Confusion is written all over his face. But then it happens. A flicker in his soulful eyes. The man has direct access into my head via my own eyes. I *need* for him to see that it's not him. There's more. And he sees. *Thank God, he sees.* "You may be doing something here," he motions behind me at the house. A growl of frustration on his part. "For now..." I shiver as he continues. "I get you have reasons, baby. Truly, I do. But you are not *with* Logan. You'll always be *with* me even when you're not. We both know who your heart has always belonged to."

"*With* you," I agree with a brave attempt at a smile that wobbles away, giving way to sadness. "I miss you and will always love you. We just can't *be* together. Not right now."

His brows are pulled together in a frown that has my heart aching. The frown is a familiar one that makes me want to tear this house apart with my own two hands. That frown is what spurs me on. "I won't wait forever now that I know where you are…"

I hold up the two eggs and force them into his hands. "I know but please trust I'll have this sorted out soon enough," I say firmly as tears stream down my cheeks. "Now go before you fuck it all up." When I bite out the last of my words, he winces at my tone.

I ache to soothe away his heartache and pain. To flay open my heart and explain everything to the man who loves me more than anything in this world.

"Si me amas, déjame." *If you love me, leave me.*

His face crumples and it delivers a final blow to my heart. Leaning forward, he presses a soft kiss to my lips. "I do love you, Nadia. Always."

All I can do is sob in return. Donovan, my best friend. My lover. My hero. My entire world. And I pushed him away without explanation aside from the vague letter I'd sent. First I left his side three years ago and now I'm trying to hide from him under Logan's roof. I can only imagine the horror that is flitting through his head right now. The thick betrayal coursing through his veins. If I could sink my teeth into his flesh and suck it all away, I would. Having Donovan seeming so devastated is almost more than I can bear. I may be strong but even warriors have a weakness.

Donovan makes me drop all of my armor.

Donovan makes me vulnerable.

Which is exactly why he must leave before I do something incredibly stupid with ripple effects that will continue to stab at my heart until the day I die.

I watch him as he storms off to his car. Once he flings

open the door to his newest black Lexus, his gaze meets mine. I expect to see anger or sadness reflected under the moonlight. But what I see terrifies me even more.

What I see is understanding.

What I see is determination.

And when Donovan Jayne sets his mind to something, he throws every ounce of himself into it until he gets what he wants.

What he wants is me…and right now, he simply can't have me.

Eleven

Kasper

"Are you Amethyst?"

A woman with a sweet smile and messy blonde hair looks up from her phone to regard me. Her nearly purple eyes—eyes that exactly match her sister's—peer back at me curiously. Despite being short like Ashley, Amethyst is built like a runway model. She has high, naturally pink cheekbones and a cute upturned nose. Shoulder-length waves of hair frame her exotic face. Her tits are small but the perfect size beneath a tight white T-shirt that reveals a black bra underneath. Jeans ride low on her hips and I'm awarded a small tanned sliver of skin between her shirt and the top of her jeans. She's all light and I am mesmerized, fucking blinded, by her sheer brilliance—like a blind man staring into the sun. I feel a reprieve from the shadowy darkness that always plagues me.

"Who's asking?"

"Kasper," I grunt out, extending my hand to her, and taking my eyes from her slender body.

She beams at me and takes my hand. For a hand so small, it saturates mine with powerful energy—the good fucking kind. This woman is pure and gentle. She's about as opposite from me as a person can get. I'm overwhelmed by the sense of need to protect her purity. I want to scold her for being so trusting of a complete stranger. "Like the ghost? You're not that spooky."

I don't respond with a smile of my own and grit my teeth. "I'm Lieutenant Kasper Grant. I work with your brother-in-law, Jason Rhodes."

"I know who my brother-in-law is," she says with a laugh that reminds me of a breeze teasing wind chimes on a warm summer day. "Did you guys drive Ash? I thought she was picking me up per her last text."

The woman is like sunshine on the cloudiest fucking day. Today is like a hurricane of terrible things and she's still coasting along shining her sweetness on everything in her path. Including me.

But shadows aren't meant to be warmed by light.

Shadows are meant to stay far away from the likes of sunshiny women like her.

I'm about to darken her world.

It's simply what I do.

"Actually, I need you to take a ride with me. I'm afraid something awful has happened. We're going to need to get to the hospital right away."

And just like that, my darkness shadows her light, eradicating it completely. Tears well in her pretty eyes making them shimmer like two polished gems. Her glossy pink bottom lip quivers as she searches my eyes for answers.

"Is she having the baby? It's too early. That's why I came

down. We were going to pick out furniture for the nursery," she explains, her voice wobbling, as if this will somehow undo the wrongs that have happened. Wrongs that I haven't yet spoken but I can tell she senses down to her very soul.

I reach for the handle of her rolling suitcase and frown at her. "It's not about the baby. I'll explain on the way."

Ten minutes later and we're flying down the road toward the hospital in my Camaro. From the corner of my eye, Amethyst is gnawing on her fingernails. She hasn't asked again and I don't want to offer the information. I don't know much about Ashley's condition. I certainly don't want to give this woman false hope.

"Is she okay?" she finally mutters.

I shrug my shoulders as I weave in and out of traffic. When the fuckers won't get out of my way, I turn on my siren. "I don't know. She was in an accident. They rushed her to the hospital."

She starts to cry softly and my hand twitches to reach over to comfort her. For someone who mostly feels disgust and anger every waking moment of the day, I'm put off by the fact that I'm feeling empathy.

I wish the woman beside me would smile again and light up this dark car with her happiness. She clasps her fingers together and bows her head. From a quick glance at her, I can tell she's praying. To whom, to what—I don't know.

But I sure as hell hope someone's listening.

Rhodes and Amethyst have gone back to see her. The fucking doctor wouldn't tell them her condition. So now, for the past half hour, I've been pacing the waiting room alone waiting for answers. My friend still doesn't know it was Dale, my stepfather. When he finds out, maybe we can hurt the motherfucker together.

"Kasper." The soft voice is nothing but a broken whisper. I turn to see a red-faced sobbing angel before she throws herself into my arms. "T-T-This can't be happening."

I wrap my arms around her and pull her against me. It feels comfortable and right holding her. "Is she okay? What about the baby?"

She tilts her head to look up at me. Her lips purse together firmly and I watch as she pulls her emotions in check. When her chin stops quivering, she speaks.

"They're gone."

"Back to surgery? Chief said he thought she might've broken her neck but people can still go on to have a good life after, even if they're paralyzed."

She shakes her head and a tear races down along the inside of her splotchy red cheek near her nose. I want to swipe away her pain but instead clench my teeth together, hoping for better answers than the ones that are coming from her mouth.

"K-Kasper. Her broken neck was the least of their worries. She cracked her skull and was bleeding internally. By the time they got her here and in surgery, it was too late. Ash passed away on the table. S-S-She's gone."

Her eyebrows furrow together and she darts her gaze all around in confusion, as if she can't even believe the words coming out of her mouth. More tears roll down silently as she attempts to make sense of it in her head.

"The baby?"

"Neither of them..." she trails off in a whisper. "Neither of them made it."

When she starts to sob hysterically, realization of the situation washing over her, I hug her to me. If this were my sister who had died and Ashley were here, she'd be the one consoling me. Ash was a good girl and my fucking stupid-ass stepfather killed her.

He killed my friend's wife and her baby.

And now I'm going to kill him.

"I don't feel so well."

Her whispered words are my only warning before she passes out in my arms. With a grunt, I scoop her light frame into my arms and stalk off toward the exit. She's been through too much.

"Kasper!"

I frown when I see Rhodes's parents rushing into the building. "Jason's with her," I clip out. "I'm sorry but your daughter-in-law—"

"No." His mother bites out the word, in denial about the death of her son's wife and child, and pushes past me. "Don't you dare say it."

"I'm sorry," I tell his dad whose face crumples with despair. "Her sister isn't well and I'm taking her to my place until she feels better. Call me if I can do something."

He nods once and trots after his wife.

Amethyst doesn't stir until I'm buckling her back into my car. "W-What are we doing?"

"I'm taking you home to rest. You're in shock I think."

She fumbles for the seatbelt but I firmly pull her hand away. "There's nothing you can do for Jason right now. His parents are there. Let them help him through this. You'll be better prepared to function after some food and a good night's rest."

Her tears the entire way home douse my flames of hate for Dale like a torrential rain of gasoline. For once in my life, I'm not fixated on my hate for the loss of my sister. Right now, I pour everything into the fact that I will exact revenge on Dale for Rhodes and his family. I'm not sure how yet, but I will destroy him for hurting them.

A warm hand on my chest awakens me. I cover it with my own and reach for the person in the darkness. My fingers thread into the soft locks of her hair which causes her to sigh. The sadness and desperation in her voice guts me.

"What's wrong?" I demand, my voice hoarse from sleep.

I'd left her to spend the night in the guest bedroom but now she's standing in my bedroom beside my bed.

"Everything."

"Do you need something?"

In the darkness, I can feel her nod. "I need a hug."

I smile, despite myself, and tug her to me. She wastes no time and crawls practically on top of me. Her slender arm curls around my ribcage as she clutches on, digging her fingernails into my flesh. I pull her against my side and press a kiss to the top of her head.

Comforting someone isn't something I'm used to.

In fact, I should feel extremely out of place here. Obsessing over shit I can't change. Plotting ways to kill Dale. Hating Nadia for ruining my entire life.

But for some reason, I can't not help Amethyst. My family is responsible for the ruin of hers. She's a nice girl who had an equally nice sister. This woman has lost someone she loves in the blink of an eye. I owe it to her to give back where I can.

Not because I have to, but I feel a strong urge to do so. Because I want her sunshine again. That brief glimpse of light in the airport she shone upon me was like a sunburn. It burned my soul a little but was worth basking in it. After a decade of cold, dark shadows, it's nice to feel a flicker of warmth, and not just in my cock. From time to time, I fuck women and it makes me feel human if only for a brief moment. And with my new plan to fuck with Nadia, I'd felt a hot fire of lust in my dick—an arousal sparked on by the desire for retribution and vengeance.

But with this woman sniffling in my arms, the heat that is warming me from the inside out is coming right from where she's resting her head against my heart.

"You can hit on her. Just don't sleep with her. She's better than a weekend fling."

Ashley's words are still fresh on my mind from earlier this evening. She'd kill me if she knew her sister was in my bed the very first night of her being here. My chest aches from the loss of Ash and the baby.

"I can't promise I won't look after her. If she's your family, then she's my family too."

My own statement carves itself as a mantra into my soul. I will look after this woman while she's here mourning her sister. I'll do it because I cared about Ashley and it's what she would have wanted.

"So you're a cop with Jason?" Her voice is soft and tickles the hair on my chest.

"Lieutenant."

"Ash told me I might meet you while on my visit." She lets out a small sob at the mention of her sister. Her voice is shaky and she sniffles but continues bravely along. "I've been studying abroad for the past few years in Peru. Thought about staying in Montana where we're from but now I'm not so sure. It's not like I can't be a mineralogist here. There are mines and mountains everywhere."

I absently stroke at her hair, the urge to comfort her almost natural. "Won't your parents miss you?"

"We never knew our dad and Mom died when we were teenagers from cancer. Ash met Jason on a college ski trip several years ago and ended up staying indefinitely. I'd planned on taking care of Mom's land in Montana but with my sister dying, I think I should be near Jason and help him through it. She would have wanted him to have someone to lean on."

The idea of her staying shoots a tiny thrill through me but I quickly snuff it out. I think her staying for Rhodes would be a good idea. Someone will need to help him process the death of his entire world. And as much as he'd probably like for that someone to be me, I know I'm not emotionally capable.

"I'm sure he'd like that," I assure her.

We grow quiet for some time, her tears long since dried. I like the way her silky hair feels when I run my fingertips through it. I've almost fallen asleep when she speaks again.

"Who is Nadia Jayne?"

My entire body jolts at her words. The old, familiar rage that had always fueled me like an efficient machine fires to

life, all engines blasting. Kasey, like Ashley, won't go on to
have a long life.

"My boss's fiancée. Why do you ask?"

She lifts up to peer down at me even though we're in
the dark. Her shoulder-length hair tickles my throat and my
dick twitches.

"I was looking for you and accidentally went into your
office. There was a file open on your desk with her picture
and name on it. Why do you have a file on your boss's future
wife?"

I groan and urge to push her away from me so I can
pace around the room. Nadia is my little secret—a secret
project I don't need the noses of anyone else into.

"Uh, I was just doing a background check on her and—"

Her fingertips graze over my lips silencing me. "If we're
going to be friends, Kaspy, don't lie to me."

"Kaspy?" The lopsided grin on my lips is immediate
and I can't stifle my laugh.

"You're so serious. I wanted you to lighten up. And apparently you like being called Kaspy," she teases, a smile in
her voice.

I smirk. "You're insane."

"I'm serious, though. Why do you have a file on your
boss's future wife?"

The death of her sister may have broken her heart—
maybe her soul even—but she's resilient and powers
through, attempting to control what she can. Just like Ash
had said. She's trying to burrow her way inside of me and
I'm already willing to flay myself open for her to see the
blackness that lives inside. Ashley warned me her sister
loved a project.

Why do I feel like I'm about to become her next one?

"It's not important." My tone is gruff but at least it isn't a lie. I would like to be her friend just so I can fucking pet her like I am now. I want to be her friend so she can burn me with her wholesome rays of sweetness. I'd love to be her friend so I can clutch onto her tiny ray of hope she's given me that I may one day have a life that isn't driven by revenge.

"It's important to me," she murmurs.

I let out a rush of air but she waits patiently, ignoring my huffing and puffing. "She was a witness to a kidnapping ten years ago."

"Oh…so what does that have to do with now?"

"Because I think she knows something she hasn't told the police. I feel like she's responsible for the girl never turning up." The bitterness in my voice can't be disguised. In the darkness, my hate wafts around us, suffocating us with its black stench.

"It's a cold case, though, right? I mean, ten years…"

I grip her wrist and pull it from my face. "If you could bring back your sister, wouldn't you chase down every opportunity to do so?" I question, my voice low and menacing. "No matter how crazy it made you?"

She lets out a choked gasp, her tears splashing my face like a rainfall from heaven, and I release her arm. The moment I do, she surprises me by bringing her lips to my ear, whispering her words in one quick, hot breath. "I absolutely would."

And suddenly I'm once again warmed by her heat.

Something unfamiliar and foreign surges through me, from my chest all the way down to my toes. Pride? No. Justi-

fication? Maybe. Confidence in another soul—a soul I barely know? Most likely.

As a weight lifts, I hug her back to me and inhale her
hair. We don't say anymore on the subject. What's more to
say?

Nadia Jayne should be pursued and badgered. *Or
should she?*

I will get answers from her. *Or will I?*

Either way, Nadia won't get off easy. I'll find out what
she's hiding, even if all she's hiding is an abusive relationship
with my boss. If my findings exonerate her in the process,
so be it. If it implicates her instead, then I'll cross that bridge
when I get there. Regardless, Nadia is still on my radar.

Amethyst's breathing levels out as she falls asleep but
my eyes are wide open in the dark. I like her, but she's shown
up a few months too soon. She's the type of girl a man settles
down with and marries. And right now, I'm not settled. Not
one fucking bit. The very idea of juggling her friendship
and my plans to figure out Nadia threatens to rip me in two.
A ragged divide between hate of the past that fuels every
cell in my body and hope for peace that seems to tickle and
tease me. For once I'd love to push away the anger and focus
on something sweet and good. Just once.

Amethyst lets out a sigh in her sleep and I find myself
smiling. I stroke her soft hair as I wonder what it would feel
like to do this every night. Is this what normal people who
aren't blinded by revenge do? Is this what Jason and Ashley
did every night?

The smile falls from my lips as I begin to drift off. I make
a silent vow to myself that I'll find the answers I'm looking
for so that I may finally move on. Even if that means helping

Donovan tear Nadia from Logan's steely clutches in the process. With Ames in my arms and the death of my friend's wife on my mind, it's easy to let go of some of the anger. To realize life is short. It's time to sort this shit out once and for all. And finally move on.

Get ready, Nadia. I'm coming for you...

Twelve

Nadia

I PACE THE KITCHEN WITH MY EYES ON THE CLOCK. FIFTY-two minutes. Logan has been on the porch consoling one of his detectives who lost his wife last week for fifty-two minutes. And I'm about to flip the fuck out. The second hand ticks by much more quickly than it should and panic causes my heart to thunder in my chest.

"What are you so anxious about?" a deep voice grumbles from behind me.

I jump, letting out a squeak of surprise, and frown to see Kasper leaning against the door frame sipping on a bottle of water. Every night this week, he's come over to work on the walls. Logan doesn't seem to notice, but I can't help but think Kasper takes his time—that he's dragging his feet on this project for a reason.

"I just really need to speak with Logan," I blurt out and cast another weary glance at the clock.

"Why?"

Jerking my gaze over to him, I gape at him with a withering stare. "I just do. He's, uh, timing something for me and the time is up in seven more minutes."

His dark brows pinch together as he assesses me. But rather than badgering me further, he flashes me a wicked grin and winks. "I'll take care of it, sweet Jayne."

Instead of cringing at the name, I watch as he makes his way to the front door. I chew on my fingernail as I see him talk to both men through the window. He motions inside and then puts his hand on the other detective's shoulder. I'm shocked when Logan comes striding in a moment later.

"How is he?" I question as he enters the kitchen. My lips pull into a tight smile in an attempt to hide my anxiety.

"Detective Rhodes? He'll be okay." He rolls his shoulders and cracks his neck. "Tragic his wife was killed."

I nod and absently swipe the countertop with a rag. "Poor guy. Is he going to be okay?"

"It's only been a week. He'll have to get over it eventually though." Logan saunters over to me and wraps me in a hug from behind. This week only continued to be confusing and torturous—not once has he hit me or abused me. I'd almost be relieved at his calmer mood, but I can't ever let my guard down around him. I don't trust him a bit.

His lips find the top of my shoulder and he kisses it softly. My heart races in my chest as I peek over at the clock. Two minutes left.

"Logan," I say in a whisper. "Did you turn it off?"

He drags his teeth across my flesh causing goosebumps to rise but never sinks his teeth in like I expect. I let out a relieved sigh when he presses a soft kiss there and then pulls away. The front door opens and closes, but all I can think about is him turning the fucker off and soon. Logan may not be hurting me—yet he is fucking with my head and he knows it. He gives me a smug grin and watches the clock for a few lingering seconds. As the time drains away, along with the color on my face, he finally lets out a grunt and pulls out his phone. I attempt to watch—to focus on those numbers—but he enters them too quickly. My stomach plummets to the floor when I realize I still don't know what they are.

For now, though, that doesn't matter.

What matters is the fact he's entered them in.

"Want to come take a look at what I've done so far?"

Both Logan and I jerk our gazes to Kasper who leans against the door frame with his arms crossed over his muscular chest. His expression feigns disinterest in our exchange, but I know better. I see the questions dancing in his eyes. The wonder.

"Yeah," Logan says as he tucks his phone back in his pocket. "Then, I need to run up to the station."

The men leave and I pace the kitchen. Could Kasper have seen?

If he did, I absolutely must get that information from him.

I see the way he devours me with hungry, almost angry, eyes. Messing with him under Logan's roof is like playing with fire in the devil's den. But all it takes is five minutes—five minutes and this could all be over.

I need those goddamned numbers.

"You hungry?" I call out once Logan's Tahoe turns onto the

road. Spinning away from the window, I hurry over to the refrigerator to start pulling out fixings for the sandwiches de miga.

Kasper appears in the doorway with a frown. "Tell me what all that was about."

"Ham, eggs, cheese, tomatoes, green peppers, lettuce, and asparagus all okay? Toasted or untoasted?"

He rolls his eyes at my ignoring him and walks over to me. When his large hands grip my hips, I let out a yelp. His head dips down so he can look at me and he growls. "Tell me."

Chewing on my lip, I let the thoughts dart around in my head. How much do I tell him? How much is safe?

"Logan uses his phone timer as a form of punishment. If I don't get him to turn it off in time, things get bad. Real bad." Not a lie. Not a lie. Not a lie.

"What sort of punishment?"

"Uh," I stammer. My hands shake with nerves and I fist them to keep them from quivering. "The worst kind actually. The kind that cuts my soul right from my body."

His eyes dart from me to my hands several times and he scowls. It's as if he's struggling with something inside of his head. "What kind?" he questions, a gruff whisper.

I shudder and clamp my eyes shut. But that just makes everything worse. Reopening them, I meet his firm stare. I'm not getting out of this conversation unless I give him some information. He's a cop. Interrogation is his thing. If only, I could tell him everything. Life would be much simpler. "He uses water to, um, hurt me." Again, not a lie.

His face darkens and his lips purse into a firm line. "Is that why there's a big ass pipe running through the wall?"

I blink at him in shock and nod slowly. "Yes."

He runs his fingers through his hair and I can see indecision warring through him. "What happens if he doesn't enter in those numbers in time? Does it have something to do with the basement?"

A ragged sigh rushes from me and my knees wobble. I can't ever think about *that* what-if in too much detail. I'm not strong enough. "Then my life is over. I cannot live with what he has planned. It's the worst kind of death. And yes," I tell him with a hiss, "it has everything to do with the basement."

His hands find my hips to steady my unstable body and I shiver. "Does that code get you *into* the basement? Or out?"

"Both." I shrug, and bark out a bitter laugh. I'm sure at this point he thinks I'm crazy. "But I don't know if the one that resets his alarm is the same one to the basement or not."

"Is this why you stay? Why you won't leave a man who beats on you? Because you're afraid of what he'll do?"

"Partially."

"So this code is very important to you?"

I nod and meet his gaze. "I would do anything for his code. Anything."

The corner of his lips curl up into a half grin. "What if I know the code? What would you be willing to do to get it from me?"

Hope, a taunting bitch of an emotion, flutters through me. "What do you want?"

"You."

His hands find their way to my throat and I frown in confusion as he holds me in place with a gentle clasp around my neck. I swallow and dart my eyes to his. "Me?"

Focus, focus, focus. Ignore your heart and use your brain.

He nods as his lips descend upon mine. His grip tightens, causing me to gasp for air and he smashes his mouth to mine, stealing my breath. When his tongue slips into my mouth, his hold on me loosens and I let out a moan of relief. I shouldn't be kissing him, but he may know the code. *That code is everything to me.* Throwing myself into the kiss, because a plan's a plan, even if it's a bad one, I fist his T-shirt and tug him closer. His hands leave my neck thankfully and travel down my body until he's gripping my ass.

"I want you," he hisses out against my lips. "Jesus!"

He grinds his hard cock against my belly and growls.

"What do you want from me? Just tell me and you can have it." Couldn't ever be as bad as what Logan demands from me on a daily basis. With Kasper, I can survive it. He could never be as cruel as Logan.

I don't get an answer but instead he twists me away from him and eases me over the counter. The world spins when he pushes up my dress over my hips and tugs my panties down. He playfully bites my ass cheek and I cry out.

"Beg," he orders.

With my cheek on the cold granite, I stare at the head of lettuce. "Please give me the code."

His fingers whisper over my flesh and he chuckles. "You really do want that number. What I meant was beg for me to fuck you."

I freeze at his words and clamp my eyes closed. I'm busy trying to talk myself into what I'm about to beg for him to do when I'm swept up into a memory. Memories of Donovan always help me cope with what I must do.

We had sex.

Donovan and I had sex.

But that was months ago. And he's avoided me ever since. I knew it would happen—the moment he pulled out of me, his cock dripping, that he'd hate himself for doing it. Selfishly, though, I'd wanted it anyway.

Now, I'm devastated and broken apart.

His calls are non-existent.

His texts are formal.

His visits are zero.

Which is why I'm going to force him to talk about us. I've prepped myself and hope he won't be able to deny me. I'm wearing a skimpy, fitted black dress that showcases all of my curves and sky-high heels. One look at me in this outfit, and he'll have no choice but to notice me.

I stop walking down the hallway to his penthouse suite to catch my reflection in the glass of a framed picture hanging on the wall. My dark hair has been curled into loose waves and I've painted my supple lips blood red. I hope he thinks about all of the things I can do with this mouth. With a flick of my hair over my shoulder, I strut down to his doorway. As soon as I reach his door and my hand is poised to knock, I hear shouts.

"I'm taking a goddamned shower and when I get back out, you better have this shit figured out."

A door slams and I freeze.

What if he's trying to work things out with Mamá?

What if he's fucking someone besides me?

I don't care, I'll make him see we belong together. With a deep breath, I twist the knob and almost squeal to see it's un-locked. I push into the room and shut the door quietly behind me. My heels make purposeful taps along the marbled entry-way floor as I head toward the living area. When I see Dan, his CFO, I can't help the smile of relief on my face.

"Where's Donovan?" I question.

Dan's gaze lifts from the mountain of paperwork that is scattered along the top of the coffee table and he glares at me. Ever since he and Darcy were busted for their relationship and he was put on probation at work for sexual misconduct with a subordinate, he's been angry. Donovan knew but never said anything. It was when one of the guests happened upon them having sex in Dan's office that it had to be addressed. Darcy broke off their fling, or whatever it was, because she was humiliated once people at the office found out. Leaving Dan a miserable and bitter man.

His lips turn up into a predatory grin. A shiver runs through me as his calculating eyes turn dark with fury. He rises to his feet and stalks over to me. "He's cooling off. Been in a pissy-ass mood for months now. Did you miss your daddy?"

I roll my eyes at him, not taking his bait, and point at the door behind me. "Donovan and I need to talk. You think you could leave?"

"I bet you're going to 'talk.' Darcy and I 'talked' all the time. Apparently, though, that was against some code of eth-ics, yet Donovan can fuck his daughter and nobody seems to bat an eye. Double standards, I tell you. Completely unfair. And filthy, if you ask me." He curls his lip up in disgust and looks me over as if I'm trash.

Not to be deterred, I sneer at him. "Good thing nobody's asking you. Now go away already."

He makes a great show of snatching up his things and muttering something about us needing to go on the Maury show or some crap. Once he's gone and the door's locked behind him, I hurry into the bathroom. I'm just stepping into the steamy room when the shower shuts off.

As soon as I see his silhouette behind the foggy glass, I nearly burst into tears. I've missed him so much. So fucking much. He pushes open the shower door and blindly grabs for his towel. While he dries his face and hair, I stare unabashedly at his thick, flaccid cock. Heat floods through me as I remember that night he made love to me. It was perfect and fulfilling. He'd told me everything about him that night.

I love him.

"Fucking hell. My beautiful girl."

His growled words jerk me from my thoughts and I meet his heated stare. "You think I'm beautiful?" My bottom lip quivers.

He pinches the bridge of his nose and scrunches his brows together. "Of course I do, baby. You kill me."

A smile tugs at my lips, especially the moment I see his cock is no longer soft but instead erect and pointing right at me. "Why have you been avoiding me?"

His silvery blue eyes snap to meet mine. They're intense enough to cut through diamonds. "Because I have to." I take a step forward and he shakes his head. "Don't."

"Why do you think you have to avoid me?" I demand. I'm on the verge of breaking down and my desperation is evident. "I thought you loved me." My voice is shrill and I'm embarrassed I sound so needy. But I am needy. I need Donovan in my life. Every single aspect of it.

"Jesus Christ, baby!" he curses and throws his towel to the

floor. "I love you more than you could ever fucking compre-hend." A groan of frustration is the last thing that comes from his mouth before he storms over to me. The moment his warm hands wrap around my waist, I throw my arms around his neck. His mouth crashes to mine and he devours me like he's starved for me. Well, I'm starved for him too.

"You can't do that to me," I murmur as he squeezes my ass. "You'll kill me if you push me away again. I need you, Donovan."

He steals another kiss before leaning his forehead against mine. "If this gets out…"

I think of the shame of Darcy and Dan's inner office af-fair. It'd be a thousand times worse with Donovan and me.

"You're not married to my mother anymore and I'm a fucking adult. Who cares?" But I know he does care.

His eyes clench closed and he groans. "I have too many enemies. They'd find a way to use this against me. If we do this," he says in a soft tone, "it has to be between us for now. I won't have anyone trying to make a public mockery of you. You don't deserve it."

"You're not hearing me," I say in frustration. "I don't care about those people. Please hear what I'm trying to say to you."

He swallows. "Baby, I always hear you. Fucking always. But do you understand why we need to keep this to ourselves?"

Right now, I'd agree to anything he says just to have him inside of me again.

"Yes, okay?" I agree. "For now. We'll keep it a secret for now."

His deft fingers work the zipper on the back of the dress and a moment later it falls to the floor pooling at my ankles. I'm completely bare underneath. He releases me to take a step back and appreciate my body.

"My God," he says with a growl, "you're fucking amazing."

I squeal when he throws me over his shoulder and strides into his bedroom. My shoes get kicked off along the way. I've barely been tossed onto the bed before he pounces on me.

"So perfect," he croons as he trails kisses down my throat to my collarbone. His hot breath tickles my flesh and I wriggle beneath him.

"You're teasing me."

He looks up at me with raised eyebrows and grins. If I had a camera, I'd forever freeze the handsome look on his face—a look I'm responsible for. I beam back at him until he starts pressing kisses all over my breasts. When he sucks one of my nipples between his teeth, I cry out.

His mouth pops off, making a loud sound, and then he drags his tongue down my flesh toward my belly button. The slow torture is driving me insane.

"Just make love to me," I beg, "please."

He chuckles and continues to go lower. His mouth covers my pussy and I whimper when he bites gently. Then, his tongue shoves its way between the lips of my sex and he searches for my clit. I moan when he connects with it.

"Dono—fuuuuck!"

With Donovan, it's like he was given a map to my body and heart. He's a master and I'm his student.

Explosive pleasure courses through me as he gives me my best orgasm to date. My body writhes beneath him as I attempt to chase the feeling until its extinction. Months ago when we made love, it was quick and ravenous. But now, he's taking his time with me. I don't ever want to leave his bed.

Once I'm weak from my orgasm, he crawls his way back

over me. His eyes have an intense glint in them that makes me crazy horny for him. When his wet-from-my-juices lips curve up into an equally evil grin, I shudder. "Make love to me already."

I wrap my legs around his waist and urge him to me. His thick, throbbing cock is hot against my wet pussy.

"God, baby," he murmurs against my lips. "I'm addicted to you. You're going to break my heart one day and kill me in the process."

Frowning, I shake my head in vehemence. "I'll never hurt you."

His mouth crashes against mine, his teeth nicking me, and he pushes his cock into me. I'm so wet and eager, he slides right in, stretching me to my limit with his girth.

"Oh God," I rasp out as he thrusts hard into me.

He sucks on my bottom lip, pounding harder and harder into me. His body completes me in a way nobody ever has. I've fallen hopelessly for this man.

"I love you so much," he grunts, his breaths becoming labored.

I clench around him when another orgasm ripples through me. Like a domino effect, his climax then explodes inside of me. The warmth of him marking me as his seems to set my soul on fire.

"If we keep making love without a condom, you're going to get pregnant." His voice is a possessive grumble, almost as if he's keen on the idea.

I smile at him as his hot cum runs out of my body. "Maybe I want to have your babies."

His eyes close and he presses a kiss on my forehead. "I love you and you're mine now, Nadia Jayne. No more games or confusion. *All fucking mine.*"

Threading my fingers into his dark hair, I regard him with an intense stare. *"It's about damn time."*

Thirteen

Kasper

SHE'S ZONED OUT. I'VE LONG SINCE STOPPED TRYING TO fuck her because the moment I told her to beg, she damn near went catatonic. With her dress still pushed up her hips and her ass bared to me, I notice yellowing bruises dotting her flesh. At least they aren't purple and black like before. Not that I should care.

But for some goddamned reason, I do.

My dick is straining against my jeans, eager to get some action but I don't let him come out to play. Instead, I drag her dress back down over her ass.

"Where'd you go just then?"

She jolts at my words and jerks her head to look at me. Her cheeks flush pink as she gives me a pouty frown. "Uh…"

Logan did say he'd knocked her upside the head one too many times…

"Untoasted."

Leaving her to collect herself, I stride out of the kitchen and down the hallway. Once I make it to the basement door,

I stare at the keypad. I'd seen the numbers he'd entered into his phone a million times but Logan doesn't seem the type to have the same code for everything. Taking my chances, I punch in the six numbers.

Nothing but a red flashing light, denying me entrance.

After a few more tries, I let out a frustrated sigh and go back to painting the trim on the door frame that leads to her bedroom.

"Kasper, I'm…" she trails off behind me. "Here's your sandwich de miga. Untoasted."

She shoulders past me, giving me a whiff of her sweet shampoo, and sets the plate on her dresser. I walk over to it and watch her as she sits on the bed.

"I'm sorry. I was just desperate for that number," she says in a wobbly voice.

I shrug as I take a bite, chewing as I talk. "Damn, this is some good shit. That code didn't work anyway. It'll work for his phone but not the door."

My words cause her to shudder and she seems to snap out of her daze, her eyes wide and blinking rapidly. "I can't believe I almost had sex with you."

Ignoring her words, I eat another bite of my delicious as fuck sandwich. "I'm going to get you that code."

Her eyes dart to mine and her plump lips part open. "You are? How?"

I crack my neck before meeting her eyes with a serious gaze. "I'll pay attention. Logan is secretive but I'm observant. Give me some time."

She nods, a small smile playing on her lips. "Thank you."

"Don't thank me yet," I say with a dark laugh. "You're

going to owe me big time." She'll definitely owe me more sandwiches de mi-something-or-other-in-Spanish. That's for damn sure. "I just haven't decided exactly what I want yet."

And the smile is gone.

My heart thunders in my chest and I get high on the power I hold over her.

Fucking high as a kite.

What can I say? Old habits are hard to break.

"How you doing, buddy?"

Rhodes doesn't look up from staring at the floor. His elbows are on his knees and he's fixated on the carpet. "Okay."

But he's not okay. My friend is losing his mind a bit. How could he not? He hasn't returned to work yet, and I'm not sure he'll ever be ready.

"Where's Amethyst?" I question as I peek in the kitchen.

"Gone to get food."

I locate a bottle of vodka from the freezer and a couple of shot glasses before making my way back into the living room. We don't speak as I fill them.

"Oh," he says in an absent manner while knocking back his glass, "I checked up on that pipe with Dad. Definitely commercial grade. They use them in a lot of the commercial properties here in the mountains because they're thick and solid and can withstand the test of the elements here. He doesn't understand why it would be in Logan's house though."

I narrow my eyes at him as I swallow the cold liquid that burns like hell going down. "Hmmm. I don't understand either."

"You know who would know, right?" he asks as he slides the shot glass across the table to me. "Donovan Jayne."

I dread having to talk to him again. He's fucking depressing to be around. It's been a week since I've seen him last, despite my duty to follow him. I'm not sure he's even left the lodge once.

"Why? Because he knows commercial buildings?"

He shakes his head. "No, because he knows Logan."

I'm still pondering his words and have decided I'll go have a chat with him tomorrow at the lodge when the front door swings open. Amethyst breezes in with her arms loaded down with bags. When she sees me, her eyes light up and her lips curl up into a breathtaking smile. The stress of the week seems to melt away in her presence.

"Nice seeing you here, Kaspy," she chirps as she carries the bags into the kitchen. I rise from the couch and stalk after her like a lion hunting an antelope. "Did you ever find what you were looking for with that file?" Her eyes flicker over her shoulder to make sure Rhodes doesn't hear. "With Nadia and what you think she might know about your sister?"

"No," I grunt, "but I've been going over to their house a lot and plan to eventually get answers."

She smiles. "Let me know if I can help."

"You have enough on your plate. Don't worry about me." I lean my hip against the counter and watch her unload the bags. "How are you anyway? How is he?" I question in a low tone. "He looks like shit."

Her smile falls and I instantly regret asking. She sets the bags on the counter to hunt for plates. Tonight she's wearing a fitted black sweater dress with some sexy-as-fuck lacy knee-high socks that stick out above her knee-length boots. Her blonde hair has been swept off to the side into a loose braid. This woman is sexy and cute all rolled into one package.

Kaspy most certainly likes this package.

"He's okay. I'm fine. We'll get through this. I'm just trying to stay strong for him all of the time."

I frown and reach for her hand. When she slides it into my open palm, I pull her to me. She lets out a soft cry the moment I hug her tight. Pressing a kiss into her hair, I murmur, "You don't have to stay strong around me. I know what you're going through."

I feel the air release from her body as she sags into me, her face buried against my chest. I inhale her hair while I stroke her back with my fingertips. After a couple of minutes, she stops crying and tilts her head up to look at me. Her cheeks are flushed and wet. The tip of her nose is red and matches her bloodshot eyes from crying. But it's her mouth I fixate on—plump, glossy lips parted just so revealing her two front teeth.

Dipping down, I press a soft kiss to her lips. When I go to deepen the kiss, she smiles against my lips and pulls away.

"Take me on a real date and you can have a real kiss."

With that, she turns away from me and starts dishing out food, her ass jiggling with every movement. If a date gets me a real kiss, I wonder what'll get me balls deep in her pussy.

"How's Rhodes today?" Logan questions as he plops down in the chair across from my desk.

I scratch the stubble along my jawline with my thumb before meeting his gaze. "He's here. Not talking much but has been anchored to his desk all day working on his backlog of casefiles."

"Understandable," he mutters, his eyes flitting to my pen—the same pen he fucked Nadia with. "Any word on Donovan? What's he up to?"

Crossing my arms over my chest, I lean back in my chair and raise an eyebrow at him. "What happened to you two? You two were tight for ages and then one day you stop speaking?"

A flash of anger glimmers in his eyes before he masks it away with an expression of ease and retrieves my pen from the holder. I watch with irritation as he plays with it. "Ever since Nadia came along, he sort of faded into the background. Kind of hard to be friends with someone who obsesses over their stepdaughter. Doesn't leave much for us to shoot the shit about. Besides, we're both busy lately."

"So you stop talking to him but then shack up with his stepdaughter behind his back? Pardon my French, Chief, but that's fucked up."

He laughs, cold and without humor. "He'll get over it."

I'm rolling my eyes when Amethyst's sunny disposition fills my doorway. For a moment, I forget about the asshole in front of me because I get swept up in her light.

"Sorry to interrupt," she says with a grin, "but I just wanted to say hi. I came to check on Jason and thought I'd pop in to see you too."

Logan clears his throat and I jerk my head to see him flashing her one of his signature charming grins that disarms every woman in this town. Jealousy ignites within me and rages through me like a wildfire.

"I'm Amethyst Gardner, Jason Rhodes's sister-in-law. And you are?" she probes, her eyes twinkling.

"Chief Logan Baldwin. Pleasure to meet you, doll." He winks at her as he takes her hand and shakes it for an unnecessarily long time.

I rocket to my feet and then stalk around my desk. Her hand is forced from his when I smash her to me in a bear hug. A sweet giggle fills the room and when I glance over at Logan, his face is impassive. But I can tell by the clenching of his jaw, he's annoyed she's spoken for.

Is she, though?

Spoken for?

Something radiates through me. Pride. Protectiveness. Hell, maybe even possessiveness. Whatever it is, I don't want him touching her. Or fucking looking at her.

A throat clears from the doorway and I release her to find Donovan Jayne standing in the doorway with a shit-eating grin on his face. Logan's grumble behind me tells me he isn't so happy to see him here.

"Why are you here?" Logan bites out.

Donovan steps into my office and Mayor Lee Dunaway follows him inside. "Well, Chief," Donovan says with a smirk, "the mayor and I were checking out some commercial properties together when he asked if you were coming to his birthday party tonight at my lodge. I told him you were probably much too busy with *my* Nadia to come, but we'd stop by to invite you anyway."

Logan rises to his feet and I can see the battle warring within him—a war between being Mr. Fake Ass and ripping Donovan's head clear off his shoulders.

"Chief," Lee says, extending his hand to my superior. "I'd love to have you and the future missus at my party at the Aspen Pine Lodge. It starts tonight at seven. There'll be dinner, drinks, and dancing. Melena, would love to meet Miss Jayne. You know she's always trying to rope the women in this town to help her with all those charity events she holds. It would please me if you could come. Heck, Lieutenant, you and your girlfriend here are welcome, too. I'll have them reserve places at my table for you all. What do you say?"

Logan's fake grin falters as he ponders the mayor's invitation. He doesn't like sharing Nadia with the eyes of anyone, but he's also smart enough to realize keeping her hidden away from everyone will raise eyebrows. And if anyone ever gets wind that he hits her, his reputation as the city's good 'ol boy police chief will be dragged through the fucking mud.

"It's a bit last minute but I'm sure we can make it," Logan responds with a tight smile.

"And I wouldn't miss it, sir." I reach for Amethyst's hand and squeeze it. "Would you like to come with me?"

She offers me a tentative smile and I decide it's my favorite thing in the entire world. Her smile. In a room full of people I'm in no mood to be around, she draws everyone in with her sweet smile. "Is this a date, Lieutenant?" she asks with a raised eyebrow.

Despite her outward smiles, I sense the sadness within

her. It practically rolls off of her in waves. She's still hurting over losing Ashley. I want to pull her into a hug and ignore the world around us until her pain lessens.

With my eyes on Logan, enjoying the annoyed glare on his face, I answer her. "I know you're probably not in a mood to party but I'd like for you to come with me. And who knows, maybe you could make a new friend here in town. Nadia's around your age."

When I look back at her, a flicker of understanding flashes in her eyes. The file. The plan. She *wants* to help. "I'd love to get out of the house for an evening. A date it is then."

Flashing her a grateful expression, I squeeze her hand once more. "I'll pick you up at six."

"Donovan is a meddling prick," Logan complains as he pushes a file across the desk to me. "Dunaway couldn't give two shits if I were there or not. But Donovan's up to something. I want you to keep an eye on him at the party. He's probably trying to get to Nadia."

His eyes darken at the mention of her name. He pulls his phone from his pocket and types in the same six numbers as before. I'm not sure what his phone controls but it has something to do with Nadia. Lately, my hate for her has dimmed to almost nothing. Now that I've been around her on several occasions, I'm starting to feel sorry for her.

What if it were Kasey in her shoes?

I'd fucking kill Logan for even looking at her wrong.

But Nadia?

They're the same age. Both with a fiery, strong personality. Two women who attract the wrong types of men in droves.

I'm not sure why my hate has waned, but it has. I've been clinging on to it for so long that I feel empty and incomplete without it. Maybe it's Amethyst who's making it too hard to remain in the shadows now that I've been blinded by her light. My heart's just no longer one hundred percent in it. Logan has already fucked her up beyond repair. Not to mention, I despise the fact that she's been spending the past decade looking for my sister too. Perhaps she's not the evil villain I've painted her to be. And that notion fucking scrambles my brain.

"You can't keep them away from each other forever," I tell him pointedly. "She's his family and he's stubborn as hell. Do you really think he'll sit by idly while you sweep her off her feet and marry her?"

He pinches the bridge of his nose and grunts, frustration wrinkling up his forehead. "I don't trust him not to try and coax her away from me. She won't go, but he'll try."

Shrugging my shoulders, I lean back in my chair, affixing him with a serious stare. "Are you good to her?"

The fucker has the audacity to smirk. "I've given her more than she could ever dream of. Nadia's not going anywhere. But Donovan's stupid enough to try anyway and it pisses me the hell off."

"Hmmm."

He changes the subject. "Talked to the DA about Dale. Slam dunk case. With Dale's prior convictions and record coupled with the accident where he killed both Rhodes's pregnant wife and the bar fly he was fucking named Gina Ratliff, he'll rot in prison. How's your mom holding up?"

I grit my teeth. I'd wanted to strangle Dale after what he did but there was never an opportunity. Prison just seems like too easy of a sentence after all he's done. "She's fine. I spoke to her on the phone a couple of times this week. All she does is rehash the entire fight she'd had with Dale beforehand as if the accident is somehow her fault. Thank fuck she's been staying away from The Lounge though. I think she's depressed but after some time away from him, maybe she can get her shit straight."

"What about Rhodes?" he questions. "He holding any hard feelings toward you?"

Frowning, I shake my head. "No, he knows how much I hated that asshole. He just wants justice for his wife and baby."

My phone beeps and I pull it up to see I've received a text from Amethyst.

Ames: I'm going to try and buddy up to her tonight when I meet her...I'll fish for information about your sister.

Her text has my calm demeanor faltering and I sit up quickly to reply back.

Me: Let it go, A. I'll get my answers eventually.

Logan, noticing my distraction swivels in his chair to face his safe behind his desk. From over my phone I pay attention as he types in the six numbers—six numbers that are different than the ones he types on his phone. Exactly backwards to be exact. My first instinct is to drive right over to see Nadia and try this code on the door. But, a part of me, the old me, still wants something in return for it. I may not necessarily want to fuck her or even ruin her, but I really want for her to remember something about that day.

Anything.

Ames: Black or red? I'm at the mall and trying to decide on dresses.

I lift my gaze from my phone and see him move a file to pull out a small handful of hundred dollar bills. After he shoves the file back into place, he slams the safe shut and jerks his head to look at me.

But my eyes are back on my phone responding back to Amethyst's text.

Me: Whichever one shows more skin…

Logan clears his throat and narrows his eyes at me. Curiosity is killing him. It's painted all over his face—his eyes nosily trying to read what's on my screen. Tucking my phone into my front pocket, I raise an eyebrow at him.

"What's with the money?"

He grunts as he stands and shoves it his pocket. "Nadia's going to need something to wear. I'm going to take her shopping. I want eyes on Donovan before the party. Make sure he isn't planning something stupid." His hand motions toward the door and I take my cue to leave.

"Donovan's always up to something. He likes to win," I tell him as we exit his office. He closes the door behind him and locks it.

"Well, I like to win too," he says with a smirk. "And this time I will win."

Donovan strides from the lodge, a glare marring his features, as he approaches my car. When he taps the glass, I roll down my window.

"Don't you think you should go get ready for the party instead of following my ass around all day? Doesn't that fucker have better things to worry about than me?" he demands and crosses his arms over his chest. "Besides, I thought we talked about this. You said you'd help me."

"No, I said I'd see what I could do. Anyway, I'm about to leave to go change and then pick up Amethyst. He's my boss, Donovan," I tell him with a shrug. "I have to do what he says."

He leans into my car and scowls. "Fine. Whatever. It doesn't matter because I have a plan."

My brows shoot up. "What sort of plan?"

"I need to get her alone so I can talk to her. Logan's gotten inside her head, and I want to find out what it is he's using against her. If this is some blackmail bullshit, I'll pay him off. I'll do whatever it takes to get her out from under his roof and back under mine." He begins pacing next to my car.

"I doubt he's blackmailing her," I say carefully, "but I have seen them together. He's kind of possessive. Do you think he hurts her?"

I've done it.

I kicked the angry hornets' nest.

Donovan's gaze snaps to mine with a murderous glare. "What are you saying? Do you know something you're not telling me? Is he fucking putting his hands on her?" he snarls in a furious rage, his shoulders heaving with each breath he takes. "So help me. If she has one single bruise—"

"I'm not saying he does hurt her," I lie. "But I'm asking what *if* he did?"

He hisses, "Then I would fucking kill him."

"You can't kill him. And don't tell that to a cop, man." I shake my head and pull out my phone. Flipping to the picture of the pipe, I hold it out to him. "Why would this be in his house?"

Donovan snatches my phone and his eyes narrow as he inspects the pipe closely. "Those are the types of pipes that bring in the water supply to this lodge and big commercial properties like hotels and chain stores. Is this behind the wall?"

I nod and hold my hand out.

He sets the phone back in my palm and lets out a rush of breath. "Why the fuck does he have such a thing in his house?"

Shrugging, I pocket my phone and regard him. He's back to pacing beside the car. "I was hoping you'd know the answer. Nadia mentioned something about Logan punishing her with water. Something's going on in that basement too. It's fitted with a keypad. Nadia wants in there badly."

I want to mention she was ready to spread her legs in order to get the code but it seems inappropriate to poke the bear when he's five seconds from slaughtering Logan Baldwin judging from the angry shade of purple on his face and the way the vein on his forehead bulges.

"This is fucking ridiculous. I knew I should have dragged her out of there when I had the chance. Jesus, I need to talk some goddamned sense into her, Kasper. Tonight, I need you to distract Logan. I'll whisk her away and pull information out of her. Please help me," he begs. His blue eyes darken with rage. "This is important."

"What do I get in return? I don't need your money."

He seems relieved I'm even entertaining the idea. "I'll

give you every lead, every contact, every detail we've un-covered over the past decade on your sister's kidnapping. I can't promise it'll be a lot but Nadia has spent the better part of the last ten years meeting with Logan to give him more information in hopes it'll lead somewhere useful."

"Bullshit," I say with a harsh laugh and shake my head. "I've seen the file. A few times. There haven't been any new details added to it. The file has been dormant this entire time."

His brows scrunch together as he stares at me incredu-lously. "I've gone with her on several occasions and listened to her recount things she remembered. We even saw a hyp-notherapist in Vegas at one point. It helped her remember some details. After that, we flew back here and went straight to Logan. It's all in the file. Or it should be all in the file."

My heart races and my palms begin to sweat. "Do you think Logan would keep a separate file on my sister? One I wouldn't have access to?" All I can think about is his safe in his office. A single file laid on top of his money and now I'm going crazy with the need to know what's inside it.

"Logan may be the king of this town," he says with a cold bite to his voice, "but he's no saint. Trust me, man."

We stare each other down for a moment before I nod. "Fine, I'll get you your moment at the party. But tomor-row, I'm going to see if this so-called separate file on my sister exists. If you're bullshitting me, I swear to God you'll be sorry."

He smiles before he takes off in a sprint toward his car, calling over his shoulder, "I'm not bullshitting you, Kasper. Thank you."

Fourteen

Nadia

"Nope." Logan's bored tone grates on my nerves. I've tried on half the store and nothing is satisfying him.

"Why not?" I demand in exasperation.

His eyes cut from his phone screen to look up at me. Anger flashes in his eyes. I immediately hate myself for snapping at him.

"Because it shows too much skin," he says in a low, clipped voice.

I let out a sigh and shrug my shoulders in annoyance. "This is stupid," I mutter under my breath and fling the door to the dressing room back open. I've barely made it inside when a strong grip is on my bicep.

Logan hauls me into the room and locks the door behind him. His eyes are rage-filled when they meet mine. I'm stunned silent wondering if he'll hit me with people nearby. But thankfully he doesn't hit me.

"Get on your knees," he hisses between his teeth. "Now."

I give him a slight shake of my head. "But what if someone hears."

He brutally digs is fingers into my throat and glares at me. When he speaks, his spittle showers down on me. "I don't give a fuck if they hear or not."

"But—"

I'm cut short when he squeezes my throat. My fingers claw at his wrist but he lifts me slightly from the ground, a snarl on his lips. "But nothing. In case you forget, doll, I can ruin your life with the push of a button. Don't fuck with me. Now get on your knees and suck my dick."

I nod as best as I can until he releases me. I'm dizzy and shaking but I drop to my knees. He's still wearing his dress slacks from work. His erection is thick and straining behind the fabric. I work quickly to free him. The moment his cock juts out at me, he thrusts it toward me. Not wasting another second, I run my tongue across his tip once before sliding my lips down over his hardness.

He grips my hair in both hands and tangles his fingers in my hair. Breathing through my nose, I attempt to relax my throat because I know what he plans to do. Without warning, he slams his dick deep into my throat. I've learned that with Logan, you don't fight it. You do whatever it takes to make it go faster. Tears roll down my cheeks and drip from my jaw as he fucks my throat. Every so often I feel the urge to gag but distract myself with playing with his balls. Anything to get him to hurry and come.

"Yes," he groans and picks up his pace.

My teeth scrape his shaft but he doesn't seem to mind. Slobber runs down my chin. A bruise begins to form at the back of my throat where the tip of his dick slams into me painfully with each pound into my mouth.

He lets out a soft groan a half second before his heat explodes in my mouth. It gushes down my esophagus. I gulp his orgasm down in an effort to hurry and get him out of my mouth. Once his cock stops twitching, he slides out of me, detangles his fingers from my hair, and pats me on the head.

"Good girl," he says with a chuckle as he shoves himself back into his pants. "Now try on the red one."

I rise to my feet and try not to shudder. When I get a glimpse of myself in the mirror, though, I do shiver. I look like shit. My hair is a mess and sticks up everywhere. The black mascara I'd put on earlier has streaked down my cheeks. And blood-tinged saliva dribbles down my chin. How long can this go on? Kasper's working on answers but not quick enough. I need out of this hell soon. Because one day I won't survive his constant brutalization.

"Hurry. We haven't got all day."

I nod as he unlocks the door and swings it open to step out. When my eyes meet with the horrified almost purple ones of a pretty blonde, panic skitters through me. She can't see me like this. Nobody can.

"Chief Baldwin?" she questions, her eyes still assessing me.

His shoulders tense and he flashes me a wicked glare before turning on his charm. "Well if it isn't my favorite lieutenant's girl, Amethyst. Are you picking up a cocktail dress for the party tonight?"

"Already got one. Just picking up shoes to match," she says with a nod but then turns to speak to me. "Are you okay? I'm Amethyst, but you can call me Ames. Are you Nadia Jayne?"

My eyes widen and Logan gives me a warning glare. One that says, *fix this shit or I'll kill you with my bare hands when we get home.*

I swipe away my tears and give her a wobbly smile. "I'm fine. I've gained some weight recently and nothing looks right on me. Just had a bit of a meltdown is all. So glad to meet you, though."

Ames shakes my hand and gives me a gentle smile. "I saw an elegant black wrap dress they were putting on a mannequin just now. It would look great on you. Chief, you should go grab her that one. It wraps around the middle and hides any imperfections by the way it cinches at the waist. Not that you have to worry about that or anything. You've got a banging figure but you might feel more confident in that one verses one of the form fitting ones."

Logan remains completely still but I give him a quick nod. With my eyes, I promise him I won't betray him. When he's satisfied, he stalks off. Ames wastes no time.

"You're bleeding," she murmurs and pulls me in for a quick hug. "Did that asshole hurt you?"

I shake my head in vehemence. "No."

Our eyes meet and she frowns. "You're lying."

"Just go, please."

"I'm sorry," she whispers. "I didn't mean to pry. You just look like you were dragged around by your hair. I tend to stick my nose in other people's business. Here, I'll give you my number."

She scrounges around in her purse until she locates a slip of paper and a pen. Quickly, she jots down the info and then shoves the paper into my palm. "Just hide this. If you need me, call me. We'll chat more at the party. I'll be moving here soon and I'd love to have lunch with you or something."

I fist the number and nod. "Maybe so. Thank you."

"Thanks for what?" Logan questions with a cold bite to his voice. He hands me the dress on the hanger and I reach for it with a shaking hand.

"She invited me to have lunch one day soon," I tell him quickly.

He glances between us. Ames smiles innocently at him. I thank God she can pick up on Logan's tense mood and doesn't try to intrude anymore.

"Hmm," he mutters. "Perhaps that will be okay."

"We'll step out but I want to see what it looks like," Ames says with giddiness that I know she's falsifying for my benefit. She even claps her hands together in excitement. Ames is disarming Logan and I'm thankful.

When they step out, I overhear her chatting his ear off about minerals of all things. He grunts his responses. Logan is normally a lot more charismatic but he's still pissed about our exchange and then her finding us. I know I'll be paying for this later.

Once I get the dress on, I decide it actually is the best looking one. It also has long-sleeves which should make Logan happy.

"What do you think?"

Logan's eyes sweep over me quickly and with mild interest. But Ames jumps up and down on her heels. "That one! Right, Chief? It's stunning and accentuates your sexy little body. I love it. You totally should get that one!"

"I like it," he agrees with a tight smile. "Now, let's go. We're running out of time and you still need to get ready."

Ames hugs me again and even gives Logan a quick side hug before bouncing back out into the store to look for shoes to match her dress. As Logan takes the dress to the cashier, Amethyst and I meet each other's gaze. Her face is serious and she gives me a nod. I don't need to hear her words because I can feel them.

I'm on your side.

And I know all about that fucker.

Logan squeezes my hand as we approach a group of people. It isn't an affectionate, loving squeeze. It's a warning. And boy do I heed it. I flash him a knowing smile before turning my attention to the people we're about to greet. Ames looks stunning in a fitted red-sequined cocktail dress. Beside her, I can see Kasper cleans up well wearing a tuxedo. His expression is serious and guarded. When our eyes lock, he frowns. Ames leans over and whispers something to him that makes him relax.

"Well, if it isn't Chief Logan Baldwin and his stunning bride to be," a robust man with rosy cheeks and a white mustache booms. "I'm Mayor Dunaway but you can call me Lee. Please, also meet my wife, Melena."

Melena, a round-faced and white-haired woman, flits over to me and hugs me. "Darling, you're absolutely stunning. I can see you turning all of the heads at this party. Are you Mexican, honey?"

I smile and shake my head. "I'm from Argentina but Colorado is my home now."

We make small talk, all the while with Logan's palm on

my lower back. He's keeping me close and also displaying to everyone around us who I belong to. Kasper's attention remains on us until Ames drags him off for a dance. As soon as the song comes on, an ache in my chest forms.

"Ain't That a Kick in the Head" by Dean Martin.

A song that reminds me of *him*.

"I believe this is our song," a deep voice rumbles from behind me. Butterflies explode to life in my stomach and I can't help the smile that forms on my lips. "Logan, I'd like to dance with Nadia for bit. You should ask Melena to dance."

He doesn't give Logan a chance to answer before he clasps my hand and hauls me away. My heart is thundering in my chest with worry about how this will upset Logan, but I refuse to look at him. Surely I can steal one moment with Donovan. We're safe here around all these people.

Once we reach the dance floor, Donovan wraps me in his arms and hugs me to him. His scent drowns away my sadness and stress. For a moment, I remember the good times.

"This is my favorite song," he says with a chuckle.

"But it's not classic seventies rock," I say with a gasp of faux shock.

His eyes twinkle. "I'm not always so predictable. My mother actually used to sing this song when she'd bake. I associate that song with good things in my life. Mom and homemade chocolate chip cookies and two greedy little boys."

We're both naked and wrapped around each other but for some reason, I want to dance. I want him to associate this song with me too. I want to be a part of the good things. "Dance with me, greedy little boy," I tease as I sit up on my knees.

His eyes twinkle and he gives me a lopsided grin. Donovan's boyish grins, such a far cry from the serious businessman he has to be most days, are my favorite. I want to bottle them up and keep them all to myself. Which, essentially I do, because our relationship has remained our little secret at this point and he only ever smiles like that for me.

"Try to keep up," he says smugly.

I swat at him but he's already dragging me out of the bed and onto the floor. He slides his palms down my bare back and clutches onto my ass. With his warm body pressed against mine as we sway to the music, I sigh happily. Life couldn't be more perfect.

"When did you know you first loved me?"

He stiffens in my arms but doesn't reply. When I lift up, his blue eyes are sad. Ashamed almost.

"Donovan," I mutter and lean forward to kiss him. "What's wrong?"

His lips meet mine and he kisses me deeply. When our mouths reluctantly pull away from each other, he regards me with a glimmer of fear in his eyes. "What if I had a secret so awful…so terrible…that you would hate me if you knew?"

Donovan's a good man. I could never hate him no matter what sort of skeletons are hanging in his closet.

"You're my other half, Donovan. Nothing could tear me away from you. Nothing. Whatever it is, we can work through it. I promise."

He leans his forehead against mine. "We better sit down."

The song has ended and I feel like whatever happiness we had is threatened by what he's about to say. But I vowed to him I'd listen. And I will. We've come too far to let anything get in the way now.

He helps me into the bed and we slip under the covers. His lips rain kisses down all over my face before I realize he's stalling.

"Tell me."

"I never slept with your mother. Not once. The only times I even kissed her were for your benefit."

I shake my head. "What are you even talking about? She was your wife. Of course you slept with her. But I don't want to think about it. It's in the past."

"I didn't sleep with her." His voice is harsh and resolute. It only confuses me further. With a sigh, he says what's plaguing him. "Look, I didn't meet your mother by chance."

"Okay…"

"Don't be upset," he grumbles, "Jesus."

I swallow and will the tears away. "Go on."

"Long before I went to Argentina, I'd been lonely. So fucking lonely. In an effort to find someone, I went on an online dating website and created a profile. Since I knew I'd be traveling to Argentina for a couple of months on business, I looked at potential people from the area I'd be staying at."

I smile. "Mamá never mentioned she was doing the online dating thing. Nothing to be ashamed of, Donovan. The whole world is online now."

He gives me a peck on my cheek. "Baby, it isn't that simple. The woman on the profile was beautiful. Fucking stunning as hell. I'd never seen anyone that beautiful before. As soon as I saw her picture, I knew I'd marry her."

Jealousy twists through me like a knife but I give him a tight smile so he'll continue.

"Through the site, we messaged back and forth. She was brilliant and wanted to go to America to further her career.

The woman wanted to travel the world. To later settle and have children. I wanted to be that man for her."

I swallow and nod. "So it wasn't Mamá? Who did you date before her then?"

His eyes close. Frustration passes over his features and he clenches his jaw. "Nadia, baby, the pictures were all of you. The profile was you. Your name, the town you lived in, your interests. The only thing that wasn't you was the age. It said you were in your twenties."

My blood turns to ice in my veins. "What? I don't understand. I never had an online dating profile. You mean to say someone stole my identity?"

"Your mother to be exact."

When I try to get up, his hands find my wrists and he pins me to the bed.

"Listen first and then you can get up. I need you to hear me out," he says softly. "I fell for you. Over the internet. We flirted and talked futures. We laughed. We spent hours together. And then, it was time for me to come see you. I was so fucking thrilled, Nadia. My life finally meant something."

Betrayal surges through me. Why in the fuck would my mother do this to me?

"As I was getting ready to meet you at the hotel, a woman let herself into my room. She looked like you but older. When I said your name, she stopped me," he says, clenching his eyes closed. "Your mother explained to me she had pretended to be you."

"But why?!" I exclaim and struggle against his grip. "Why would she pretend to be me? This makes no sense."

He frowns. "Because she was doing it for you. Selene's rent on the apartment had gone up and the hotel she worked for was downsizing. She could barely afford to keep a roof over your head, much less send you off to college like you deserved. Your mother had big dreams for you. Dreams that included you living and working in America."

I gape at him in shock and he presses a soft kiss on my mouth.

"Shhh," he coos, "let me finish."

But I don't want him to finish. I'm not sure I can take much more of what he's saying. In an effort to distract myself, I hook my legs around him and urge him to me. He lets out a grunt but I can feel his cock harden between us. A few uncoordinated slides against me and then his cock is stretching me wide as he fills me. But instead of fucking me, his eyes find mine and we remain physically connected while he continues his story.

"Once she explained everything, I still wanted to see you. It was fucked up, especially once I knew you were only seventeen, but I craved to take care of you. To touch you. To hold you. To protect you. She told me her plan that we'd play it off as a marriage to get you and her the proper citizenship, but that the marriage would be a farce. I went along with it because I only wanted to help you."

He slides in and out of me slowly causing me to moan.

"So your plan was to make me fall in love with you?"

Donovan grins and my pussy clenches around him. He drives himself all the way in to the hilt. I cry out before digging my fingernails into his shoulders.

"No, baby," he murmurs as he kisses me. "I told her I'd take care of you despite what she did to trick me. I was in love with you and if that meant it had to come from being your stepfather, then so be it. But I was taking you home with me.

I had no plans to pursue it any further. I just wanted you safe and near me. I wanted you to come back to Colorado and do whatever you wanted with your life. If you found some nice guy in college, I would have paid for your wedding and been there for you."

My body tightens around him when he quickens his pace.

"I didn't want you to fall in love with me because it wasn't right. I'm nearly twice your age and essentially in a position of power over you. But then we did fall, baby. We fell so fucking hard."

I gasp as my orgasm slices through me. I'm sure I'm drawing blood from his shoulders but he doesn't complain. Seconds later, his heat pours into me. As soon as dick stops twitching, he relaxes and kisses me on the nose.

"I'm sorry," he says, remorse in his voice. "I'm sorry about how it began but I'm not sorry for how it ended. In the end, we have each other and that's all that fucking matters."

I smile at him through my tears. "I'm going to kill her. But, Donovan, you're right. It was fate. You're my best friend. I love you and I can't imagine not loving you."

"Baby?" he murmurs.

I open my eyes, still lost in my memory, and stare into the silvery blue ones of Donovan Jayne. "I've missed you," I admit in a whisper.

He lets out a frustrated breath and I can tell he's dying to kiss me. But he won't. Not in front of all these people. Not in front of Logan. Donovan knows me well enough to know what would do me in. Kissing me in front of all of these people would fuck everything up.

"I love you, Nadia," he tells me in a fierce voice before resting his forehead against mine. "You've always been mine and you always will be. I don't know what the fuck is going on but I'm going to figure it out. Then, you're coming home to me for good. Got it, baby?"

I close my eyes and nod. "I want to believe your words. God, how I do."

"Then believe them. When it comes to you, I can't stop. I refuse to stop. I'll always do whatever it takes to keep you. And if I truly believed you loved Logan, I'd let you go. But you don't," he says almost viciously at the end. "Because you love me. You can walk away from the mess you got yourself in. Whatever hold he has over you, we can find a way to get rid of it. I swear to you we can."

I'm about to speak when a firm grip on my elbow jerks me from Donovan.

"May I have this dance?"

My entire fantasy world comes crashing down around me when my gaze meets the murderous one of Logan Baldwin. Back to reality.

Shit.

Fifteen

Kasper

DONOVAN STALKS OVER TO US WITH HIS HANDS FISTED at his sides, his rage barely concealed. When he reaches me, he loses it.

"I'm going to kill that motherfucker. I am going to put a bullet in his skull and dump him in the goddamned lake," he snarls under his breath, completely ignoring Ames at my side.

"Calm down," I urge.

He scrubs his face with both palms and his shoulders hunch forward. I've never seen him so dejected. "Why can't she just let it go, man? I've funded her searches, stood by her, and even sacrificed my business at times to help her. She's made it her life's mission to find your sister and it absolutely consumes her. I know this has something to do with Kasey. It *always* has something to do with Kasey with Nadia. But she jeopardizes her own safety for her cause. This is too much, though. I'm not going to be able to sit by and watch him destroy her, all so she can accomplish her goal…whatever the hell that may be."

The more Donovan speaks of Nadia as an advocate for my sister, the harder it is for me to focus on everything I've tried to piece together all these years. Anger and hate have fizzled. Determination sets in. I have the urge to bring both Nadia and Donovan down to the station, open Kase's file, and demand answers. Real answers. Not whatever bullshit that I've been working with this entire time. Then, I can confront Logan and find out what he knows too.

"Jesus Christ! What am I going to do?" he demands.

Ames reaches out and touches his shoulder. If I didn't think Donovan was obsessed with Nadia, I'd be jealous. But he is obsessed. Borderline manic.

"He's a lunatic. I'm pretty sure he was hurting her today at the mall. When women are abused, they're afraid," Ames tells him. "My sister, Ash, was in an abusive relationship in high school. I know the signs. It took a long time for me to convince her to leave him."

Donovan swivels on his heel and I can see he's about three seconds from attacking Logan. I grab on to the back of his suit jacket and jerk him backwards.

"Not here," I rumble. "I'll get you your moment in a little bit and you can try to talk some sense into her. But clobbering his ass on the dance floor will only make things worse for Nadia. Trust me."

He snaps his gaze over to mine but gives me a clipped nod. "Room three seventeen. Find a way to get her there without Logan seeing. Please."

When he storms off, I frown at Ames. "I'm sorry our first date couldn't be a little more romantic."

She smiles. "I prefer adventure over romance. I climb

mountains, explore mines, and dig in dirt for a living. Romance is overrated," she says with a wink.

Her purple colored eyes glitter with mischief, and for a moment, everything around me fades into the background. For the past week, amid all the chaos, Amethyst has had a way of making me forget the past ten years. She brings me fucking happiness just by being her.

"Then you won't mind me doing this," I say with a smirk, grabbing her ass with both hands and pulling her against my now hard cock. I slip one hand around her neck, just under her jaw, and hold her in place while I go to kiss her. My kiss isn't soft or sweet or anything romantic. It's hungry and desperate. Needy. It's a kiss that promises adventures to follow.

Her hands, starting at my waist, running up my chest are enough to drive me mad. I've almost convinced myself to bend her over a table and fuck her right here when the notion is quickly snuffed out by the idea of anyone other than me seeing her naked. *Fuck that.*

A giggle erupts from her and I reluctantly pull away.

"What?" I grumble but can't help but smile back.

"You," she says, with a half-smile. "I like it when you're a caveman. I like playing in caves so we kind of fit together."

I tug her to me again and ravish her mouth. Eventually, I release her with great reluctance. Her pink, swollen lips are driving me fucking mad. "I'll show you how we fit together later, Lames," I tease.

Her eyebrow lifts up. "Ugh, Lames? Really?"

I chuckle. "Kaspy and Lames. Kind of has a nice ring to it."

"Fine, I'll give you that," she concedes. "It is cute." Her

smile is radiant. "Better not disappoint me, though, Lieu-tenant."

I'm about to respond when my gaze falls to Logan and Nadia. I look over just in time to see him forcefully gripping her hips in a way that is more than possessive—it's preda-tory. So much so that it causes her to wince. My mind is once again on the fact that she's been trying all these years to help find Kasey but my asshole boss decided to keep this information from me. Maybe he was trying to protect me from what I'd find. Or, maybe he knows I'll find something they screwed up on when they worked the case. Whatever it is, I need to know.

"I have to stop this. He's fucking hurting her," I snarl. I may have a thing for Ames but I still have a sense of protec-tiveness over Nadia I can't explain.

"This is our chance. I'm going to, uh," Ames says with a stutter, "start some trouble and create a diversion. When it all hits the fan, sneak Nadia away. I'll meet you outside his hotel room door."

Before I can ask what she means to do, she disappears into the crowd. I start making my way over to Nadia and Logan. He's bitching her out under his breath but stills when I walk up.

"Mr. Dunaway was asking for you," I lie.

Logan's nostrils flare in anger. "Of course he was. Keep an eye on her," he spits in Nadia's direction with a jerk of his chin. He's practically coming apart in front of all these peo-ple. This town's good 'ol boy is having trouble keeping that perfect mask in place. "We're not done talking." He storms off and I turn to look at Nadia.

"Room three seventeen," I hiss. "Go."

She frowns at me. "What? I can't go—"

Grabbing her shoulders, I give her a tiny shove toward the door. "Don't be stupid, girl. Just go. Donovan's waiting."

At the mention of his name, her face crumbles and she runs off. Weird as fucking hell, that woman. I'm just striding over to Logan and Mr. Dunaway when a couple of women start screeching from the doorway that leads outside.

"There's a car on fire in the parking lot! Chief! I think it's your Tahoe!"

My eyes widen in shock. Logan curses and trots toward the exit while I make a hasty retreat to the third floor. When I make it out of the elevator, Ames is leaning against the wall with a shit-eating grin on her face.

"Room three twenty-eight," she says and waves a room key at me. "Come on."

She slips off her shoes and carries them in her hand while I follow her like a lost puppy. What the fuck is it about this girl that makes me crazy?

Once we slip into the room, she beams at me. "How was that for a distraction?"

Shaking my head at her, I can't help but smile back. "Um, *illegal* comes to mind. What the fuck were you thinking, you little pyro?"

She snorts and waves me off like I just reprimanded her for going five miles over the speed limit. Not setting our police chief's car to flames. "I don't like that guy. He had it coming." She unzips the side of her dress and I nearly choke when she lets it drop to the floor. Her ass is all but bare in a red thong and I crave to mark up those cheeks with my teeth to make it match.

I clear my throat and try to find my voice. "Guess I better stay on your good side, huh?" She tosses me a playful look over her shoulder and I feel it all the way down to my fucking pinky toes. "Besides," she continues as if I hadn't even said anything. "Did you see the way Donovan looks at Nadia? Swoon. They're in love."

I gape at her. "Said the self-proclaimed non-romantic. You do realize that's his stepdaughter, right?"

She looks at me through the mirror and unhooks her bra. It falls to the floor without a sound. When she bats her eyelashes at me, I nearly pounce on her. She stops short, though, and crinkles her nose. The expression makes her look adorable. "Wait, so he's married?"

"Not anymore. He and her mom divorced a few years back."

"Ah," she says triumphantly as if she just won an argument. "Well, you're blind if you don't see what's really going on there. They're in love and we helped them. I bet he's making love to her right now."

Curling up my lip in disgust, I shake my head. "You're nuts."

"Yeah, I guess I would be nuts to want to have sex with you," she says with a yawn.

A growl rumbles in my chest as I work at the bow tie at my throat. "How did you even pull that shit off? You don't smoke. You wouldn't have a lighter in your purse."

I shrug out of my jacket and toss it onto a chair. My fingers fly through the buttons as my dick tries to escape my slacks on its own. She walks over to the window, her back still to me, and peeks out the curtains. An orange glow lights the parking lot below. "I told you, I work in mines and caves all day. A woman like me must always be prepared.

You'd be surprised at what I have in my purse. Besides, I didn't use a lighter. I used one of those tiki torch things by the walkway out front. Broke his window with a rock and tossed the torch inside. Lit up like the fourth of July."

"You could have been hurt," I grumble as I shed my dress shirt and undershirt.

She giggles and looks over her shoulder at me again. "But I wasn't. Nadia, however, was being hurt."

Her gaze falls to where I'm unbuckling my belt and her smile falters. I pause to regard her with a frown. "I thought you wanted to do this. What's wrong?"

Slowly, she walks over to me. Her perky tits bounce slightly with her movement and I'm eager to suck on them until they're red and sore.

"I do want this, Kasper," she says and pushes my hands from my belt. Her slender fingers begin working to get my pants undone. "But I'm not usually a love 'em and leave 'em kind of girl."

I thread my fingers into her hair and tug back so I can look into her sparkly eyes. "One night would never be enough for me. Besides," I say with a smirk, "you'd probably set my car on fire too if I did such a heinous thing."

She scoffs, already poised to say something back, but I attack her lips with mine. Her mouth parts open and I taste this sweet woman. A hint of the wine we drank earlier lingers on her tongue. I want to get drunk from licking off the remnants. While I kiss her, I let one palm slide down to her breast. She lets out a whimper when I pinch her nipple between my thumb and forefinger.

Her lips pull from mine and she regards me with furrowed brows. "Actually, that's the thing," she says, her voice sad. "I can't really give you more than one night right now. After what happened to Ash, I'm so…"

"Heartbroken?" I ask, cupping her face in my hands. Of course she fucking is. I'm a dick for thinking anything different.

Her lip wobbles and she nods. "But I'd like to just turn off my heart for one night. I'd like for you to make me *feel*… anything other than the never-ending ache in my chest. Make my body feel good. Can you do that? Please? Just one night."

A pang of disappointment ripples through me but I'm not going to be selfish. If she needs this, I'll be more than happy to give it to her. I won't make any promises about afterward, though. Her heart is something I've grown quite fond of. And I'll earn a piece of it eventually…when the time is right.

"Of course I can," I assure her and drop my mouth to hers. "Tonight is ours. I'll make you forget about the pain. Even if only for a little while."

My hand slips beneath her silky thong as I kiss her deeply. Her moan nearly does me in the moment my finger connects with her clit.

"You like that, Lames?" I hum against her lips with a satisfied smile as I massage her. "Can you *feel* that?"

She nods and her breathing becomes ragged. "Y-Yes. Don't stop."

Smiling against her mouth, I pick up my speed. "I won't stop until you're coming all over my fingers."

Another whimper.

Her body writhes and squirms at my touch but I keep my promise, only intensifying my efforts with each passing second. When she lets out a yelp before shuddering in my arms, I suck on her bottom lip and draw out her orgasm as long as I can.

"I haven't had one of those in a long time," she says in a breathy voice. "Far too long."

She drags her fingertips along my hardened chest. My cock begs for attention but I remain still. When her eyes meet mine, I raise an eyebrow at her.

"Want more?"

Her smile is immediate. I love the way her cheeks are slightly pink from the orgasm I gave her. The way her pale flesh colors so easily has me wanting to mark her up all over. An odd sensation comes over me...one I've never felt before. Is this how normal people feel with someone they like? Do they want to brand them? Hardly seems normal but it's such a far cry from the norm for me that I welcome the change. I've never wanted something to be mine so badly in my life.

And I want Amethyst to be only mine.

If I could write my name in hickeys on her stomach, I would.

"I don't know if I will be able to stop at one night," I admit as I push her panties down her thighs. I kneel to pull them off her ankles. Her fingers thread into my hair when I kiss the inside of her thigh. "Actually, I'm quite sure of it. I have an obsessive personality...and you're all I can think about."

She's quiet for a moment but then laughs. "Let's not worry about all that right now, Lieutenant. I'm wet and ready. Now. Enough talk already. Show me what you got. You can talk about your precious feelings in the morning," she teases.

With a chuckle, I stand and hug her, only because I want to swat her bare ass. As soon as the slap echoes in the room, she squeals. "Hey! What was that for?"

I smirk and shove down my slacks. My boxers are gone in the next instant. "Get on the bed, smartass. I'm about to show you what I've got. And I can assure you in the morning you'll still be talking about that. Not my feelings."

Her eyes snap to mine and she watches with parted lips as I retrieve a condom. I take my time rolling it on my dick because I like her hungry gaze on me.

"You truly better back up that arrogance with something special," she murmurs.

Ignoring her, I pounce on her. She cries out when my teeth find her nipple. My cock is eager to push inside of her but first I want to mark her up a bit. Like normal people do. "I'll show you something special."

"Oh, God," she whimpers as she fists my hair.

I suck on her tit until I'm good and sure she'll be bruised for a week. With my elbows caging her in, I tease her wet pussy with the tip of my dick. Dragging it up and down along her slit, I drive us both insane with the act.

"Just fuck me already," she begs, her fierce gaze locked with mine.

My lips curl up into a half-grin. "Humor me and tell me we'll do this again."

She wriggles beneath me in an attempt to get me to push into her but I remain strong. Her sigh is resigned but the fire in her eyes still remains. "Fine, if you're as good as you say you are, then we'll do this again, you caveman."

I chuckle as I ease my cock into her, inch by blissful

inch. Ames is tight and wet and going to drive me insane with pleasure. With a final thrust, I drive myself all the way into her.

"Jesus, you feel so fucking good," I praise and then steal her lips with mine.

Our tongues duel for ownership in each other's mouths. I fuck her like a man possessed—certainly obsessed—until she's screaming my name. When her pussy contracts around my cock with an all-body consuming orgasm, I climax right after her. Together we chase the high until it fizzles into ashes. Relaxed and sated, I collapse onto her tiny frame and suck on the lobe of her ear. My dick softens within her but I don't pull out just yet.

"Ames, I'm glad you're here. It's fucked up *why* you're here but I'm glad you are. I can't think straight when I'm around you. My job and motives and obsessions are unimportant. Basically, I'm one hundred fucking percent content with staring at you. And now that I've had you, I won't be content unless I'm nine inches deep inside your hot little body again and again."

Her entire body trembles with a snort and then dissolves into cackles of laughter. "Nine inches? Did you actually measure it?"

Lifting up, I grin smugly at her. "Could be ten. I've got a monster cock."

"You've got a monster ego," she teases.

"Don't *laugh* at it! You'll anger it." I dip my mouth to hers and kiss her softly, her body still trembling with silent laughter. Her heel digs into my ass, urging me to stay firmly planted inside of her. "Ready for round two already, Lames?" I slip my fingers between us and touch her clit. She jolts and nods her head.

"If you've got a monster cock, *Kaspy*, you have to back it up with a ferocious sex drive. It's just how these things work," she tells me, voice matter of fact.

With a rueful shake of my head, I slide out of her hot, greedy body to deposit the used condom and hunt for a new one. When I return, she's staring at me with furrowed brows.

I slide another condom on my cock before crawling back into bed with her. "What's got you frowning? You miss my monster already? This will be a complicated relationship if I can't get two minutes away without my cock inside you. I don't think we have 'Take Your Girlfriend to Work Days' at the station."

She rolls her eyes at me. "No, brat. And I'm not your girlfriend."

Yet.

I lift a smug brow at her.

"Do you and your monster and your ego need a bigger hotel room?" she asks with a shake of her head. "I was thinking about Nadia and Logan. About how you said she was there when your sister was taken but couldn't remember anything. He's abusive to her, I know it. Do you think he is blackmailing her somehow?"

My dick softens and any light-heartedness from a few moments ago slips away. I want to grumble in annoyance, but instead, I consider her words. "Donovan says she's had some answers. Stuff they've told Logan. Today, I noticed he had a file in his safe. I'm going to find out what it says. He's clearly either hiding something or trying to protect me in some way from what I'll find."

Her fingers whisper over my cheek and her eyebrows pinch together. "I feel sorry for her. I want to help you help her, Kasper. I know you're angry with her for not giving you answers about your sister's disappearance, but we can't just sit around while he hurts her. If your sister were here, would she be okay with you standing by and watching that happen to her friend?"

"No, she'd kick my ass," I admit. "Plus, my mom was a victim of domestic violence. It sort of hits too close to home."

"Tell me more about her. Your sister."

I close my eyes and remember my sister. She was always watching everything I did. Following me wherever I went. And eventually fell for my best friend. My sister was just always around, watching with wise eyes. God, I miss her.

"She was an old soul. Didn't really fit in anywhere except as my little sister. Once I finished college, the plan was to get a place she could move into with me. I wanted her out from under Dale's roof," I tell her. She flinches at the name of my stepfather. I hate that his stupidity killed her sister. That his senseless presence killed so much good while he is all bad, but still filled with life. "But I never got the chance. She was just gone."

She pulls my head to her chest. I rest my ear between her breasts and listen to the sound of her steady heart pounding inside.

"We have to help Nadia. If it were Kasey in her shoes, you'd want someone to help her. Despite Nadia's lack of memory, she's still someone's daughter. Someone's true love. Someone's friend. While you may not necessarily like her, it doesn't change the fact that she doesn't deserve to have someone like Logan controlling her every move."

Rage festers in my chest at the thought of Kasey in Nadia's place. I'd fucking blow Logan's head off with a god-damned shotgun if he were to treat my sister the way he treats Nadia. And the fact of the matter is, Nadia has been trying all these years, despite my original observations, to remember things from the crime scene. Evidently, she's come to the department on multiple occasions in attempts to keep the case warm and to breathe life into it with new details.

I need that damn file.

"Tomorrow I'll get with Donovan. I'll take a look at the file and confront Logan. Then, I'll help Donovan get her out of there. You're right," I say with a sigh. "If it were Kasey, I'd be infuriated. Now that I've gotten to know Nadia over the past couple of weeks, I know she doesn't deserve what Logan does to her. No woman does. She won't speak of it at all—believe me, I've tried—but I've seen the bruises and lacerations. He controls her with his glares and menacing attitude."

"Thank you," Ames says, petting my hair. "You're a good cop. And a good man."

I lift up and quirk an eyebrow at her. "I don't know how good of a cop I was tonight. Don't good cops punish criminals?"

She scrunches her nose at me, looking too fucking cute for this world. "Are you saying I'm a criminal?"

"Yes, that's exactly what I'm saying, pyro. Maybe I should arrest you." My dick twitches in agreement.

"What if I try and escape, Kaspy?" she taunts.

"I'll catch you, and get to see my cuffs on you, Lames."

The little hitch in her breath tells me she likes that idea as much as I do. Which is a fuck of a lot. She squirms in my arms, but I quickly flip her onto her stomach and pin both of her wrists at the small of her back. With my free hand, I slide my dick between her thighs until I find her slick opening. She moans when I push into her perfect pussy from behind. Her legs are pushed together and I love the way she feels from this position. Ames is becoming the perfect distraction from my crappy life. She's a bright fire that I want warming my cold, busted up heart.

"Oh, God," she gasps, her voice muffled as she buries her face into the comforter.

I thrust into her deep and slow. When she squirms and moans loudly, I slap at her pale ass. Her pussy clenches around me so I slap her ass again and again until she's coming all over my cock.

"You're all mine, Lames."

When I feel like I'm about to come, I pull out quickly and yank off the condom. I grip her ass with one hand while I fist my dick with the other. Soon, a thick, ropy shot of my semen splatters on her ass. Her red bottom glistens with my cum. So fucking hot.

"You're such a caveman," she groans, but I hear the smile in her voice.

I chuckle. "Just making sure you won't forget this in the morning, criminal."

Once we're cleaned up and I have her wrapped in my arms, she speaks again. All jokes and amazing sex are a thing of the past.

"I'm serious about what I said. Tonight, it was nice to find a distraction in you. But I can't promise tomorrow I won't be struggling." Her words aren't sad or broken. Simply resigned.

I drag my fingertip along her arm and kiss her shoulder. "Stop thinking about tomorrow. I'll be here when you're ready. I'm not going anywhere."

And it's true.

This woman has cracked open my blackened heart and seeped her light inside of it, brightening the dark, hate-filled parts of it. Now that I know the damn thing is capable of beating in my chest, I'm not eager to let that sensation go. If she needs to go slow, I can be a fucking turtle.

But this?

There's no stopping this…

Sixteen

Nadia

"TALK TO ME, BABY."

I've stood here for far too long simply staring at him with my back pressed against the door. What am I doing here? What happens when Logan discovers I slipped away?

Donovan checks his phone and smiles. It's his wicked, evil grin he reserves for the business deals he completes, properties he buys, and assholes he fucks over. I love that smile.

"Looks like we've been bought some time. There was just an unfortunate fire involving Logan's Tahoe."

My eyes bug out of my head as he approaches me. I don't flinch or run. No, I simply melt when his arms envelop me. It feels like being home being back in Donovan's arms. Seeing him tonight, at the lodge of all places, was already messing with my head. Reminding me of better times. More innocent times. Times *before* Logan Baldwin and his wrath came into my life. For a moment, I want to pretend that it is just he and I here, up on his mountain, away from the world. Nothing but our love surrounding us. Like old times. "Get out of your head, Nadia. Please. I need you here with me right now."

Tears swim in my eyes and I meet his gaze. His silvery eyes are glittering with shards of bright blue. Determination is a sexy look on Donovan Jayne. He cups my cheeks and slips his thumbs over my bottom lip. His gentle touch is something I've craved for a long time. I want him to hand me a shovel and help me dig myself out of this gigantic hole I've burrowed into.

"Baby…"

"I should leave."

Pain flashes in his eyes and my throat seizes. I hate that look in his eyes. I hate even more that I am the one who put it there. If it were up to me, I'd never see that look again for as long as I live.

His mouth descends upon mine and he kisses me tenderly. I want his lips all over my body erasing the past three years.

"Tell me how I can fix this," he begs, his hot breath tickling my lips.

"You can't," I tell him simply. "Unless you can get inside Logan's head and give me something I need."

His body stiffens as he pulls away, eyebrows pinched together in confusion. "That's all you want? Information? All of this is for information on Kasey."

I laugh bitterly. "Something like that."

"Come on, talk to me. Stop shutting me out, baby."

My lip wobbles. "I'm so sorry. I just…"

An animalistic growl that makes its way straight to my

core rips through him as he kisses me again, harder. His mouth claims mine. He makes nonverbal promises to right all of the wrongs. I wish it were so simple.

"Let's go. Tonight. We'll leave all this shit behind and I'll take you to Paris or Vancouver or wherever the fuck you want to go. It'll just be us. I'll marry you, we'll have babies… Let it be our turn, Nadia. Please."

His words slice me open and gut me. Tears roll down my cheeks as I sob. "I-I-I want that, Donovan. I truly do. But, it's not always about me. There's something I need from Logan. Let me get it and I swear to you we can be free together."

He scrubs his face with one hand before staring at me with red eyes. I've never seen my love so broken in the entire decade I've known him. With a lingering look, he lets go of me and turns away, leaving me cold without his imposing presence there to cage me in. His fingers thread behind his neck and his body tenses as he says, "And how are you getting these answers out of Logan, Nadia? How much longer am I supposed to just stand on the sidelines and wait?"

Flinching, his words leave me raw. They're exactly the reason I'd stayed away from Donovan for as long as I have. I feel the shame warming my cheeks. My knees give out, and in a second, he's back at my side, like he's always been, to catch me. His strong, capable arms scoop me up to carry me over to the bed. Once he lies me down, he crawls in beside me.

"I'm sorry. I'm so sorry, baby."

I shake my head at him. "D-Don't be sorry. None of this is your fault. J-J-Just trust me I'll sort it out. Then, I'll come back to you. We can be a family like you said. Promise me you'll love me, even when I'm broken and used."

He holds me tight against him as I cry. "I swear to fucking God, I'll wait for you. But I can't just sit here and let him hurt you. He's out of his mind. If he lays one hand on you, I'll—"

"It's too late, Donovan. He's already crushed my body and my soul. But it was my decision. A part of my plan. I won't let all this suffering and time lost between us be in vain. Let me finish what I started. Then, we can pick up the pieces together. I'll never leave your side again, I swear."

A choked cry rattles from him which successfully smashes the last bit of my being. I hold him against me, praying we can find a way to the other side of this. Together.

"Te amo con todo mi corazon. Mi amor. Mi unico." *I love you with all my heart. My love. My only one.*

He grows silent but digs his fingers into my ribs, pulling me closer to him. His warm lips drop kisses on my collar bone and throat. "Oh, sunshine. What a fucking unfair mess this is." And he doesn't even know the half of it.

His phone vibrates in his pocket and he grumbles when he pulls it out. With a curse, he shows me the screen.

Logan: Get Nadia back to me now. I know she's with you. I know you're behind tonight, too.

Swiping at my tears, I take a deep breath. "We need to do as he says, Donovan. Please."

He clenches his jaw and unmasked fury darkens his features. "Only because you seem so adamant. Trusting you was always easy, baby. And that's why I'm fucking going against every red bell ringing in my head right now."

I throw my arms around him and kiss him. Our tongues tangle together as I straddle him. What I wouldn't give to have one intimate moment with Donovan. Just one. I grind against his growing erection, the friction raising goose bumps all over my body. He clutches my ass with a death grip.

God, I miss this.

"I have to go," I murmur against his mouth.

He sighs but nods. With reluctance, I climb off his lap. His eyes stay on mine as he stands and takes my hand. "I won't let him continue with this charade for too much longer, baby," he states and kisses the back of my hand. "I can barely keep from smashing in his face with my fists. If you don't get this shit figured out soon, I'm going to intervene. I don't know what this means for your plan or whatever it is you're trying to protect or hide, but I will step in. It's in my nature to look after you and keep you safe. Three years of fucking agony is what I endured without you by my side. I won't let it continue on. If I have to slit his goddamned throat, I will. So be ready. I'm giving you a chance to save yourself before I come in and save you anyway."

I throw my arms around his neck and press my lips to his throat. "Thank you, Donovan. I'm so close. Kasper's helping me. Just let me fix this."

Letting go of him, I hurry into the bathroom to fix my makeup. Once I'm fairly certain I look presentable, I turn to regard Donovan. He's leaning on his shoulder against the doorjamb staring intently at me. His strong jaw clenches but he remains silent. If things were different, we'd both be naked and lost in each other.

But things are complicated.

And first things first.

Logan.

"We should hurry," I tell him as I breeze past him.

His hands find my waist and he pulls my back up against his front. I let out a whimper when he kisses the side of my neck. "There's not enough time. I wanted more time with you, baby."

I turn slightly to accept a kiss from him. "We have all the time in the world..." I trail off with a sigh. "After this."

He kisses me once more before reluctantly releasing me to lead me downstairs. When we turn the corner, Logan is pacing the entryway like a lion with no prey—starved and pissed at the unfairness of it all. I'm terrified of the rage rippling from him. His dark, hate-filled eyes meet mine, and I freeze in my tracks.

His eyes jerk to my side for a half a second, surely to Donovan, before settling back on me. "Time to go," he barks and stalks over to me.

Donovan is tense beside me. I swear I can hear his teeth grinding together. Logan snatches my wrist in his brutal grip, hauling me behind him toward the parking lot.

"What happened?" I question upon seeing a firetruck through the windows.

"Like you don't know," Logan snaps, squeezing my wrist hard enough to nearly make me cry out.

"I don't know, actually."

"Someone set my goddamned car on fire, that's what!"

My eyes flicker to Donovan's. His face remains emotionless but I've known him long enough to see triumph in his eyes.

"In that case, allow me. My Lexus is this way," Donovan grunts and starts in the direction of the parking lot, before Logan intercepts him by grabbing his wrist which was resting casually in the pocket of his tuxedo pants.

Donovan doesn't miss a beat—the complete personification of cool and collected. Only his eyes drop to his wrist, where Logan has the cuff of his tux jacket crushed in his hand. "Careful there, Chief. Your faithful citizens can see."

Donovan's words seem to hit their intended target as Logan loosens his grip, taking a perfunctory glance around the lobby. "I don't know what the fuck you think you're up to, but let me give you some *friendly* advice," Logan hisses, careful to keep his voice low. "Back the fuck off."

The unfazed look combined with the easy shrug in Donovan's response seem to only fuel Logan's rage further. Although, in this moment, I think I love Donovan even more, if that's even possible. He's trusting me, like I asked him to.

"I'm afraid I'm not sure what you're referring to, Chief. I was just having a word with my stepdaughter. Saying hello. That's not against the law, is it?" And with that, he ambles out the door toward the parking lot. Logan yanks me along behind him.

My eyes flit over to Logan's smoking vehicle as dozens of firemen stand around it, assessing the damage. Donovan Jayne is not to be fucked with apparently. God, I love that about him.

Once we arrive at the Lexus, Logan loads me into the backseat behind Donovan, surely so that he can watch me from the front seat. As the car is put into drive, panic begins to surge through me. Logan is insanely furious and I'm terrified of what he'll do once we get back to his house.

Think of silvery blue eyes.

Focus on that.

Focus.

When a hand touches me, I nearly yelp. I can't see it in the darkness, but I know it's Donovan reaching behind him between the seat and the door. His fingers whisper over my bare leg. The touch is soothing. It fortifies me and gives me the strength to endure what's ahead.

The drive, although Donovan takes his sweet time, is all too short and soon we're pulling up in front of the house.

"Selene and I spoke on the phone yesterday, Nadia. She's coming in for a visit soon and we'd love to take you to dinner at your favorite Italian restaurant. You won't mind, will you, Logan?" His question is threatening and it causes me to shiver.

I squeeze Donovan's hand one last time before he pulls it away.

"We'll see," Logan barks. "Nadia. Let's get inside."

As soon as Logan pushes open the door to the house, panic really sets in. Donovan's comforting protection that I'd always relied on is once again torn from me. I'd love nothing more than to reminisce about his loving touch and sweet kisses but there's no time. Logan's hell storm of fury is clouding the air around me. It's thick and black. I can almost taste the evil radiating from him. I need to think.

Our shoes echo on the hard wood floors and neither of us speak. His breathing is ragged. Heavy and uneven. I'm terrified that anything I say or do will provoke him. He's already been poked too much tonight.

Focus. Focus. Focus.

A chill shudders through me when he turns on a lamp. The living room lights up in a yellow glow but it does nothing to calm me. My heart has skittered up into my throat, rendering me speechless.

He slowly raises his arm and points down the hallway. I can't help but glance toward the darkened master bedroom.

"Now!" he barks.

I squeak and jump, rushing to obey. His footsteps are slow but steady behind me. Once we're in the bedroom, he turns on the light and begins tugging at his bow tie. I drop my gaze to my feet as my mind creates awful scenarios he's no doubt planned for me.

"Undress." This command is quiet but no less threatening. Once I'm naked, he points to a chair. I don't utter a word as he searches in his box full of kinky fucked-up treasures and retrieves some rope. Remaining relaxed while he ties me to the chair is nearly impossible.

Don't provoke him any further.

Go with it.

Focus. Focus. Focus.

"Do you remember that day you came to see me?" Logan's voice is cold and low. A shiver ripples through me. I want to look up at him, to implore him to calm down, but I'm afraid of what I'll see. I'm afraid that this might be the time he snaps completely.

"Yes."

And I do remember it clearly. That was the biggest mistake of my life. The point when I chose to be a vigilante and not inform my partner of my next move. I'd had a breakthrough. But instead of telling Donovan, so we could deal with it together, I acted on impulse and came in search of answers immediately. Answers Logan promised to give me. A file with details and information. Safe in his home. So he'd told me.

What a stupid, stupid woman I was.

"You were happy. Probably just finished fucking your stepdaddy, huh?" he sneers.

This time, I do lift my eyes. He's pacing in front of me. His bulky frame is bare from the waist up and his muscles ripple with each movement. A hair falls into my eyes tickling the side of my nose. If my wrists weren't bound behind me, I'd shove it away. I have to settle for blowing it out of my view. My ankles are tied to each front leg of the chair I'm sitting on. Squeezing my naked thighs together is a fruitless endeavor. They won't move any closer, leaving my pussy open to him. I'm not sure what his plans are but something tells me they're going to make me scream.

"No."

His malevolent eyes meet mine and he shakes his head. "Don't even try that fucking bullshit on me. Everyone in this goddamned town knows you and Donovan were sleeping together. Such sick shit, if you ask me. He's a pervert, Nadia. You're lucky I saved you from him."

I clench my teeth together in an attempt to keep my emotions in check. The last thing I need to do is reveal my weakness to him. Logan would expose it, tear it apart, and feed it back to me.

"You're wrong." My lip wobbles.

Fucking weakness.

His gaze zeroes in on it and he grins. It's far from warm and another shiver quivers through me. "Liar. Perhaps we should play a little game, sweetheart. A little lie detector game."

I'm shaking my head no but he's already sauntering over to his chest and digging through it. Moments later, he returns with a TENS unit. The earth shakes beneath me and a shudder wracks my entire body.

"Please…"

His eyes are narrowed in concentration as he peels the plastic from the sticky part of one of the patches. The wires that lead to the device wiggle with his movement. "You're not getting out of this interrogation."

With a lifeless grin, he proceeds to apply one patch to each of my nipples. When he finishes, he slides one between my legs, bypasses my pussy and presses it against my anus. The final patch, he applies to my clit making sure to wrap it tightly around my sensitive bundle of nerves. Once he's satisfied, he sets the unit on the chair between my legs and trots off. He returns with another chair and places it right in front of me.

"Now, let's begin." He grabs the TENS unit and leans back in his chair. Our eyes meet and I ignore the way the sticky patches tug at the hairs on my most sensitive places. "Did you fuck Donovan the day you came to see me?"

I clamp my eyes closed and shake my head. "N-No."

A tiny click is my only warning before my nipples zap to life. He's barely got the thing turned up and I'm screaming for him to quit.

"Lie," he says simply and turns the dial back down.

Beads of sweat form on my forehead and I tremble in fear. "I'm sorry, I just—"

"Next question," he barks. "Did you fuck Donovan to-night? You smell like him, whore. You fucking reek of that prick."

Tears stream down my face and I meet his gaze fiercely. "Logan, I swear to you I didn't have sex with him tonight."

He holds my gaze for a long while before he nods. "Truth. But you still fucking smell like him. Did you let him touch your pussy? Did Daddy Donovan lick your cunt?"

"No! Jesus, Logan. He didn't touch me, okay?"

His fingers twitch over the dials as if he's pondering my answer. "Truth, I think. Did your daddy stick his tongue in your throat? Did he taste your sweet lips?"

Snot dribbles down over my upper lip and I sob. "N-No. We just talked."

The back of his hand comes so quickly, I don't have time to react. His knuckles crack against my cheek bone causing my head to jerk to one side. "Lies! Did you want him to fuck you?"

"No!"

This time, my vision goes black as intense, electric fire explodes between my legs. I jerk at my bindings to push the pain away but I'm completely immobile. The only thing I can do is scream and scream until I'm hoarse. When I think I may pass out, the buzzing ceases.

"Logan, please," I beg, my teeth chattering as slobber runs down my chin. "Just stop this. Make love to me." My normal words have no effect on him. Typically, I can coax him into fucking me but not tonight. Tonight he's getting off on torture.

"Why should I? You want him," he says simply.

"No."

He leans forward and slides a finger past the patch. When he finds the opening of my pussy, he pushes his finger into me. I'm dry. Not at all ready for his next act of punishment. As he begins his probing, I hide. Mentally. Like always. I flee to the safe place in my mind.

Donovan.

Always Donovan.

"I'm scared. What if it hurts?"

He chuckles and rubs my ass with his palms. "For someone begging to try this, you're suddenly apprehensive. If it hurts, tell me. I'll stop. I want you to feel good, baby. Not be in pain. We can do it another time if you—"

"No. Do it now."

I've already downed several shots of tequila in anticipation of this moment. We've played with toys and his fingers. I always get off. I know he'll feel good there too.

I hope.

We want to share every part of ourselves with each other.

"Touch your pussy, beautiful."

With a nod, I slip my fingers between my thighs. I massage my clit while he spreads my cheeks apart. The sound of a cap being opened makes me take pause, but when he slides the slippery head of his cock against my anus, I focus on getting myself off.

"You ready?"

"Yes," I whisper. "Go slow in case it hurts."

His lubricated cock begins pushing against the tight hole of my ass. I let out a grunt of pain the moment he breaches the opening.

"Ahh!"

"What do you want, baby? More or out?"

I take in a deep breath and close my eyes. "More. Slowly."

Donovan must have the patience of a saint because he

does exactly as I ask. His thick cock fills me more and more with each passing second. The pain is there, the pressure is intense, but it's not something I can't bear.

"Nadia, baby," he hisses once his cock is completely seated inside of me. "I'm afraid to move because you feel so good. I might come just from how tight you are."

The desperate need in his voice—the slight tremble—makes me hungry for him. I want to please him and give him whatever he wants. Massaging at a quicker pace, I urge him on. "More, Donovan. Fuck me."

The words feel dirty to say, but I mean them. At first, I couldn't even think them without turning as red as a tomato in front of Donovan. But like he's taught me, sometimes people in love make love. And sometimes they fuck. There's nothing wrong with us voicing our desires to each other.

He groans and begins a slow assault on my ass. "Mmmm, that's my girl. Tell me what you want." As he thrusts into me with gentle movements, it sends unusual quivers of pleasure racing up my spine. "Like that? Do you like it when I'm in your ass?"

"Yes, I do."

The pain is intense but the rush of breath coming from him spurs me to take it. I want him coming deep inside of me. I want the poised and put together Donovan Jayne coming apart at the seams—all because of me.

"Fuck!" he grunts. "This is too fucking much, beautiful."

The foreign sensation within me becomes less about pain and more about pleasure. I focus on the feeling, lose myself to it. Stars glitter in my vision as an orgasm deep within me cuts through me like a sharp knife.

"I'm coming!"

"There!" Logan barks, jerking me from my memory.

His finger is fucking me hard. My memories are laced with what he's doing and I come with a painful shudder at his hand. "Oh, God!"

"Where the fuck do you go that makes you go from dry to gushing like Niagara Falls? It isn't here with me, doll."

I tremble and meet his eyes with a weary stare. "What? Nowhere. I'm here with you."

He growls, rage contorting his features into something hateful and wicked. "You're lying again. It's with Donovan Fucking Jayne. It's him you run to in your head. Just like it was him you ran to tonight. You playing me, bitch? Did you really think you could sweet talk your way out of that basement and into my life? For fucking what? To escape? That's bullshit because you've had a thousand chances if that was your motive. Why the fuck are you playing me, Nadia?"

When I don't answer, he rips the patches from my body, causing me to scream. Then, he storms off. I'm sobbing when he returns with a sharp knife.

"Logan…W-what are you doing?"

The psychotic glare in his eyes tells me all I need to know. Instead of answering me, he begins sawing the rope from my ankles. His movements are uncoordinated, causing him to nick me a few times with the knife. Then, he stands so he can cut the rope from my wrists. Once my hands are free, I open and close them several times to get blood circulating. If I have to run, I need my extremities working.

A clicking sound jerks my attention back to him. He dangles the handcuffs in front of me. Before I can even think of escaping from his wicked grasp, he wrangles me into the handcuffs and secures my wrists tightly behind me.

"Logan—"

"NO MORE!" he booms and shoves me toward the bed.

I stumble and land face first on the duvet. His belt jingles behind me and I can hear him unzip his slacks. He's poised to fuck me from behind. And once again, I retreat inside my head. But just as I close my eyes, his hand is on my jaw.

"Look at me," he snarls, spit showering my face. His fingers bite into my jawbone and he turns my head to a painful angle to look back at him. "Eyes on me. This is about us, not Donovan Fucking Jayne."

His eyes are almost black with rage and I'm terrified. With nowhere to mentally run to, I panic.

"No," I cry out, "Please stop."

A harsh, bark of a laugh rings out from behind me. "Fuck you."

With those words, he begins to force himself into my pussy. I scream and squirm but he doesn't stop until he's all the way in.

"Watch me fuck you, Nadia," he hisses. "Watch me."

Tears spill out and I stare at him as he brutally pounds into me. I'm powerless to stop him. All I can do is look right into his two dark windows into hell, all the while praying for a savior. But my savior isn't coming. I pushed him away and told him I had it handled. And now, I can't even close my eyes and go to him. The burning inside of me from Logan's rape is too much to bear without my Donovan. I pray for him to come soon and end this terror.

"Dios, ayudame," I murmur. *God help me.*

And he does because a moment later, Logan spills his

demon seed into me. Luckily for me, on one of my random pardons from his prison, I made sure to protect myself with a birth control implant. I'll never birth one of Logan's children. Ever.

"Now, sleep on the floor. I'm not done punishing you, bitch."

I shriek when he rolls me off the bed and I land painfully on my shoulder. Rolling onto my stomach, I attempt to bury my face into the carpet to hide from him.

Donovan, my salve.

As my eyes flutter closed, blue silvery ones rush in and envelop me. He does save me. Every single time.

Seventeen

Kasper

WHEN I PULL INTO THE PARKING LOT OF THE STATION, I'm alerted to someone standing on the side of the building. Groaning, I climb out of the car and put my hand on my piece as I approach. The last thing I want to do is start the day with bullshit.

I'm still high after a night of fucking a woman who mesmerizes me. This morning, we'd gone back to my place and I'd had sex with her against the shower wall. Despite her previous words, she didn't seem too enthusiastic to let what we started end with one night. In fact, she seemed all too eager for my monster when I woke up with her lips around it. She promised to visit me for lunch after she ran some errands. Until then, I plan on figuring out what the hell is in Logan's safe. One way or another.

"That's a restricted area," I call out as I walk toward the figure.

The man lets out a puff from a cigarette before tossing it into the grass. When our eyes meet, I frown to see Bart

Stokes staring glumly at me.

"Stokes," I say with a sigh, placing my palms on both hips. "Chief let you go, man. You know you can't hang around the station all creepy as fuck."

He grumbles and runs a shaky hand through his greasy hair. The man looks like utter hell. "I'm here to warn you. That asshole's off his rocker."

I give him a sympathetic nod. "I get that, man. I think we all get that. And I appreciate it, but I don't need your warnings. Not worth you taking the risk."

He takes a step toward me and holds out his hand. I reach out and pluck two bullet casings from his palm. "What's this?"

"Evidence," he states plainly.

I cringe. "Okay. Why do you have *'evidence'* that won't matter in a court of law anyway? Spoliation of evidence is obstruction of justice. I could arrest you for such a charge. You know that, Stokes."

"Exactly. Your boss man has been having me do shit for him for the better part of six years. Collecting evidence like this from crime scenes to keep certain local politicians and businessmen out of trouble." He runs a hand through his greasy hair and scratches his scalp. "And then he just fires me. I do his goddamned dirty work and he lets me go for doing shit he told me to do. He's the dirty cop, not me. I was just following orders."

Tensing up, I grit my teeth before speaking. "You have anything to back up these claims? These are hefty accusations—accusations that could land you in prison because of your part in them."

He scoffs and throws his hands in the air. "You think I

give a fuck about that right now? Word on the street is Chief fired me because I checked out his woman. Can you believe that? The actual bogus shit he fired me for isn't what got back to my wife. No, Sandra hears this stupid rumor about me lusting over some chick and decides to leave me. Took my boy with her. Says I'm a cheating manwhore. I ain't slept with nobody but her in sixteen years, Ghost. So now I've got no job *and* no wife."

I sigh and pull out my phone. "There're ways we handle this. Internal Affairs deals with this stuff all the time. I'll call Mark and—"

"No," he grumbles and waves me off. "Chief has all his friends in high places. Mark Smart is another one of his fucking minions. This whole town is full of crooked bastards hiding mistresses from their wives, money from the IRS, and crimes from the police department. Logan Baldwin carries the broom. He sweeps it all under the rug. For the longest time, I lifted that rug. Helped him do his dirty work."

I raise my eyebrows at him. "So what do you want from me?"

"I want a clean cop. I want someone to involve the Feds and bring him down. The motherfucker should go to prison."

Turning away from him, I stalk to the corner of the building and peek around. Satisfied that nobody is watching or listening, I stride back over to him. "So you want me to bring this information to the Feds? I need substantial proof, Stokes. If he's dirty like you say, and I honestly believe you, then we need unmitigated evidence against him."

"We have it," he says in a triumphant tone. "Storage

shed near the airport. He pays rent on the thing. Was always sending me out there. The place is damn near full of all the skeletons he's been paid to hide. I know this because I was his fucking errand boy."

I narrow my eyes at him. "We'll need a warrant and—"

"And who the hell you think you're getting a warrant from, Lieutenant? Judge Ackerson? The man got a seventeen-year-old girl pregnant. You think he's going to help you when Chief Baldwin got rid of the statutory rape case filed by her parents? Or hell, maybe you think Judge Miller would get you that warrant. Well, funny thing is, her son Josh should have more DUIs than any normal person and should have gone to prison years ago, but somehow that guy still drives a bus for the school district. His record is clean. Who do you think 'handles' Josh's mishaps?"

"I see your point," I grumble. "So you have the number to the storage unit? What about a key?"

He lights another cigarette and sucks in a drag. With a smoky exhale, his eyes meet mine. "It's in his safe. Whenever he needed me to run something out to the unit, I came and got the key. Afterwards, I was to give it back. For my troubles, he always paid me in cash, under the table. It really helped out because with Kenneth playing varsity ball, we could afford to send him to tournaments and on trips. I ain't dirty like him, Kasper. Just did my job."

Of course Logan would have someone doing his deeds for him but also kept a careful eye on the fact it was secure.

"I'll get in his safe. But he always locks up before he leaves. I'll need you to distract him so I can get in there. If I go through all this trouble and there is no key or storage unit, I'll have one of the unis bring you in for falsely accusing an officer of the law."

He takes another drag of his cigarette and hands me a sticky note with a number written on it. "The key's there man and here's the unit number."

"Fine. I'll get it today."

Stokes flings yet another burning cigarette into the grass before stalking off toward the back of the building. When he's out of sight, I stomp both of the butts out and head inside.

Lena regards me with raised brows when I pass by her desk. "Chief is on a tirade today. Did you hear someone set his Tahoe on fire last night? He's like a raging bull. I'd steer clear of him if I were you, Ghost."

Rolling my eyes, I say, "I can handle myself."

I make my way straight to his office. When I enter his doorway, I stealthily cram the sticky note into the latch catch of the door and lean against it to hide my evidence. "Any leads on the perp?"

Logan's rage-filled eyes meet mine and he grumbles. "Security footage conveniently lapsed during that time. Fucking bastards. I know Donovan had something to do with this shit. I'll get to the bottom of it."

My body is tense but I try to school my features. I'd put an entire magazine of bullets in his skull before I even let him breathe in Amethyst's direction.

"We can send some unis to interview some of the staff and guests from the party. I'm sure something will come up," I tell him.

A screech behind me has Logan and I looking out into the hallway. Lena is hurrying toward us.

"Chief, I'm so sorry to interrupt you but it's Bart Stokes.

He's outside swinging a baseball bat. Took out three sets of headlights on some squad cars out front before I could even gather my thoughts to come get you. I don't think he's done either!" she blurts out quickly.

Logan's face turns bright purple and he looks like he wants to turn over his desk at any moment.

"Get some unis out there now!" he barks as he grabs his gun and holster from the desk. When he stands, he eyes me warily. "I still want eyes on Donovan. Get on that, Lieutenant."

I nod and step out into the hallway. He carefully takes the time to lock up his office before trotting after Lena toward the parking lot. As soon as he rounds the corner, out of eyesight, I pull out my pocketknife and wedge it in near where the latch is supposed to connect. But since I stuffed the sticky note inside, I'm able to pry open the door easily. The moment the door pops open, I push my way in and head straight for the safe.

"This better work," I mutter to myself.

I attempt the numbers from yesterday I'd seen him enter and it unclicks, gaining me entry. There isn't much inside except for stacks of cash, a file, and a key. I swipe both the file and the key. Once I've shoved the file into my zipped-up jacket and pocketed the key, I open his desk drawer and find a random file to replace it with. Then, I yank off one of my keys from my ring that opens the supply closet in the back. Once I'm satisfied that nothing looks amiss, I close the safe and tidy up any evidence that would indicate I was here. The last thing I grab is the sticky note from the door latch and lock the door, pulling it closed behind me.

There is all sorts of commotion in the lobby, but I head

straight for my office. Once inside, I lock the door behind me and take a seat at my desk. Pulling the file from my jacket, I set it down so I can stare at it. It's thick and bulges with paperwork. My stomach turns when I see my sister's name scrawled on the tab.

That motherfucker.

This file is four times as thick as the one I'd checked out of storage on her long ago. Fury bubbles deep inside of me but I contain it at the moment. I refuse to let my anger cloud my judgment.

With a deep breath, I flip open the file. The first few pages are the same as in the file I have. Nadia Jayne's testimony. Her million fucking "I don't knows" and "I can't remembers." But then, I come across another statement. And another. And another. Each one a tiny detail. One little morsel she'd remembered. A lead she'd researched and thought the department should follow up on. All kinds of leads.

I pull up another handwritten statement in her girly flourish.

I'd gone to a hypnotherapist to help me remember. She'd helped get me back to that day. I could still smell the lingering scent of the cigarette she'd thrown in the street. The way the grass tickled the backs of my thighs. Everything seemed to go in slow motion. A black vehicle, a Suburban, with a lift kit and gigantic tires. On the windshield, it had red vinyl angry eyes. Like a beast.

My body ignites with a hate so furious, I can barely control myself to continue reading. I know that goddamned vehicle. I flip the page to another statement that had come several months later.

I woke up from a nightmare but I'd remembered some-

*thing. Something important. The man had on black slacks.
And his boots were the kind you'd wear with a uniform. He
even had something silver that glinted in the morning sun at
his belt. I think it was a badge. I'm worried he may've been a
policeman or a fireman or a member of the military.*

My rage blinds me for a moment.

Focus, Kasper. Fucking focus.

Flipping the page, I find one dated the day Nadia disappeared off my radar.

*He had a tattoo. Something colorful and artfully done. I
couldn't make out what it was but it had peeked out between
the bottom of his long-sleeved shirt and his wrist. Feathers
maybe? Fire? I'm not sure but I feel like this is useful information.*

It's useful for sure.

I'm still flipping through the file trying to make sense
of this shit when I realize several hours have passed. I scrub
my face with my palm and pull my phone out to let Ames
know I won't be making our lunch date. When I open the
display screen, I see I've missed some texts.

**Ames: I'm going to talk to Nadia while Logan
is at work. I'll find out what I can from her
about Kasey and also give her the number to
the women's shelter. See you soon, handsome.
Turns out I do miss that monster cock of yours,
Kaspy. ;)**

This text was sent not long after I left her at my place
this morning. Not even a half hour later, about the time
Stokes was pulling his crap, I missed another text. This one
from Logan.

Chief: Something came up at home. I'll be out

**for the rest of the day. Keep your eyes peeled for
Stokes. He drove off before I could get to him.
Also, keep Donovan in your sights like we talked
about.**

I'm already rising to my feet before I even finish reading
his text.

Fuck!

Quickly, I dial Donovan. When he picks up, I start
barking at him. "Meet me at Logan's. Right fucking now.
Some shit is going down."

"Leaving now," he bellows back before hanging up.

Fuck! Fuck! Fuck!

I drive twenty over the speed limit the whole way there with
my lights flashing. Motherfuckers still drive like shit and I
nearly run a couple off the road. As soon as I pull into Logan's driveway, I'm glad to see a sleek, black Lexus pulling in
behind me. We both clamber out of our vehicles. Upon first
inspection, the garage door is open but only one vehicle remains in the three-car bay. His white Ford is missing along
with his ruined Tahoe.

"It's Logan. I found the file on my sister. That motherfucker has kept all this shit from me. I can't fucking believe
this," I grumble as I pull my 9 mm from its holster. "His
truck isn't here, but that doesn't mean anything. Keep your
eyes peeled."

Donovan shocks me when he pulls a Glock from the
back of his pants and holds it at his side. I give him a nod
before silently climbing the steps. Once on the porch, I slip

past the windows and try the door handle. It turns easily to which I push through.

"Nadia?" I call out.

The house remains quiet aside from the heavy breathing from both Donovan and I.

"Nadia? You here? Is Ames here?"

This time, I hear a muffled moan. Donovan and I both dart toward the back of the house. The moment we enter Logan's dark bedroom because of the heavy curtains hiding the afternoon sun, I fumble for the light switch.

As soon as the room is lit up, Donovan lets out a choked gasp. "Nadia!"

My stomach roils in disgust at the scene before me. Nadia is naked and handcuffed. Her cheeks are stained from the mascara she wore last night having bled off from crying. The normally pretty hair on her head is matted and tangled. She's bleeding from several lacerations all over her badly beaten body. But the disgusting thing is the metal stuck in her ass.

"Is that a fucking hook?" I demand.

Donovan is kneeling beside her, his hands roaming all over her flesh, and I can see him working out what to do next. How to help her. "How the fuck do I undo this shit?" His voice is hoarse and emotion-filled.

I take in the ball gag stuffed in her mouth. Slobber runs down her chin. The hook that's stuck in her ass is attached to a chain that travels up her spine, around her neck, and hooks on through a loop of the ball gag. A lock holds it all in place.

"What in the ever loving fuck?" I mutter and run my fingers through my hair.

"I-I-I need something to cut through this chain," he says as he strokes the hair out of her eyes. "Baby, I'm going to get you out of this. Just stay calm, okay?"

But she's not calm.

Her eyes are on me as tears roll out. Muffled cries. Pleas maybe. Whatever she's trying to convey to me isn't coming through.

"Is Logan here?" I question.

She starts to shake her head and lets out a scream behind the gag. The stupid goddamned contraption pulls at the hook in her.

"Jesus," I bellow. "Don't move. Don't fucking move. One blink for yes and two for no."

She blinks once showing her understanding. I wish Donovan would look around for a key or something but he's about three seconds from having a meltdown. He just keeps stroking and kissing her.

"Is Logan here?"

Two blinks.

Good.

"Is Amethyst here?"

One blink.

Shit.

"Where?" I demand.

Tears spill out as she glances past me.

"In the basement?"

One blink.

When I start for the doorway, she starts screaming through the gag, effectively halting me. Two blinks. Two blinks. Two blinks.

"Can he see us right now?"

One blink.

"Fuck!"

"I need something to cut through this, Kasper. Do you see a key lying around anywhere?" Donovan demands, desperation making his voice husky.

I frantically start flinging drawers open. Nadia is screaming again, so I turn to her. "Do you know where the key is?"

One blink.

I sink on my knees beside her. "Where is it?"

She sobs and I hate that I can't help her.

"Is it in this room?" I try again.

One blink.

"Am I close?"

One blink.

"Fuck, does a handcuff key work?"

A sob but one blink.

Scrambling at my keys, I locate the one that will work.

"What's that sound?" Donovan shouts.

I'm focused on trying to unlock the padlock without tugging on the fucked up hook thing it's attached to. She starts screaming again and I think I've hurt her.

"KASPER, WHAT THE FUCK IS THAT SOUND?"

I pause to listen.

Gushing.

Gushing.

Gushing.

Sounds like water.

I twist the key in the lock and thank fuck it unlatches. As soon, as I unhook it and pull the lock off, I tug the ball gag from her mouth.

"Kasper, go! Before it's too late!"

Donovan takes over unwrapping the chain from around her neck and then gently removes the hook from her body. I was right. A thick, metal hook shaped device with a round ball the size of a butt plug at the end was shoved up her ass. At least it wasn't sharp.

"What are you talking about, Nadia?" I question and toss Donovan my pocketknife as I stand. He sets to sawing the rope binding her knees together.

"He finally did it. We have to get down there. Tell me you have the code!"

"Is Ames down there?"

"Yes, and they'll drown if you don't get down there now!!"

I'm already sprinting down the hallway before the words leave her mouth. With shaking fingers, I unsuccessfully enter the code.

Denied.

Denied.

Denied.

Fuck!

I enter it again, forcing myself to slow down.

Click.

Donovan is helping a naked, hobbling Nadia down the hallway just as I get the door open. "Get her out of here, Donovan. I'm going to save Amethyst!"

He nods and starts past me with Nadia but she starts screaming. "No! I have to get down there! I have to help save them!"

Them.

Them.

Hope, a bitch of an emotion, floods through me as I stomp down the steps, adrenaline coursing through me.

"Ames!" I call out.

The basement is pitch black and I fumble for the small flashlight I keep on my belt. The sound of water rushing is loud. I can't hear anything over it. It sounds like it's rushing from several different locations.

"Ames!"

I locate my flashlight and push the button right as ice grips my ankles. Light illuminates my path in front of me.

Water.

Cold ass water.

And lots of it.

Coming up the bottom few steps.

"We have to save them!" Nadia shrieks as she shoves past me, wading her naked body right into the icy abyss. Donovan is on her tail and I follow after them, trying to light the way. Nadia seems like she knows where she's going. The water is already to her chest and about waist deep for Donovan and I. I don't understand where exactly the water's coming from but it shows no signs of stopping.

"There!" she points to an open doorway under the stairs. "Shine the light there!"

I wade over to her and follow her inside. My small beam of light flashes across the bedroom fashioned with a large bed. When my gaze lands where she's gesturing frantically to on top of a dresser, my whole world spins. Everything around me tilts and whirls. Like I'm on some stupid ride at a carnival.

Hope, that useless emotion, isn't so useless after all.

My eyes meet the terrified ones of my sister.

Kasey Grant.

Older but still my baby sis.

No fucking way.

But what sets my world on fire with rage and utter confusion are the other sets of small eyes. A boy, no older than
seven or eight clutches on to another child, a toddler, also
a boy. And Kasey, holds a bundled up infant to her chest.

What the fuck is happening?

Eighteen

Nadia

"I T'LL FILL UP FAST," I YELL AT KASPER. OF COURSE I know this. Logan drilled it into my head for three fucking years to keep me in line. Icy water, funneled in straight from the lake via six gigantic pipes, would drown innocent people—people I love—in a frigid tomb within twenty-seven minutes.

And we've already wasted too much time.

"Donovan, take the baby. You're tall enough to keep her dry. Hurry. Kasey, get Tay out of here," I instruct, my teeth beginning to chatter. "Amethyst is somewhere down here. You have to find her, Kasper!"

At the mention of her name, he hands me the flashlight and then splashes away calling for her.

"Come here, baby," I coo. Van's frightened eyes light up when he sees me.

"Mamma, I scared."

His sweet voice is music to my ears and I reach for him. "I know, sweetheart. We're going to go someplace dry." He lets me pull him into my arms and I squeeze him tight. I inhale the scent of him that I haven't allowed myself to think about or obsess over for several months.

All part of the plan.

Even if it nearly killed me in the process.

"Climb on my back, Tay," Kasey says, her voice calm despite the terrorizing sound of the water rising quickly in the basement. She hands Kassie to Donovan who wears a stunned expression on his face. But as soon as he has her in his arms, he holds her against his chest high above the water.

He starts out of the room and toward the stairs with Kasey right behind him. I hold the flashlight beam in front of me to lead the way.

"MOTHERFUCKER!" Kasper's voice rings out above the rushing water that nearly deafens us.

"What?" I call out to him in the darkness and quickly sweep the light across the watery abyss.

"She's stuck! She's fucking cuffed to a goddamned pipe!"

Panic ripples through me but I remember the key is still on the floor in Logan's bedroom. "Stay with her, Kasper! I'll be right back with the key!"

When I make it to the stairs, Donovan is waiting for me. His hand reaches for me and he helps me out of the water. The six of us climb up the stairs, shivering and the kids whimpering. As soon as we're at the top, I set Van to his feet.

"Donovan, take him and get them out of here. Don't let him out of your sight. Promise me!"

He scowls at me. "You're not going anywhere!"

Pushing past him, I run to the bedroom and snatch the key. When I return, he's clutching Van's tiny hand and glaring at me.

"I can't let you go back down there, baby."

I give him a quick peck on the lips. "Too bad, I can't let her drown. We'll be right out."

He growls but I'm already bounding down the steps. I put the flashlight between my teeth and jump into the frigid water, which is already much higher than it was when we first came down here. In another fifteen minutes or so, it'll be completely filled with lake water.

"Kasper!" I cry out around the flashlight.

I don't see them.

Shit!

"Kasper!"

His head emerges from the water and he's frantically tugging at the pipe. Amethyst is nowhere to be found. Diving under the icy water, I swim to where I can see her arm attached. She's clawing at her wrist as she attempts to free herself, bubbles of air rushing from her with her panicked exertion.

With the key in hand, I work to unlock her. She wiggles and I lose my grip. The stupid key flutters to the floor. I clutch onto the pipe and launch myself to the floor to search for it. My palm flits over the carpet for a few seconds until I grasp onto the metal. Once I have the key back in hand, I float back up to where she's attached.

She's stopped moving and her body goes limp.

The banging as Kasper attempts to pull the pipe right from the wall echoes beneath the water.

Hang in there, Amethyst.

As I work to unlock her again, my mind is back on this morning. When everything went to hell.

"Nadia?" a soft voice calls out, pulling me from my nightmares.

I crack my eyes open to see an angel staring down at me. My entire body aches and burns from Logan's ruthless attack. After he raped me and forced me to watch as he did so, he'd shoved me to the floor and forgotten about me. I was in and out of consciousness as he made breakfast, went downstairs to visit Kasey and the kids, like he does every morning, and then as he dressed for work. He never offered to un-cuff me or feed me or anything. Hell, he didn't even speak to me.

"Nadia, oh God," Amethyst murmurs as she kneels beside me. "What has he done to you? I'm going to get you out of here!"

I've come-to enough to realize it's already too late. He'll see her on the video feed. Logan doesn't leave loose ends. Amethyst's fate is about to match that of Kasey and I.

"Go! Amethyst, you have to leave right now!" I croak. "He'll come back!"

She shakes her head as she helps stand me on my feet. "Let me grab you some clothes and we'll leave. Together. End of story. I'll call Kasper once we leave."

Time ticks by way too fast as I beg for her to leave. She ignores my pleas and shoves items into a bag.

"Where does he keep the handcuff keys?" she questions.

"You mean this handcuff key?" a deep voice booms from the doorway.

We both jerk our gaze to see Logan's giant body leaned against the doorframe. I'd expected to see rage or hate, but instead I see amusement. Just like that first day I came to see him for information. The day he'd easily lured me into his house, hit me upside the head with the butt of his gun, and

I'd woken up in the basement to Kasey tending to my wound.

"You're a monster," Amethyst hisses and her eyes skitter around in search for something.

"Semantics," he said with a shrug. "Do you really think you're going to save my pet, hero girl?" he taunts and aims his gun my way. "I don't think so."

"I should have burned your car with you inside of it!" she snaps.

His eyes darken and his jaw clenches. I know the look— the look right before the devil emerges.

"Logan, I'm not going anywhere. Just let her go," I plead in a calm voice hoping to distract him.

Amethyst makes a dive for her purse which jolts Logan into action. She's barely retrieved a knife from it when he tackles her to the floor.

"Stop!" I screech and throw myself at him. My arms are still cuffed but I have to try and help her. Everything happens quickly. He rips the knife from her grip, shoves her away, and then yanks at me by my hair. The cold bite of the metal pierces the flesh on my throat and I feel blood trickle down.

"You're going to do exactly as I say or I'll cut her to fuck-ing chunks right in front of you," he snarls as he quickly moves to his feet with me in his grip.

"Just run," I choke out. "Run!"

The knife is pulled away from my throat and an instant later pain bursts from my thigh as he slices it across the skin.

"Chunks..."

Amethyst meets his glare with a teary one of her own but doesn't try to move, clearly heeding his warning. "Kasper will come for you. He knows I'm here."

His breathing is heavy behind me and I know he's furious. "So fucking what. He'll find nothing. Nadia won't speak a word of it. I'll toss you down there with Kasey and things will keep going as planned. Nobody will miss you."

She flinches, like she's about to attack, and he slices at my flesh several more times. I scream in agony. When I start choking on my sobs, he tosses me face first down onto the bed so I can't see her.

"Over there," he barks out.

I hear a shriek and soon he walks to the other side of the bed, clutching at her hair.

"No, Logan! Don't do it!"

He ignores me as he wrangles her into his guillotine contraption. She fights him off but he manages to slam the wood down over her neck. Our eyes meet and hers are tear-filled yet angry.

"It's my fault. Leave her alone and punish me, Logan, please."

He ruffles her hair and grins at her. "Your lucky day, hero girl. Nadia over here wants to take your punishment. She's kind of a masochistic bitch like that. Haven't laid a heavy hand on 'ol Kasey in months. I'd never been with someone before who begged for such intense pain and humiliation. If it wasn't so fucking fun, I'd deny her simply for the fact she so desperately craves it."

In a way, he's correct. I'd always felt responsible for losing Kasey. For nearly a decade, I've blamed myself. The punishment he doles out, though, feels like retribution for all the years she's had to suffer while imprisoned by him. If anyone deserves his rape and beatings, it's me.

She curses at him but he ignores her to dig around in his chest of horrors. Once he pulls out the ball gag and anal hook,

I start screaming to distract him. I hope to God those are for me and not her.

Again, my cross to bear. Not hers.

When he makes his way to me, I let out a gasp of relief. I try to go to my happy place—to my Donovan—but I can't take my eyes off of Amethyst's terrified ones. Stay with me. Focus on my eyes. We'll get through this together.

Logan does what he does best, all the while with Amethyst watching in horror, and soon I'm ready for his next act.

"Now watch me punish her, hero girl. You did this to her by trying to save her. Look into her pretty brown eyes and see her pain. Pain you rained down on her. Fucking watch, bitch."

She sobs and I try to tell her with my eyes it'll be okay. When I hear his zipper go down, I close my eyes for a brief moment. For one second I try to grasp at Donovan. But when she starts screaming, I have to look at her.

Fire rips through me as he pushes his dick into my dry pussy. The metal ball at the end of the hook presses against his large cock through a thin membrane inside of me. This isn't the first time I've endured this type of brutalization so I breathe and focus. Anything to keep my mind off the pain.

Blue, silvery eyes.

I love you, Donovan Jayne.

"Fuck," *Logan grunts behind me and snatches a handful of my hair.* "Always such a good slave."

Amethyst is shuddering as sobs wrack through her. All I can do is pray he comes quickly. He doesn't try to get me off. His only goal is to savagely fuck me to torment her.

A few moments later and his heat fills me. My entire body relaxes in relief. He's done—he's fucking done. When he pulls out of me, he drags me by my hair and tosses me into the floor.

I can hear her screaming at him but everything is hazy and confusing. My eyes roll back in my head but I can feel him tying my knees together with rope.

I black out before I even know what he plans to do with her.

Click.

I snap out of my daze the moment the key unlocks the handcuffs. My fingers quickly release her and together, I swim us to the top. Seconds have passed but time is dripping slowly like molasses from a tipped jar. As soon as we hit the surface, I gasp for air.

"K-K-Kasper, she needs help," I chatter to him.

His strong arms steal her from my grip. The water has risen more and I can't reach the floor anymore. I'm not sure he can either because he's struggling to get her back over to the steps. Eventually he's able to set her down.

"Ames, babe, stay with me!"

Nineteen

Kasper

MY LIFE IS A LIE.
A goddamned fucking lie.

For ten years I hated a woman who just risked her life to save Amethyst. It's bullshit. All of it. And Logan has been at the root of all of it. His utter fuckedupness. His abusive, asshole, controlling ways.

I laughed.

I fucking laughed when I found out Nadia got what she deserved.

What a nightmare.

"Breathe, Ames," I murmur against her lips as I blow another huge breath into her lungs.

She makes a gurgling sound, so I quickly turn her head to the side. After a croaking cough, she spews the water she'd swallowed.

"Oh gracias a Dios," Nadia murmurs from behind me.

"Nadia," Amethyst rasps. "You're okay."

Nadia starts laughing, an incredulous look on her

face. "Yes, you loon. You're the one we were worried about. Thank God you're okay."

"Come on, the water's still rising," I grunt as I scoop Amethyst's weak body into my arms. We climb the stairs, and as soon as we emerge into the hallway, Nadia runs toward the back of the house. I wait for her to return, which she does shrugging on a robe, before we head out of the house.

We're just passing the living room headed toward the door when an infuriated voice roars at us. "Where the hell do you think you three are going?"

I snap my gaze over to lock eyes with the wild, enraged ones of Logan. He's leaned against the wall, a twelve gauge shotgun pointing at the couch, his chest heaving with fury. His face is hardly recognizable now that it's twisted into a psychotic red scowl. Kasey sits with the older boy in her lap. Donovan is next to her holding both the baby and the toddler. Both are soaked on the bottom half of their bodies. While my sister seems distraught, Donovan seems three seconds from murdering Logan with his bare hands.

"Game's over, Logan," I say through clenched teeth, wishing for my gun that's in the holster on my belt.

A guttural rattle in his throat, much like a lion about to devour his prey, echoes in the room as he stalks over to the armchair across from them to sit. "This game doesn't end until I win. I've been playing this game for a long time, Ghost. You don't get to fucking waltz in here and change the goddamned rules."

I glare at him and grit my teeth.

"Come here, son." He motions for the older boy to come to him. And shockingly enough, he yanks himself from my sister's arms and runs to Logan. Logan pulls him to his side and kisses the top of his head. "This is Taylor or Tay as the girls like to call him. He's your nephew. We named him after your best friend and 'ol Donovan's brother. Kase always had a thing for him until he blew his head off, you know."

"Enough of this." A growl rumbles from me. "You don't have to hurt anyone. Let them all go."

His eyes blacken. "Nobody is going anywhere. In fact, I want you to sit your hero bitch down right at your feet and keep your arms crossed in front of you where I can see them. And Nadia, my pet, I want you at my feet," he seethes, "where you belong."

When none of us moves, he waves the barrel of the shotgun at the couch. "What, do I need shoot their fucking brains out for you to obey one simple command?"

At that, I slowly lower a shivering Amethyst to the ground. Nadia hugs her arms to herself, water rivulets dripping from her and splashing to the floor, as she makes her way over to Logan. Once she's seated, Logan pets her. Fucking pets her.

"Perfect. Now," he says and cracks his neck. "As I was saying. If you haven't figured it out yet, I took your sister. Someone responsible had to look after her. Your dumbass stepdad traded her for sex, Kasper. Let Donovan's dad fuck her for payment. If you ask me, that shit's messed up. Taylor was smart in smothering 'ol Frank's ass."

I gape at him in shock. "You're a fucking idiot…"

"No, you're a fucking idiot. Dear old Donovan and I covered up their father's death long before Taylor killed himself. He'd asked his brother in his suicide note to come clean about it to the newspapers. To reveal how fucked up his family was. He also wanted to make sure I kept her safe. And I did. She's been safe ever since."

I tear my gaze from him and glance over at my sister. She hugs the small boy to her and her chin quivers. Last time I saw her, she had black hair. Now, her natural strawberry blonde hair is cut into a cute bob. Her face is free of makeup making her look every bit as young as she was the day she was taken. But gone is the disdain for the world. The hurt and hate for things others had taken from her. Now, my sister has purpose written all over her face.

"Did you know about this?" I choke out to Donovan.

A muscle in his neck twitches with anger. "What the fuck do you think?"

Logan laughs. "No, dumb shit didn't know I stole his precious girl right from under him. He kept sending her to me over and over again. Every time I'd see her succulent lips, I'd imagine them sucking my cock—"

"Logan, the children," Kasey hisses.

He meets her glare and has the sense to look ashamed. "Sorry, Kase. This shit just pisses me the hell off. We had a good thing going until the fucking cavalry showed up."

I roll my neck on my shoulders. My hands twitch to snatch my 9 mm and put a bullet through his skull. But I can't risk him hurting my sister.

"Anyway," Logan continues, his hand reaching out again to stroke Nadia's soaked hair. "This little doll shows up on my door step wanting to see the file I'd promised. She'd seen my tattoo in the process. Said it reminded her of one she'd seen long ago. When realization and the utter betrayal sunk in, she tried to run. But, my sweet girl here..." He yanks on her hair and she cries out. "She's got the shortest damn legs.

Never made it very far before I dragged her ass back into my
house and knocked her upside her pretty little head. That
night she finally got her wish. She found your sister."

"Stop," I cut him off. "What do you want? I'm already
tired of hearing your bullshit story time. Money? Donovan
has plenty. I'm sure he'd give you whatever the hell you need
to get out of town. You've been found out. You can't hide
all of us. Eventually, people will come looking. So what the
fuck do you want, asshole?"

He shrugs his shoulders. "I want things to go back to
the way they were before you and stepdaddy Donovan over
there and your nosy ass girlfriend started prying into my
life. I want my family safe and my fuck toy primed and always ready. That's what I want."

Nadia's gaze meets mine and she implores me with her
eyes. *I'll distract him*, she mouths. I nod slightly my understanding, pointing my focus on remaining alert.

"Junior over there isn't related to you but little Kass is
your niece. Kasey has a thing for naming her kids after the
ones she loves," Logan says with a smile and winks at my sister. If I didn't think I'd get her killed the instant I moved, I'd
have already launched myself at him. "But Junior is named
after me. Logan Baldwin, Jr. And that boy is a product of
Nadia and me. What does that make him to you, Donovan?
Your step grandson?"

Donovan's gaze is on Nadia. Hardened.

"He's not his grandson," Nadia says with a cold bite to
her voice as her eyes flicker to me and then back to the child
on the couch. "What's your name, baby? What do Mamma
and Aunt Kase call you?"

The boy looks up at my sister and she nods. "It's okay,

sweetie."

"Van."

Logan snarls. "Excuse the fuck out of me?"

A harsh laugh pierces the air and Nadia looks up at him with venom in her eyes. "That's right. He's a junior, but not yours, you psycho prick. He's Donovan Allen Jayne, II. We call him Van for short. I was pregnant when you dragged me down into that basement. Pregnant with his," she points at a shocked Donovan, "child." She glances at me once more and blinks purposefully at me. Yes.

All hell breaks loose in the next instant.

Nadia grabs the middle of the shot gun and drives it upwards. I've already drawn my gun when the blast rings out. Ignoring the fact that his weapon was just pointed at my sister, I focus on taking down the perp. He's no longer Logan, my boss. He's a psychotic, unhinged, kidnapping rapist. Nadia jerks Taylor into her arms as I tackle Logan. I drive the barrel against his throat as I wrench the shotgun from him.

There is screeching from behind me but I focus on this fucker. I'm going to paint the ceiling with his brain matter. I've made the decision to do so when someone tugs at me from behind.

"Please don't kill him, please Bubba."

Bubba.

I halt at my sister's request.

"Why the fuck not? After all he's done to you and Nadia?" I hiss.

She hugs my middle and I choke back tears.

"He's my children's father. Don't let them see that."

Logan's smug stare makes me want to do it anyway. But the image of those three kids having to witness such a horror stops me dead in my tracks. I'm an officer of the law. A good fucking cop. This ends now. And the right fucking way.

Jerking from him, with my gun still trained on him, I start barking out orders. "Donovan, get to my car and call for backup. Kasey, get the girls and the kids out of here."

She releases me and I wrestle Logan into the floor. I yank my cuffs from my belt and hook them around his wrists tight enough to make him grunt.

"You have the right to remain silent. Anything you say can and will be used against you in a court of law. You have the right to an attorney. If you cannot afford an attorney, one will be provided for you. Do you understand the rights I have just read to you? With these rights in mind, do you wish to speak to me?"

He doesn't answer after I Mirandize him but I don't give a fuck.

His life is over.

And he's going to spend the rest of it staring at the grey walls of a ten by ten cell.

Good fucking riddance.

"Thank fuck they finally got that pipe shut off," a federal agent grunts as he splashes past me. "The whole house is damn near flooded."

The Feds are crawling all over the crime scene. Normally, I'd have my panties in a wad over the whole ordeal, but after what Stokes told me, I hardly trust anyone. Well, aside from Jason Rhodes.

"I think they can wrap it up from here. You've all given your statements. It's probably best if you take my sister-in-law and get the hell out of here before she falls asleep standing up," Rhodes says with a grunt.

He was the first person I called. It was him who called the Feds rather than bringing in our own people. The case is too close to home and I wasn't willing to risk any evidence disappearing in case Logan had any other minions on his payroll.

"Thanks, man. And have them check this out." I hand him the key to the storage unit and tell him the number. He nods before heading back over to the lead investigator.

I step outside to search for my family. Two ambulances are parked in the driveway. The EMT is checking over everyone, but so far, nobody seems hurt too badly. Thank fucking God. Amethyst has her arm wrapped around my sister's shoulder and is whispering things to her. The sight is one I'd like to see more of. It cracks through my black, hardened heart and kick starts it to life. All of the hate I'd armored it with flicks away like weathered paint, until it all blows away.

When I look over at the other ambulance, Donovan has the boy—his boy—sitting on his hip as he regards Nadia with an intense gaze. I guess Ames knew what she was talking about after all. The love. I see it one hundred fucking percent right now. With a sigh, I stride over to Nadia.

"Thank you."

She lifts her gaze to mine and she smiles. "You're welcome. I had it handled."

I scratch at my jaw and raise an eyebrow at her. "You did. I'm sorry I…" I trail off as I try to regain my composure.

My chest aches with sorrow. The things I tried to do to her. To hurt her. Hell, I even tried to fuck her all to get even. It's goddamned sickening to think about.

She shakes her head with tears in her eyes and throws her arms around me. "Shhh, we'll talk about this later. Okay? Get them all home and take care of them until then. I promise we can discuss this at another time."

I squeeze her once more before I release her. Bending over, I place a soft kiss on her forehead. I'll right this wrong one day. It might take weeks or month or years, but I'll make it up to sweet Nadia Jayne for paying such a huge sacrifice for my sister. That, I can bet money on.

When I step away from her, I regard Donovan. His smug, all-business exterior is gone. The wind tousles his messy hair and dark bags are forming beneath his eyes. I feel sorry for the guy—to learn he's a father the same day we barely rescue the love of his life from Logan's dark clutches.

"He looks just like you," I say with a smile and attempt to joke to lighten the mood. "Poor guy. Only thing we can hope for is he has your taste in music."

He presses a kiss to the boy's head and his eyes are rimmed in red. I've never seen him so vulnerable. Right now, he reminds me so much of his brother, Taylor. My best friend who took his life all too soon.

"Thanks, kid," he mutters and juts his hand out to me.

I shake it brusquely before leaving them to get back to my sister.

"Come here," I say with a grunt and tug her into my arms.

She hugs me tight. Her body is tense and I rub at her back to relax her. After a few moments, she breaks down.

Sobs wrack through her as she lets go of a decade's worth of pain.

"I'm so sorry, little bit. So fucking sorry."

Twenty

Nadia

WHEN I EMERGE FROM THE SHOWER, A TOWEL wrapped around my body, I find Donovan asleep with Van in his arms on the couch. Those two took to each other rather quickly. I think it helped that ever since he was born on a rug in a basement, delivered by Logan and Kasey, I would whisper tales of his heroic daddy named Donovan Jayne. Van knew from the get-go he was to be polite to Logan but that he wasn't his father. So when I introduced Donovan as his real daddy, he was thrilled to finally meet him.

And Donovan, once the shock wore off, has only focused on making up for lost time. For two days now, he's stayed glued to our boy's side. I told him if he caters to our two-year-old's every whim, he was going to spoil him rotten. Donovan just laughed me off and said he didn't care.

I sit on the coffee table and watch them. Both of them look so peaceful. Kasey kept her promise to me and I kept my promise to her. I'd had to do the unthinkable. Renounce

my child for Logan. To convince him I wanted more than to
be trapped in a basement with a kid stuck to my hip. I told
him I couldn't stand being down there. Kasey and I came
up with the plan to tell him it was postpartum depression.
As soon as Van was born, we planned and plotted. It was
during one faked suicide attempt, that Logan finally took
me to a doctor outside of Aspen. She'd taken one look at us
and asked him to step outside—that it was her practice to
see her patients without an audience. I didn't expose him—
that would be a threat to Kasey, Taylor, and my son's life.
Instead, I had her implant me with a birth control device
and begged her for a low-dose medication for my supposed
depression.

Then, I worked my magic on Logan.

While he was at work, I played the parts for the cameras
in the basement showing how depressed I was but would
hold my baby at night and whisper sweet nothings to him.
I told him stories of his real father and promised I'd get him
out of there one day.

One day, several months ago, Logan took me upstairs
much to both Kasey and my surprise. He was drunk and
horny. Kasey always had a way about making him feel bad
about doing anything sexual around the kids. It was my opportunity and we pounced on it.

That day, I begged, pleaded, and pretty much forced
him into keeping me upstairs. I cleaned and cooked. I
sucked his cock like I was starved for it. I played a role just
for him. Eventually, he liked me up there. Late at night, he'd
question why I didn't love our child or why I hated Kasey.
I'd simply shown him how much more I loved him instead.

He thought I was crazy.

Crazy for him.

But every time he'd bring a tray of food downstairs to have a meal with his family, I'd slip notes to Kasey underneath the rubber mat on the tray written inside a folded napkin.

I'm getting him to fall for me.

We made progress.

I met your brother. He's perceptive. I can work with this.

Your brother knows something's up. Thank God!

He keeps kissing me. I hate leading him on but it's necessary.

Donovan knows I'm here. I nearly died having to send him away. I'm broken.

Logan made love to me in the shower. The fucking fool is falling for it!!

Kiss my son and tell him I love him. God, I love him.

Kasper's girlfriend saw Logan hurting me. Almost there, Kase...

The plan moved slowly forward. Piece by piece, we were able to position ourselves. With enough people taking notice, and Kasper's keen detective skills on our side, eventually it would all come to a head. And it did.

We made it to the other side. Alive. And with our children in tow.

"We're going house hunting this weekend. I hate having to make him sleep in that portable crib. He's too big for it. It doesn't even look comfortable," Donovan murmurs, dragging me from my thoughts.

I smile and scoop my sleeping baby into my arms. His mop of dark, thick hair is one of my favorite things about him. But when he opens his eyes and peers at me with those silvery blue orbs like his daddy's, I simply melt for him. "He'll be okay until then. I promise."

Kissing my son's forehead, I make my way over to his bed. Once I've tucked him in, I find Donovan standing in the doorway with his arms crossed. A smoldering look on his face has my entire body igniting with need. It's been two days since we were rescued from that animal, and I think Donovan has been afraid to touch me. Meanwhile, I'm desperate to connect with my love. To erase the past with Logan once and for all.

"It makes me crazy fucking insane to try and wrap my head around all of this, baby," he says with disgust in his voice. "To think, this whole time I could have…I should have…"

Shaking my head, I make my way over to him and slide my palms up his chest, stopping him from saying any more. He's wearing a simple white T-shirt and it fits him well. I've been dying to tear it off of him all night. "Listen to me right now, Donovan Jayne. I love you. And not once have I ever felt disappointed by you. It was you," I murmur and stand on my toes to kiss his soft lips, "that kept me going. Your memories. Our love. Tu, mí amor."

His eyes close and he looks up at the ceiling. I run my fingertips along his Adam's apple as he swallows. He's having a hard time keeping it together emotionally. I've caught him on several occasions with tears in his eyes.

"Donovan," I say as I kiss his throat. "You can't punish yourself any longer for this. Neither of us can. It's our turn now, remember? It's time to let this go."

He tilts his head down to me and a million emotions flicker in his eyes. Regret. Sadness. Fury. Longing. Desperation. Sexual hunger. Love. "He nearly broke you. If he would have killed you…"

I press my thumb to his lips to keep him from finishing that thought. "Make love to me. I want to replace the pain within me with you."

His fingers tangle into my wet hair and he groans before his lips meet mine. Hungrily, he devours me. Our tongues duel each other but his is winning. Owning. Claiming. Marking. I let him take the control he so desperately needs. When I let out a moan, he tugs away from me. His glare confuses me for a minute.

"What?"

He runs his fingers through his hair and gives me a pained look. "I'm afraid I can't be careful with you. What if I do something you don't like? That reminds you of *him*?" He says the last part with a vicious hiss.

I yank at the towel and toss it to the ground. Then, I grab his hand and guide him into our bedroom. Under the bright light, I let him see. His furious, heartbroken eyes take in each and every scar Logan Baldwin put on me. "These bruises will fade. The cuts will heal. And the emotional damage will be dealt with over time. But you can't hurt me, stupid man. You're the only one who can help me. If I haven't broken already, I'm not ever going to break."

His hand reaches out and his touch flutters over a bruise on my breast. Then, he leans forward and kisses it. I let out a happy sigh when his tongue flicks out. He runs the tip of his tongue over the sore bruise and then teases my nipple. I'm craving him desperately.

But I know, just like me, he'll have his own demons to sort out. I'll give him what he needs so that we may move forward and leave the past behind us. At last. I thread my fingers in his hair when he moves over to my other nipple. His teeth gently graze the flesh causing me to suck in a harsh breath of air.

"Did I hurt you?" he murmurs against my flesh, his hot breath tickling me.

I laugh. "Quite the opposite. You're driving me wild, handsome. Te necesito." *I need you.*

He rises back up to his full height, regarding me with narrowed eyes. I love being under his scrutiny. Like I'm some never-before-seen creature that needs understanding. That I'm a hypnotic drug. Rare. Precious even. I want to be the only one who he'll ever look at this way with a beautiful mixture of lust, love, and undeniable attraction.

His fingers find the bottom of his T-shirt and he peels it effortlessly from his body revealing a nicely sculpted chest for a forty-five year old man. Donovan has aged well and doesn't look a day over thirty-five to me. He's every bit as sexy as the day he stormed into our lives. After he tosses his shirt and begins working at his belt, I can't help but think about Mamá. She'd found Donovan *for me.* Played a masterful game of deception that could have backfired drastically *for me.* Because of her desire for me to be happy and successful, she plotted *for me.* When she gets back from her cruise, I'm going to have a long sit down with her. I'll explain to her everything that's happened. There'll be tears but then I will present her grandson to her. A product of her unconventional matchmaking. A child created in love.

"You're smiling. What're you thinking about?" he questions, his voice husky and deep.

I chew on my lip and let my eyes scan over his perfect

body—strong and filled out in all the right places. His cock hangs thick and alert. Eager to be inside of me. A shiver of delight runs through me. "Just thinking about Mamá. How she's going to freak out once she realizes she has a grandson."

He chuckles and raises an eyebrow at me. "We'll never get to see him again. She'll fatten up our boy with her choripan con chimichurri and keep him all to herself."

When we stop laughing, our eyes meet, both hungry for the other. I don't get a word out before he pounces. His hands grip my ass and he lifts me, carrying me straight for the bed. We fall together, my head bouncing once before his mouth is back on mine.

I've missed this.

So fucking badly.

"I thought about you every second of every single day," he growls against my lips before nipping the flesh of the bottom one. "Always you, baby."

His dick slides against my bare pussy causing me to whimper and mewl like a little kitten. I need him inside of me like yesterday.

"Donovan…"

"I'm going to fuck you and suck you and devour every goddamned inch of your body. Once I take you, there's no going back. You're mine forever," he tells me, his voice deep, dark, and delicious.

"Forever," I agree, my words a breathless promise.

His cock pushes against my slick opening and then he drives all the way into me. I start to cry out but he silences me with a kiss deep enough to steal my soul. With Donovan, he can have it. It belongs to him anyway.

"So beautiful. So fucking beautiful," he coos as he thrusts into me, brutally and uneven. No rhyme or reason to his lovemaking. Just desire and need and love guiding his body.

I melt at his touch and his tender words. With every pound into me, I soak up his love. I can feel him in my nerve endings. My every thought. My heart.

His teeth nip at my lip again causing me to cry out. I want him nipping at me everywhere. My neck and ears and tits. Everywhere all at once. He's too much and not enough. It drives me insane with need.

"Donovan…"

He pulls away from our kiss and rests on his palms on either side of my head caging me in. Our eyes meet as he thrusts slowly, almost lazily into me. I love the intensity he stares at me with. That although his gaze is heated and borderline scary with need, the love and protectiveness over me shines through, comforting me.

"I'm fucking you, Nadia Jayne. It will always be me."

I nod and stare into his beautiful orbs that let me peek at his good soul. If I were capable, I'd climb inside of him and cocoon myself with his love.

"Touch your clit while I fuck you. I want to watch you come all over my dick, pretty girl."

His words ignite a match within me and I eagerly slide my fingers between us. My sensitive bundle of nerves is throbbing with the need to come and I'm all too happy to help out the cause. Me, touching myself, while he devours me with his hungry gaze has me soon writhing beneath him.

"Look at me when you come, beautiful. Say my name

when you do it." His commands are breathy and hoarse. He's barely hanging on by a thread. I crave to yank at it and unravel him forever.

"Oh, God," I murmur as the exhilarating sensation of an orgasm born by love begins to spread like wildfire.

"Say. My. Name," he grunts, his thrusting becoming more powerful.

"Donovan!"

The second I cry out his name, I am sucked into the vortex of an all-body consuming orgasm. Years of stress and pain, melt away as pleasure and love whip around me. His heat floods through me as he too loses himself and his thrusting slows until he all but collapses on my weakened body. We lie conjoined, our bodily fluids mixing together as if they were created to do so, and remain motionless. Our heavy breathing is the only indication we're both still alive and here on this earth.

"Te amo." My words are soft and but a whisper.

But he hears them.

Even with time and space and questions separating us, I felt like he always heard me, especially during the worst of times. Times I'd been a victim of Logan's brutality. It was always Donovan cutting through the haze of my hate and pain. He was the voice of reason. My comfort. My sanctity.

"I love you too, baby," he murmurs, his face buried somewhere in my hair.

I smile and run my fingernails up and down his shoulders.

"Donovan?"

He lifts up and regards me with a lazy smile I want to lick. "Yeah?"

"Will you marry me?"

His laughter fills the room and warms my soul. "Crazy girl, you're not supposed to be the one asking."

I pout when he slides out of my body and climbs off the bed. His ass, all firm curves and muscle, tightens as he strides over to the dresser in the room. He opens it and retrieves a small blue box I recognize as Tiffany's. I'm going insane with need to see what's inside but he disappears into the bathroom. When he returns, the box is gone but he's carrying a wet cloth. He's already wiped himself clean so when he sits down on the edge of the bed, he gently wipes away any remnants of our lovemaking from me.

I'm antsy and can't sit still any longer. "What was in the box?"

He flashes me a smile. "Before you disappeared, I bought you this." His palm reveals a dainty solitaire diamond ring. It's not flashy or gaudy but it's not small by any means. It seems perfect.

"You held on to it all this time? Without knowing if I'd ever come back?" I question with tears welling in my eyes.

He grasps my hand and slides it on my ring finger. "I knew if I could ever get my hands on you, you'd let me put this ring on you too. Just had to find you first." His wink has my heart fluttering around in my chest.

I admire the ring and beam at him. "I love it. But…"

He scowls and it's so cute. "But what?"

"Won't people think we're crazy? You marrying your stepdaughter? Like you used to worry about?"

His hand tugs mine and he brings it to his lips. He kisses the knuckle above the ring he just gave me. "Fuck those people. Since when do we care? It's always been the Donovan and Nadia show. If they can't accept us, they can fuck off."

I sit up on my knees and attack him with a kiss. I'm straddling him with him inside of me again before my next breath.

"Fuck me, Daddy," I tease with a wicked glint in my eyes. "And then tomorrow take me to the courthouse and marry me."

He slaps my ass with both palms and urges me to ride him faster. His teeth find my tit and he bites down. When I moan, he chuckles. "Anything for you, dirty girl."

I fucking love Donovan Jayne.

Twenty-One

Kasper

A LOT CAN CHANGE IN THREE WEEKS. IN MY LIFE, *everything* changed. The dark burden I've carried for nearly ten long years has been lifted. Every single day, I find *her*, my sweet baby sis, in my kitchen cooking breakfast. I still have to rub the sleep out of my eyes and pinch myself to make sure I'm not dreaming.

"Uncle Kasper? Can you stay home and play Minecraft with me?" Tay questions from the bar while he watches his mother flip bacon.

I walk over to him and ruffle his light brown hair. He's a cute little kid, even if he does look mostly like Logan and is a painful fucking reminder of what transpired to bring him into this world. Kase hasn't recounted what happened in detail to me, but I've read her testimony. Rape. Torture. Physical abuse. All things Nadia suffered from as well. Although, once Nadia came along, my sister was spared from almost all of that.

A pang of guilt washes over me. I still haven't spoken to

Nadia like I want. There's so much I need to say to her.

"Sorry, little man. I'm swamped up at the station. Maybe you, your mom, and your sister could come visit me for lunch, though. We could go to that diner you like so much where the chicken nuggets are shaped like dinosaurs."

He shrugs his shoulders. "Will Ames be there?"

My heart swells at the mention of my girlfriend, that's what she is despite her eagerness to not "label" what we are. "She meets me every day. I know she'll be glad to see you again. When I talked to her on the phone last night, she said she had a geode for you."

His nose scrunches up. "What's a geode?"

"It's a rock. Kind of ugly on the outside but beautiful on the inside. She says it's purple. Do you like purple?"

He nods, a toothy grin spreading across his cute face.

"Eat up, sweetie," Kase says and sets a plate full of scrambled eggs with a side of fruit and bacon in front of him.

When he starts eating, she finds her way into my arms. I hug her to me. My sister is finally here. After all this time, I'm still completely fucked in the head over this.

"Any plans for the day, little bit?" I question, my voice hoarse with emotion.

She nods and pulls away to dish up more food on a plate. "Mom is going to come over and see the kids for a bit. She looks better than I remember."

"Now that Dale's out of the picture, she's finally getting her life put back together."

I accept the plate and sit down to eat. We're all quiet, each of us lost in thought. I've made sure Kase and Tay have been put into counseling—the best our city has to offer thanks to Donovan. They go twice a week and I hope it's helping. Tay seems like your typical seven-year-old. But Kase sometimes walks around with a glazed over look in her eyes.

If I ever speak out against Logan, she completely shuts down. Ames tells me you can't help who you love…even if that person is a psycho prick. And unfortunately Kase loved Logan in some warped way. He did father her two children but I don't see how she feels anything in her heart for him.

Once breakfast is over and I've kissed them all good-bye, I head out to my Camaro. Again, thanks to Donovan, I haven't been bombarded by the media or nosy citizens. Apparently, his umbrella of protection really does cover my family too. When our story first hit the news, this town was a goddamned circus. But Donovan coordinated a one-day media event with CNN. He and Nadia handled the interviews, giving the media something to sink their teeth into, which kept them away from my family. All requests and correspondence goes through him. In a nutshell, they all stay the fuck away from me, my sister, her kids, and my girlfriend. I'm not complaining and am thankful for Nadia's bravery.

Today, the air is extra brisk. A snow storm is on the horizon. Tay's never seen snow so I'm hoping he'll get his wish.

I sink into my seat and fumble with my music. Once I've turned on "Free Bird" by Lynyrd Skynyrd, I put my car in drive and cruise toward the station. It still feels weird sitting in Logan's office. I'm interim Chief until Mayor Dunaway officially appoints the position to me. With good music starting my day, the drive to the station is a quick yet relaxing one. The stress I used to carry with me is no longer present. Soon, I'm hustling into the building to escape the freezing ass wind.

"Mr. Jayne is waiting to see you," Lena says as I enter.

I nod my head and stride down the hallway. Sure enough, Donovan leans against the doorframe of my office. "Hey man," I say as I unlock my door. "What's up? Any word from Logan's attorney?"

Our biggest concern is Logan tearing the lid off what happened with Frank's death and the cover up that followed. Since Logan broke federal laws that also implicated some local judges and his case is such a high profile one, the Supreme Court took the case. He's being held in a maximum-security penitentiary in Florence, Colorado until his hearing. With five counts of kidnapping, five counts of attempted murder, two counts of non-consensual sexual acts using violence or force including non-consensual sex with a minor, multiple counts of racketeering, and the countless laws he broke while in his employment as a government official, he'll no doubt be put away for life. Donovan and I both hope they'll execute him by lethal injection but our attorney says he hasn't done anything hefty enough to warrant that judgment.

"Actually," he grunts as he follows me into the office. "Yes."

I shed my coat and then take my seat. "What is it?" Anxiety swells in my chest. Donovan has the best attorney this side of the US but I still worry. He doesn't deserve to go to prison. Nadia and Van need him.

He tugs a folded piece of paper from his pocket and pushes it toward me. I frown as I pick it up to read it. The outside has Donovan's name scrawled in Logan's familiar handwriting.

> *Donovan,*
>
> *I know you don't understand my reasons and you hate me for everything I did to the woman you love. I'm not about to explain myself to you or anyone else. But, I'm betting you're sweating it right now. Wondering what I will tell them about the past. Here's the deal... We may not be friends right now. And we certainly haven't been for a while. Yet, that night, you were my brother. That night, I'd have done anything for you. I did do everything for you. I have no regrets and like we vowed outside Len's Tatt shop all those years ago, we take it to our grave. My tattoo reminds me each day of that. Just like your brother's name we both have inked on us. You have my word.*
>
> **Harmony after annihilation.**
>
> *I hope you have finally found the harmony you had your sights set on. Please take care of my children. And Kasey is your responsibility now. Look after her. Taylor would have wanted you to carry that torch since I'm no longer able to.*
> *PS – I never would have allowed them to drown...*
> *Logan*

I read the note three more times before I look up at him. His jaw clenches and his eyes darken.

"I guess we have our answer," I say with a huff. "But my sister isn't some burden. I'll take care of her, Donovan. You have your hands full with your family."

He carefully folds the letter once I give it back to him and tucks it in his front pocket. "I will always make sure you guys are taken care of. That's what family does for one another."

I laugh and can imagine Taylor looking down on us with a triumphant smile on his face. "Is that what we are? We're one big pretty fucked up family then, huh?"

He chuckles. "That we are."

"It's snowing!" a cheery voice chirps from my doorway.

I lift my gaze and lock eyes with Nadia's molten chocolate ones. I've never seen the girl smile so much in her life. She's happy. Truly fucking happy. And that makes my heart swell.

"Tay's going to be thrilled," I say as I stand and grab my coat. "Do you care if I steal your wife for coffee?"

Donovan darts a questioning look at Nadia and she nods.

"Just drop her off at the lodge when you guys are done. I have some work to get caught up on," he agrees.

He draws her to him and kisses her lips so gently, as if he thinks she's made of glass. Their love is thick and palpable and fills the space around us. A month ago, I'd have said it was perverted and sick, considering their age difference and what he was to her when he was married to her mother. But like Ames says, they're in love. And I'm jealous of that kind of love. I wonder if Amethyst and I will have anything remotely as intense one day. With the way things ignite anytime we're near each other, I'd say we have a pretty good shot.

"Coffee, huh?" Nadia questions as I usher her out the door. "Is this where you kidnap me? I've gotta say…been there, done that. You'll have to do better than that."

I roll my eyes. "Not funny."

She laughs as we head to my car and I find myself laughing too. Once we get inside my warm car, I hand her my iPhone.

"Play something good," I say with a growl.

She bites the end of her glove and tugs it from her hand. As if she knows which song she's searching for, she scrolls down through my selection. This. Our love for the same kind of music. That's Donovan's doing. He pushed that shit on everyone.

Carly Simon's husky voice fills the car as she sings "You're So Vain." I cut my eyes to Nadia and her face is bright red as she giggles. She forces me to endure her over the top, loud-ass, off-key singing of that song as she uses the iPhone as her microphone to sing it to me the entire way to the coffee shop. When it ends, I flip her off.

"You're a dick."

She swats at me. "I learned it from watching you."

We both smirk as I pull into the Mocha Bean, a quaint little coffee shop on Main Street. This is what's so weird between us. I like her. I truly like her. She's funny and self-less. When Kase breaks down crying, Nadia is over at my apartment in like eight minutes flat. I can't help but love her for how she loves my sister. Their friendship had been brief and budding that first day before Kasey was taken but they picked right back up the day Nadia was forced down into that basement too. Their bond is tighter than mine and Kase's is and we're siblings. I'm thankful for Nadia. So fuck-ing thankful.

Once we're settled on a low comfy couch with a steamy

cup of coffee each, I turn to regard her. She's so serene and settled. It's a good look on her. Her wedding ring glistens in the warm light. I still can't believe she and Donovan went down to the courthouse and got married a couple of weeks ago on a whim. It was a surprise to everyone.

"Where's Van?" I question.

She beams. Pride and adoration paint her pretty features. "With Mamá. She came over to the lodge this morning so Donovan and I could run some errands. He loves her so much."

I grin back at her. Guilt, the ever present emotion, though, floods through me. Letting out a sigh, I narrow my eyes at her. "Nadia, we need to talk."

She pats my knee and sets her mug down. "Water under the bridge, Kasper."

I shake my head and run my fingers through my hair in frustration. "No, we need to talk about this. I'm sorry. For everything. I hated you for so long. Blamed you for something that was out of your control. It was fucked up. I'm fucked up."

Her gaze hardens and she purses her lips together. "Your sister was stolen from you and I was the only witness. It's understandable."

I huff and set my mug down on the table beside hers. Taking her hand in mine, I squeeze it gently. "It was over the top. I turned into a fucking monster. Every day I thought up new ways to fuck up your life. To ruin you. Hell, I even tried to use you for sex. Don't you see what an asshole I was?"

She arches up a dark eyebrow and smirks. "Was?"

I chuckle and roll my eyes. "I'm being serious. I kissed you. Put my hands on you. It wasn't right, Nadia. I took advantage of you."

"You weren't the only one with guilt. When Kasey and I plotted on how we'd get out of our prison, we discussed in great detail how we'd involve you. I was prepared to sleep with you and make you fall in love with me if it meant you finding a way to get us out of there. We all played parts that we're ashamed of."

I groan. "I just feel so stupid. So fucking blind."

"It is what it is. I have only ever loved one man and you only carried hate for me. It would have been awkward and weird even if we had gotten the chance. Luckily, you're good at your job and put together the pieces before I was forced to see your 'monster.' That's Ames' cross to bear, thank God."

Heat floods through me. I'm going to kill my girlfriend. "What the fuck, Nadia?"

She bursts into a fit of giggles earning us a glare from a college student studying at another seating area. "Who names their cock 'monster' anyway? Is it hideous or something?"

I yank my phone out and text Ames.

Me: You're in so much fucking trouble, Lames.

When Nadia finally calms down, she sips her coffee and turns her twinkling brown eyes on me. "Thank you, Kasper. Thanks for seeing past your hate for me and being open to a bigger, invisible story. Without that, I could still be under Logan's hateful thumb and they would still be down there." Her smile falls and tears well in them. "You saved us. So quit your shit about feeling guilty. You're my friend and if Donovan ends up traveling next month for an acquisition in California, I'm going to need someone to go see Aerosmith with. I can't even take my best friend. Kasey likes country.

Country!"

We both shudder at that dirty word.

"Okay," I extend my hand to her.

"When we leave here, it stays. Got it?"

I nod. "Got it."

My phone chimes while we shake and when she lets go, I pick it up.

Ames: Apparently your monster's reputation has gotten out... Jason works tonight. Maybe you should stop by and give me a spanking. I'll cook your favorite. :)

Me: I want you bare assed and ready.

Tay got his wish. It snowed and I got a kick out of all the pictures Kasey sent to my phone throughout the afternoon. My heart is full having her back in my life with her two kiddos in tow.

I shiver as I trudge through the snow up Jason's front steps. Amethyst has been looking for an apartment but is staying with her brother-in-law until that time comes. We've hardly found any moments alone in the last few weeks. A stolen quickie here or there. But tonight is all ours.

When I raise my hand to knock on the door, it swings open. My beautiful blonde stands there looking sinful as hell. Her wispy hair has been braided into two schoolgirl braids on either side of her face. She's makeup free tonight except for a pink, shimmery lip gloss that coats her full lips. But it's her outfit that makes me crazy. Her lips tug into a grin as she spins for me to see. And boy do I see.

"Don't you think that skirt's a little short, missy?" I say with a growl. It's a red and black flannel pleated skirt with a buckle on the side. The damn material barely covers her ass. Her white knee socks are sexy as fuck. She's a naughty girl.

Her cheeks tinge pink and she flutters her eyelashes at me innocently. "Oops."

My gaze falls to her white button up shirt that's been undone to reveal her pert tits spilling out of a black bra. I'm seconds away from ripping the damn thing off of her. When she shivers, I remember it's cold as fuck out here and she's barely wearing anything.

I stomp the snow off my shoes on the porch before coming inside. Once I've kicked off my boots and shed my coat, I gather her into my arms. She smells like garlic from the lasagna I know she's cooking.

"I missed you, beautiful." I bury my nose against her neck and taste her soft flesh. She lets out a needy moan that sets my body on fire with desire.

"I missed you too, Kaspy."

With a smile, I nip at her flesh and feel her tit up through her shirt. "I talked to Nadia today. Apologized for everything. But you know that already don't you? Since you two seem to share...everything."

She giggles which makes me growl. Pulling away from her, I snatch her wrist and then guide her into the living room.

"Time for that spanking I owe you."

She squeals when I push her over the back of the couch and shove up her skirt. Sure enough, she's bare beneath the fabric. If I know my girl, she's probably dripping with want too. I slip my finger between her thighs and push it into her pussy. A moan escapes her and my finger slips right in. So wet. I start fucking her with it until she's squirming and about to come. Then, I pop it out of her.

"How do you feel?" I question, my voice low.

She whines. "Unsatisfied."

I grin and smack her ass. "Good. Are you going to kiss and tell anymore, Lames?"

She wiggles and shrieks. "No! I swear!"

Smacking her once more, I revel in the way her pale ass turns bright red in the shape of my big hand. "Beg for me to fuck you."

I push my finger back inside her and she moans. "Fuck me, Kaspy!"

God, she's so fucking cute. Only she could get away with calling me something so stupid at a time like this. When she's about to lose control once more, I pull my finger from her and yank at the buckle on my belt. As soon as my dick is out and sheathed in a condom, I tease her opening with it. "Say you want my monster."

She giggles so I smack her ass again. "I want your monster, caveman."

Grasping my thick cock, I drive into her hard and fast. This is what she and I do. We fuck like a couple of horny cavepeople when we get the chance. It's not long before she's coming all over my dick and I'm exploding inside of her.

"I miss her."

Her fingertips tickle over the hair on my chest in her dark bedroom. I cover her hand with mine and draw it to my lips to kiss her palm. "I know you do, babe."

She's quiet for a few minutes before she speaks again. "I feel guilty some days. Her life was stolen from her and here I'm just finding mine. It doesn't seem fair. I should have been the one to die that night, not my sister and her little girl."

A growl thunders in the room as I roll on top of her naked body. I press my lips to hers and run my fingers through her hair. "Don't say shit like that, Ames."

She sniffles and I swipe away a hot tear as it slides down her cheek. "I told you I'd be no good at this relationship thing."

"Shhh," I coo against her lips as I begin pressing kisses on her flesh to her throat. "You're perfect. And you're mine."

Her entire body stiffens. "I don't belong to anyone, Kasper. We're just having fun."

My cock twitches in agreement with the fun part. I spread her thighs apart and tease the tip of it as I slide between the lips of her pussy. "You belong to me. We're most definitely having fun but you belong to me."

She lets out a kitten-like growl of protest but it dies in her throat when I push my dick into her slowly. We don't go slow, she and I. We're always in a needy, eager rush to come. But right now, I want her to feel how we belong together.

"You make me a better person, Ames. From the moment I saw you in that airport, I've been tethered to you by some invisible rope. I have only ever been under that dark cloud of bitter hate. But then you showed up, tugged on that rope, and brought me into your light. You made me want to shine right along with you. Together we make rainbows. Don't you see?"

She starts to sob. "Y-Y-You'd choose now to be sweet and make me cry."

I suck on her bottom lip and then bite her gently before pulling back away. All the while, I thrust into her with slow, even movements. "I don't want to make you cry. I want to make you fucking happy, woman."

Her fingers thread into my hair and she smiles. I don't have to see it in this dark room because I can feel it in my soul. "You *do* make me happy."

Sliding a hand between us, I massage her clit. Her small gasps of pleasure ignite a raging fire within me. "And I'll continue to make you happy. I don't want to mess what we have up. I need you to tell me if I'm fucking things up. Promise, Lames?"

Her body quivers as her orgasm nears. "You're not fucking things up."

Closing my eyes, I groan when my balls draw up as I start to come. She lets out a moan as her climax overtakes her. Her sweet pussy clenches around me and forces out my own release.

"That was different," she whispers, her fingertips drawing circles on my shoulder blades. "Good different."

I smile and press a kiss to the corner of her mouth. "It was different because I just made love to you. Because I do love you. I love you a whole fucking lot."

She chuckles and lets out a ragged sigh. I don't miss the sadness and guilt her voice but there's a hint of hope too. A hope of a happy future. With me. "I love you and your monster a whole lot too, Kaspy."

My heart aches and bleeds but in the best kind of way. This is what love feels like. This is where any lingering hate

at myself for what I've done completely dissolves away. I'm
light now. Cloaked in her warmth. I am floating. Like a goddamned ghost, go figure.

I'm finally fucking free.

Epilogue

Donovan

Two years later...

"NEED ANY HELP?" I QUESTION FROM THE DOORWAY of our open-plan kitchen. This kitchen is what sold us. Well, Nadia at least. I was sold on her smile when she saw it. Knew right then I'd buy it for her on the spot if she wanted me to.

"You can pull out the ensalada de pepinos," she says absently as she stirs the sauce on the stovetop.

Today she's fucking glorious in a fitted sweater dress that shows off all her delicious curves. Every delicious curve. If we didn't have company chatting it up in the next room, I'd already be balls deep inside her. When it comes to my wife, I'm a man possessed. Insatiable when all I want to do is devour her completely.

"Everything okay, beautiful?"

She turns to regard me, a smile gracing her lips. My eyes skim over her plunging neckline that reveals her gorgeous breasts. Nadia's pregnancy tits are what porn stars dream of having. Full, supple, bitable as hell. All mine. Her belly is round and I go crazy if I don't get to touch it at least seven hundred times a day. Like now, I'm already reaching for her. To connect with my daughter—a healthy, bouncing baby girl inside.

"Everything's perfect."

And I believe her. Our lives have gone from confusing and heartbreaking and uncertain to fulfilling, joyful, and whole. My family is my entire fucking life.

"Why don't you go and sit down?" Selene's voice chirps from behind me. "I can finish up in here. You look exhausted, mi hijo."

Nadia flashes her mother a relieved smile. Those two are inseparable. I was sure when Nadia finally confronted her about what Selene had done for her, there would have been claws and tears. Instead, my brave wife thanked her mother. Told her how much she appreciated the sacrifices she made in her own life to ensure the happiness of her daughter. Selene told her she'd do it again in a heartbeat if it meant Nadia would have the full life she has now. I'll forever be grateful for Selene's unconventional ways that brought my love from halfway across the world and into my heart.

"Come on," I say as I wink at Selene. I grasp Nadia's hand and guide her into the living room where our guests are shooting the shit.

"Mamma!" Van shouts from the floor where he and Tay and Kass are playing. "Unkie Jason showed me how to wiggle my ears."

She laughs and starts for him, but I pull her back to me to steal a kiss.

"Don't you two ever quit?" Kasper groans. "Ow!"

I grin at his fiancée, Amethyst, who's just slapped him upside the head. When Nadia walks away, I glance over at Kasey. My wife's best friend. Those two have spent hours on the phone crying, whispering, and screaming in the past two years. Together, they work out the hate they had for Logan but they also talk so openly about forgiveness. That, I struggle with. How they can forgive a man who took so much from them. I'm still tender from the place where he tried to cut my heart right from my body. To think that someone who I trusted and damn near loved like a brother was capable of the sick shit he did. And he even justified it in his goddamned head. Some nights, I toss and turn trying to make sense of it. Forgiveness isn't even on the table as far as I'm concerned.

"Hey, Donovan," Kasper says as he stands and strides over to me. "Can I talk to you for a second?"

I nod and wave for him to follow me into my office. We both step over Van's trike that sits in the doorway and sit down in the two chairs opposite my desk.

"What's up?"

His features harden and he scowls. "Kasey's gone to see him."

"Who?" I demand with a growl.

"Logan. And Rhodes went with her. What the hell is up with that?" He scrubs his face with his palm in frustration.

"Closure maybe?"

He shakes his head. "It wasn't the first time. In fact, she goes about once a month. She told me she wants her children to know him. When I blew a gasket, she informed me this was her life and her decision. I swear, you'd think I was trying to be her damn father or some shit. I'm just worried that she's in love with Logan or something."

I think about how I walked in on Jason and Kasey in a more-than-friendly embrace last weekend. In fact, his tongue was down her throat. There's no doubt in my mind she's moving on from her past.

"Fighting with her about it won't solve a damn thing. Believe me. Nadia and I have come to blows about this shit over the past two years. You just have to give her the space to make her own decisions. Trust me."

He grumbles but nods. "I guess. Did Nadia tell you the news about Ames?"

I smirk when a shit eating grin spreads across his face. "That you knocked up your girlfriend?"

His laughter booms in the room. "God, there's no keeping any fucking secrets between those three women."

Scratching at my jawline with a fingertip, I narrow my eyes and regard him seriously. "You know, Jason's a good guy."

He picks at a piece of lint on his sweater and considers my words. "Apparently he's the best. He's known as Lieutenant Rhodes now," he says with a sarcastic drawl.

"Technically he's the second best," I reply with a wicked grin, "Chief."

He groans. "I hate that title."

"But not the job."

"No, not the job. The job's badass, getting to tell everyone what to do. But that title reminds me of…"

Our eyes meet and we both frown.

"Dinner's ready," Jason's voice booms from the doorway. "Nadia sent me to get you."

Kasper stands and strides over to him, the trike the only thing between them. "Hey you, be straight with me, man. Are you sleeping with Kase?"

Jason's jaw drops and he cuts his eyes to mine for support. I shrug my shoulders. Not getting in the middle of that one. "I, uh… maybe you should talk to her or something—"

His words evaporate the moment Kasper grabs him by the front of the shirt and jerks him forward. Jason stumbles over the trike and looks up at Kasper as if he's lost his mind.

"Listen, Ghost—" Jason starts.

"No, you listen to me. That's my baby sis in there. You fuck her up and I fuck you up. Got it, motherfucker?" Kasper's words are a venom filled threat.

"I, uh, yes," Jason spits out, "Jesus fucking Christ. We're just taking it day by day, man."

Kasper narrows his eyes at him, doing that police shit he's so good at. After a moment of careful scrutiny, he releases Jason's collar. "Don't hurt her."

Jason growls as he straightens his shirt. "I wouldn't dare."

Little Kass interrupts their exchange from the doorway, clearly annoyed the trike is in her way. Her little button nose scrunches up and she whines. She reaches up her chubby arms for Jason. Without hesitation, he scoops her up and rescues her from the obstacle in her way. When she lays her head on his chest and rubs her eyes, Jason smiles.

"Look, man," Kasper says with a huff of resignation, shocking Jason and I both. "I'm just happy to see your ugly mug smiling again. You, after Ash and the baby. And her, after Taylor, and then that monster Logan. I just want you *both* to be happy."

"Here's to hoping." Jason nods, with a very sleepy toddler in his arms, and walks away. When he's gone, I let out a laugh.

"You're an asshole. You knew?"

He rolls his eyes. "I'm a perceptive asshole. Of course I fucking knew. I knew the moment she started dropping in for surprise visits to see me a few months ago. Kasey sees me every day. She and the kids live with me and Ames, for crying out loud. Kase didn't come to see me. Apparently she's been lusting after the good lieutenant."

I pick up the trike and move it from the doorway before turning to regard him. "You turned out okay, kid."

He slaps at my back as we start out the door. "So did you, Donovan."

Together we make our way back to our family—an unusual combination of blood, friendship, and unbreakable bonds between a group of unlikely people.

As we gather around the table, I pull Nadia into my arms with her back pressed against my chest and kiss the top of her head. Her hair smells of garlic from cooking and I want to bury my face in it. If all these people weren't here, I'd do just that. Of course we'd be naked too.

"She's kicking," Nadia purrs, her voice thick with happiness.

I splay my hands across her swollen belly. My daughter rolls around inside and a thrill shoots its way straight to my heart.

"I love you, sweet Jayne."

Her hands cover mine and she rubs her thumbs across them. "Yo tambien. Te quiero, mi amor."

Most days, I don't know what the hell she says when she

speaks in her native tongue. For all I know, she could have told me she had a craving for dill pickles and chocolate ice cream.

But I *hear*.

I always *hear*.

It never fails to send the same message to me no matter what she says.

I fucking love you too, Donovan Jayne.

Kasey

Three years after rescue…

The cold metal table under my forearms causes me to shiver. I'm nervous to see him today. It's not like I haven't been to the supermax US penitentiary in Florence County before, where Logan is serving two consecutive life sentences. In fact, I come about once a month unless I've been informed Logan is in solitary for doing something stupid, like fighting. Today, though, I'm good for a visit and my nerves are shot.

It's just Logan. Breathe.

Closing my eyes, I let my mind drift to happier times before his actions caught up with him.

"My kids already in bed?" Logan's deep voice rumbles, startling me awake on the couch.

I sit up and glance at the clock. It's after midnight. When my eyes find his, my heart sinks. He looks terrible tonight. Something is weighing heavily on him.

"*Come sit,*" *I urge.*

He kicks off his shoes and yanks off his tie before slumping down on the couch. Once he's settled, I straddle his lap and palm his cheeks. His dark eyes, shame flickering in them, find mine.

"*What happened?*"

He tears his gaze away from me and focuses on my hair as he tucks some loose strands behind my ears. "Donovan came over, looking for Nadia. Things got pretty bad. The house is all fucked up."

My heart thunders in my chest. This is what she and I have been working toward. We need for people to notice we're here. Sounds like all her hard work is paying off.

With a frown, careful not to let my hope shine through, I regard him. "Logan, baby, it's just Donovan. What's he going to do? You already said you announced your engagement. They can't tear your house apart on assumptions. Nadia is convincing is she not?"

He nods. "Yeah. Your brother is getting nosy though." When his eyes meet mine again, he swallows. "I'm sorry. I know it upsets you to talk about him."

I run my fingers through his hair and kiss him. "Stop worrying so much. Nadia is obsessed with being your wife and living up there in the house. She doesn't even care about Junior. There's no way she'll leave you or alert anyone to the fact we're down here."

He hugs me to him and buries his face against my chest. "I love you, Kasey. You have to know that."

And I do. At one time, I didn't understand how. But after all this time, I feel his love for me. I don't understand him when he loses control or becomes abusive. I don't see how keeping us captive in his basement is okay in his mind. I certainly don't get how he can fuck two women exclusively and be at ease with that.

But I do feel his love. It's strange. It's dark. It's wrong. Yet it's there.

"I love you too," I assure him. This too is true. Nadia despises his very existence but that's because her heart always belonged to someone else. Mine belonged to Taylor until he left me. Now, I feel like Logan owns it through and through. The day I held baby Tay in my arms, my heart became inexplicably intertwined with Logan's.

"Do you need anything for the kitchen? Clothes for the kids? Toys? I can pick some things up next time I'm out," he says, his tone gruff as he clutches onto my ass.

I look past him at my home. The basement has long been converted into a comfortable living space. We have a nice bathroom with a bathtub where I bathe the kids. A small kitchen complete with a range, oven, sink, and refrigerator. There's a bedroom off the living room with enough places to sleep for everyone. Nadia and I used to share the bed until she moved upstairs. This is my home. It's small and I can't leave, but I do okay here.

"I need..." he trails off as he tugs at the hem of my dress.

I lift my arms and allow him to peel it from me. He unlatches my bra and tosses it away. Ever since Nadia had Van, we've stuck to our plan. She provokes him so he'll leave me and the kids alone. Not once has he ever laid a finger on our children, but we don't give him a chance. Of course he and I have had sex over the past few years but it's different than the in beginning. It's consensual and actually enjoyable.

"God, you're so beautiful, doll."

My cheeks warm as he lowers me down on the couch beside him. I watch with an eagerness I can't explain as this beautiful demon of a man strips down and reveals his perfect body to me. He then peels away my panties before climbing on top of me.

"Don't forget the condom," I murmur.

He frowns but pulls one from the pocket of his slacks. Once he's sheathed, he spreads me open. I let out a soft gasp when he pushes his length inside of me. "I want to have another baby with you. Nadia hasn't gotten pregnant again. Maybe I'll take her to a doctor soon to get her checked out, now that everyone in town knows she's my fiancée. But until then, maybe we could try again."

A flare of jealousy thunders in my chest but I quickly push away those senseless thoughts. Nadia is my partner. Not my enemy. Logan just confuses me sometimes.

"Kassie is too little. I can barely take care of her by myself. Maybe in another few months, okay?"

He agrees with a slight nod before crashing his lips to mine. Our bodies, completely used to one another after a decade of being together, melt into one. His cock hits me in all the right spots as he makes love to me. A delicious and long overdue orgasm slices through me and I bite my lip to keep from crying out and waking the kids. He groans as his cock throbs within me. Then, he relaxes and buries his face against my neck.

"I'm sorry this isn't your ideal life, Kasey. But this is mine. Having you and my children here together. I'm happy, doll."

I hug him to me. "I'm happy too." And in this exact moment, that's not a lie. With his heart thundering in his chest against mine, I find peace. Even if only for a little while.

A buzzer sounds and I jolt back to the present. Another shiver courses through me the moment I know his eyes are on me. I look over my shoulder and see his massive, shackled frame hobbling over to me. Darkness has settled over him and a scowl mars his handsome face. He looks just like Kass when she doesn't get her way. Once he's settled in his seat, the guard walks away to give us some privacy.

"Hey," I whisper.

His coffee-colored eyes flit to my lips and he cracks a small smile. "Hey, beautiful. Your hair's getting longer."

I absently tug at a strand and my hand trembles. When my gaze finds his, he's frowning again.

"What's going on? Kass and Tay okay?" The overprotective, fatherly growl warms my heart. He'll always be their dad. Always.

"Yeah, they're fine. Taylor had to do a report about his father in his class…" I trail off.

Shame flashes across Logan's face and my heart aches a little. "And what did he say?"

I reach across and briefly skim my fingertips over his cuffed hands before bringing them back to my lap. Lifting the paper Tay drew, I slide it across the table. "He still brags to anyone who'll listen about how you're the best Minecraft creeper killer in Colorado. When the kids asked how you got so good, he told them because you used to be a cop and learned at the academy. Apparently they all think that is cool."

We both smile.

When he looks down at the paper, his jaw clenches and a tear rolls out splashing it. I want to hug him and comfort him but it's simply not allowed.

"Who's the little monster with the wild hair he drew that's frowning?" he asks, his voice choked with emotion.

I laugh and point to Tay's rendering of Kass. "That'd be your baby girl. She's kind of a terror these days."

He stares for a long time at the picture. The man in the picture is Logan holding Tay's hand. The woman is me and I get to hold the unhappy monster's hand. Except in the picture, there's not a sun or clouds or the family standing in front of a house. No. In the picture, we're in the living room of the basement. The grey walls are neatly colored in around the figures.

"Did you drive here alone?" he asks, his eyes never leaving the picture.

My entire body tenses. "No, Jason brought me. Like usual."

His gaze lifts to mine and he looks me over. At one time, his scrutiny terrified me. That was before I loved him. But I'll always love him to some degree, so he doesn't scare me anymore. What I have to tell him—words that will break his heart—that's what scares me.

"I wanted to tell you this in person. Not through our letters. Jason and I..." Tears well in my eyes and my lip trembles. "We're pregnant. He wants to marry me, Logan."

His jaw clenches and another tear streaks down his cheek. When he doesn't say anything, I bring a couple of photographs from my lap and slide them across to him. Mostly they are of the kids. A few are of me and the kids. One is Jason holding Kass on his hip at Tay's baseball game.

"Does he make you happy?"

I nod and reach for him again. He lets me touch his fingers. "Very. It's been a long road for us. There're still days we both have trouble dealing with certain things from our past. But this is good news to us. A baby is always good news."

His Adam's apple bobs in his throat as he swallows. "Do you love him?"

"I do. He's so good to our kids too. You know what a nice guy he is."

He stares at me as if he wants to memorize every freckle on my face. I wish the stupid guards would just unshackle him and let me hug him. "No man ever wants to give his blessing for the mother of his children to move on from him…"

Sniffling, I nod and fortify my heart to say my next words. "I know. And I'm not asking for your blessing. I'm telling you, Logan. I choose this for myself. You weren't a choice but I learned to love you anyway. Because of your actions, I was given two children I would die for. I'm grateful for what you gave me. But please realize this is not me asking. I love you. I always will. If you love me too, you'll make peace with this. Our children deserve this. *I* deserve this."

He regards me with a tortured expression. It slices through my heart but I knew it was inevitable. This had to be said.

"You have three more minutes," the gruff guard mumbles from somewhere behind me.

We both flinch at the realization that the visitation is nearly over.

"Does this mean it's over? That you'll stop coming to see me? That my children will eventually forget who I am?" His voice wobbles with each word.

Shaking my head vehemently at him, I meet his stare with a firm one of my own. "Absolutely not. It may go

against my brother's and Nadia's wishes, but I won't abandon you. I'm probably the only person, besides the kids, on
this planet who cares about you. It would be impossible for
me to ever fully let you go. I promise I'll visit you. We'll still
send pictures and updates. The kids look forward to when
you send them letters. Nothing is changing as far as that
goes. But I am going to move forward with Jason. We're going to go on and have a good life together."

His tears don't stop but he doesn't argue. He just stares
at me as if he has the ability to keep me here forever. At one
time, he had the power to keep his little doll all to himself.
But now, his little doll is grown up. She's standing on her
own two feet and doing things her way.

"Time to go, inmate," the guard says.

I stand as he helps Logan to his feet. The guard groans
but allows me to press a chaste kiss to Logan's cheek. His
dark, pained eyes stay trained on mine as he's ushered away
from me without so much as a goodbye. My chest hurts but
I also feel lighter. The news is still fresh and he'll be upset
but eventually he'll learn to accept it.

The walk out of the facility and into the lobby is a blur.
When I push through the doors and the warm sunshine hits
my face—a feeling I still feel grateful for every day—I clutch
my stomach and pray I don't lose my lunch. But when two
strong arms wrap around me from behind, I finally relax.

Jason's presence blankets me and I feel safe.

"Everything go okay?" he questions, his palms splayed
out on my small baby bump.

I cover his hands with mine and nod. "It was hard. Just
like we knew it would be. But I'm ready. Ready to move forward."

He removes one of his hands and shoves it into his pocket. When he brings it back, he's holding a small gold ring with a tiny cluster of diamonds that shimmer around a larger diamond. I bite my lip to keep the tears at bay as he slips it on my finger.

"Marry me, angel."

Twisting in his arms, I wrap my arms around his neck and stand on my toes to kiss him. He wastes no time tangling his tongue with mine. Jason tastes like cinnamon and hope and love all rolled into one delicious kiss.

"Is that a yes?" he questions against my lips, a smile breaking out on his face.

I pull away from his kiss and hug him tight. He lifts me from the ground, spinning me in a slow circle. The high cinderblock walls and barbed wire fence may be the background of his proposal but the sun shining down on us is all that matters right now.

Everything was once all screwed up and terrifying and confusing. At times, I didn't think this life was even worth living. But all the bad got me here. To the now. From darkness, my two adorable children were birthed in perfect light. Eventually, I was given a chance at a full, satisfying life, despite the long and downright awful journey to get where I am now.

Was it worth it?

"Yes."

Every single moment was completely worth my eventual happy ending.

And lucky for me, my happiness doesn't end here.

It's only beginning.

The End

Playlist

*Listen to the entire playlist here
(open.spotify.com/user/12130346590/
playlist/02IYfWudpmhXXSbTMLxUYk).*

Sweet Jane – Cowboy Junkies
Crimson and Clover – Tommy James & The Shondells
Take Out the Gunman – Chevelle
Hotel California – Eagles
Tainted Love – Marilyn Manson
Fade Into You – Mazzy Star
Love is Not Enough – Nine Inch Nails
The Way – Saigon Kick
Crown of Thorns – Mother Love Bone
Stargazer – Mother Love Bone
Ain't That a Kick in the Head – Dean Martin
Wonderwall – Oasis
Killing Me Softly With His Song – Fugees
Kiss From a Rose – Seal
Truly Madly Deeply – Savage Garden
Crazy – Aerosmith
Stairway to Heaven – Led Zeppelin
(Don't Fear) The Reaper – Blue Oyster Cult
You're So Vain – Marilyn Manson

Acknowledgements

Thank you to my husband, Matt. You wash clothes and feed mouths when Momma Bear is hard at work. I couldn't have picked out a better man. My love for you never wanes. Only grows stronger with each day.

A huge thanks to Nikki McCrae. Your support and help is what keeps me going. I know I can always count on you to set me straight and remind me of who I am when I'm not being Author K Webster. Thanks for always bringing me back to reality. If it weren't for you, my head would always be in the clouds and I'd probably forget to eat breakfast most days. You're my voice of reason.

Thank you to Sunny Borek. You've become a great friend to me. I appreciate that you always let me throw ideas at you, no matter how weird and wild, and then wave your pom-poms in the air to cheer me on. You make me happy when skies are grey.

I want to thank the people who either beta read this book or proofed it early. Nikki McCrae, Elizabeth Clinton, Ella Stewart, Jessica Hollyfield, Amy Bosica, Shannon Martin, Brooklyn Miller, Robin Martin, Amy Simms, Rebecca Graham, and Sunny Borek, (I hope I didn't forget anyone) you all gave me great feedback and the support I needed to carry on. You all give me helpful ideas to make my stories better and give me incredible encouragement. I appreciate all of your comments and suggestions.

A big thank you to my author friends who have given me your friendship and your support. You have no idea how much that means to me.

Thank you to all of my blogger friends both big and small that go above and beyond to always share my stuff. You all rock! #AllBlogsMatter

I'm especially thankful for my Krazy for K reader group. You ladies are wonderful with your support and friendship. Each and every single one of you is amazingly supportive and caring. I love that we can all be weird page sniffers together.

I am totally thankful for my author group, the COPA gals, for being there when I need to take a load off and whine. Y'all rock!

Vanessa Bridges, you're my hero. You totally somehow see the greater vision within my story and pull it to the surface. I'm grateful that you can understand what it is I'm trying to convey. I love that you aren't afraid to cut my story up until it's hemorrhaging, only to guide my trembling hands in stitching it back up to perfection. It comes out raw, real, and thought provoking because of your work on it. The wounds and scars only show the fight of how the story came to be. Keep your blade sharp and I'll keep offering my bloody heart to you over and over again. And, Manda Lee, you always help my story become so much better with your helpful feedback and notes. Finally, thank you, Jessica D. I'm glad to have your eagle-eyes on the last pass. Love you ladies!

Thank you Stacey Blake for taking my hard work and shining it into something pretty. Your magic is the finishing touch that turns my bloody, scarred up project into the belle of the ball. Love you!

A big thanks to my PR gal, Nicole Blanchard. You are fabulous at what you do and keep me on track!

Lastly but certainly not least of all, thank you to all of the wonderful readers out there that are willing to hear my story and enjoy my characters like I do. It means the world to me!

About the Author

K Webster is the author of dozens of romance books in many different genres including contemporary romance, historical romance, paranormal romance, dark romance, romantic suspense, and erotic romance. When not spending time with her husband of thirteen years and two adorable children, she's active on social media connecting with her readers.

Her other passions besides writing include reading and graphic design. K can always be found in front of her computer chasing her next idea and taking action. She looks forward to the day when she will see one of her titles on the big screen.

Join K Webster's newsletter to receive a couple of updates a month on new releases and exclusive content. To join, all you need to do is go here.